CW01081103

The Curious Case of Cut-Throat Cate

The 2nd Case for Inspector Capstan

David Blake

www.david-blake.com

Edited and proofread by Lorraine Swoboda

Cover design by David Blake

Published in Great Britain, 2016

Disclaimer:
These are works of fiction. Names, characters, businesses, places, events and incidents are either the products of the author's imagination or used in a fictitious manner. Any resemblance to actual persons, living or dead, or actual events is purely coincidental.

ISBN: 1533128677
ISBN-13: 978-1533128676

DEDICATION

For Akiko, Akira and Kai.

THE INSPECTOR CAPSTAN
SERIES INCLUDES:

1. The Slaughtered Virgin of Zenopolis
2. The Curious Case of Cut-Throat Cate
3. The Thrills & Spills of Genocide Jill

CONTENTS

Acknowledgments   i

Act 1, Scene 1   Leg of Lamb   3

Act 1, Scene 2   With some reservation   10

Act 1, Scene 3   The body in the bin   20

Act 1, Scene 4   Selling, door-to-door   30

Act 1, Scene 5   Nothing to see here   36

Act 1, Scene 6   Can you take your shoes off please   45

Act 1, Scene 7   Do you know anything about computers   54

Act 2, Scene 1   Fifty pounds and a box of Ferrero…   61

Act 2, Scene 2   Another good idea   72

Act 2, Scene 3   How does your garden grow?   76

Act 2, Scene 4   A boat, a boat. Does anyone have a boat?   85

Act 2, Scene 5   Put that ship down   95

Act 2, Scene 6   A difference of opinion   104

Act 2, Scene 7   You have the body of a dog and the IQ of…   110

Act 2, Scene 8   What does it look like?   119

Act 2, Scene 9   Are you insane?   124

Act 3, Scene 1   Murder, Death, Kill   133

Act 3, Scene 2	They shot me, the bastards!	143
Act 3, Scene 3	Drugs, Cash and Gold	150
Act 3, Scene 4	School trip for obese children	159
Act 3, Scene 5	Good shot	163
Act 3, Scene 6	Are you French or English?	170
Act 3, Scene 7	You must have heard it wrong	176
Act 4, Scene 1	An eye for an eye	183
Act 4, Scene 2	An inspired idea	190
Act 4, Scene 3	Headline News	198
Act 4, Scene 4	Special Ops	210
Act 4, Scene 5	Kill or be killed	219
Act 5, Scene 1	They're all dead, Captain	225
Act 5, Scene 2	Penetration is the best form of attack	233
Act 5, Scene 3	I'm not sure that was such a good idea	239
Act 5, Scene 4	Loitering, or something	245
Act 5, Scene 5	The Spoils of War	254
Act 5, Scene 6	I like this girl	258
Act 5, Scene 7	A Suit and a Case	266

ACKNOWLEDGMENTS

I'd like to thank my family for putting up with me and my rather odd sense of humour.

I'd also like to thank my Editor and Proofreader, Lorraine Swoboda, for making sure that what I write makes sense, sort of, and that all the words are in the right order.

Act 1, Scene 1
Gigot d'agneau
Leg of lamb

"Now is the winter of our discontent."
King Richard III, Act I Scene I

COCOONED IN HER warm, cosy double bed, Cate gazed up at the ceiling, listening to the central heating turn itself on. It was Tuesday morning, she was still on holiday, the sun had yet to rise and she had absolutely no intention of getting up.

A loud knock penetrated her peaceful serenity.

'Oh, for God's sake,' she moaned to nobody in particular, still lying motionless and hoping that whoever was at the front door would go away.

There was another knock, but this time a little louder.

'Coming,' she groaned as she heaved back the duvet, slid into her slippers and pulled on her dressing gown before making her way down the stairs.

At the bottom she turned the hall light on, glanced into the mirror, gave her hair a prod and opened the door, just enough to peer out into the wintry gloom.

The postman stood there.

'Sorry to bother you, Miss, but there seems to be a, er, body lying outside your house,' he said, looking rather cold and somewhat apprehensive.

'Really?'

She'd forgotten about her husband. The previous night, she'd decided to kill him. She'd actually made up her mind to kill him the year before, around the time of their first wedding anniversary; but she'd made it one of her New Year's Resolutions that she'd definitely do it, and just as soon as the opportunity presented itself. She'd also promised to keep the house tidier and do more exercise, but killing her husband was definitely top of the list.

Last night the opportunity *had* presented itself - well, the incentive, anyway. He'd phoned her late "from work" again, obviously completely drunk, again, to say that he'd be home late, again.

She'd had enough, especially as he'd just interrupted her favourite *Poldark* on TV. So she'd immediately instigated her plan of murderous intent by storming into the kitchen, filling up a saucepan with cold water and pouring it out over the hard concrete steps that led up to the porch. Then she'd slammed the door shut and returned to watch *Poldark*.

The postman was now staring directly at her with a clear expectation of some sort of emotive response to the body that lay face up on the path.

'Oh, my God!' she exclaimed, covering a smirk with her hands. 'It's my husband! He didn't come home last night. He must have slipped on the steps and hit his head.'

It had happened exactly as she had hoped. His skinny little body lay on its back, his arms splayed out on either side, and after the night's heavy frost he sparkled festively in the street's yellow light. He looked like either a huge fairy who'd fallen from a giant

Christmas tree, or a frozen skydiver who'd forgotten to pull his chute. She couldn't decide.

'Shall I call an ambulance?' asked the postman, in an attempt to move things along.

It was then that the body twitched and groaned a little.

'My God, he's still alive!' exclaimed the postman in excitement and incredulity.

'My God, he's still alive!' repeated Cate, but for different reasons. 'Wait there,' she said, and dived back into the house, leaving the postman stranded out on the path.

Not sure what to do next, he took off his heavy postman's bag, made his way over to where the man lay, and, crouching down, eased the mumbling head to rest gently in his lap.

A moment later, Cate re-emerged from the house with a frozen leg of lamb.

'Yes, that's it,' she said, treading carefully down the still-icy steps. 'Sit him up straight and let's have a good look at him.'

The postman was confused as to why she wanted to have a good look at someone who she must have seen before, given that it was her husband, but he did as he was told and heaved the gurgling body into a sitting position.

'Right, mind out the way,' she said, placing her feet shoulder-width apart and holding the leg of lamb with an overlapping grip. She wiggled her hips a little, as if to tee off, swung back and then violently forwards to make a sizable dent in the back of her husband's head, which slumped forwards to rest unnaturally on his chest.

Having seen all this happen right before his eyes, the postman sat, open-mouthed and unable to stop staring at the caved-in skull and the thick goo that oozed out from it.

'Wh…What have you done?'

'Finished him off, I hope. Now, help me shift the body,' she said, regaining her balance and tossing the murder weapon casually onto the front lawn.

'I won't do anything of the sort!'

'Yes, you will. You're an accomplice to murder now, so man up!'

'Jesus! Don't be absurd! How can I possibly be an accomplice to murder?'

'Well, it was you who lifted him up for me to get a good swing at, so you're as much involved as I am.'

'But, I, er…' spluttered the postman, attempting to follow her argument whilst trying to think of a plausible excuse.

Not giving him the chance, Cate said, 'Now come on, help me pick him up. Grab his legs.'

At a complete loss as to what to say, the postman stood up, walked over to where the legs were, and secured his hands firmly around the ankles.

'Right: one, two, three and LIFT!' and they picked up the recently deceased so that he lay suspended equally between them.

'What now?' asked the postman.

'We'll stick him in one of the bins.'

'Which one?' he asked again, looking at three of them standing innocently beside the path.

'How do you mean?'

'Well, one's for general waste, one's for recycling and the other's for food waste only.'

'Yes, I see your point. The food waste one is far too small, and I can't imagine anyone wanting to recycle him. We'll stick him in General Waste.'

With that, she dropped the top half of her late husband back onto the path with a thud, re-adjusted her dressing gown, and carefully made her way down the slippery path to fetch the large black General Waste wheelie bin that seemed to have been designed for such a macabre purpose.

She rattled it down the drive and parked it as close to the body as she could before pulling the lid up and over, so that it fell backwards to leave a large, body-shaped sort of a hole.

'Right, we'll stick him in there. It'll be collected soon, which will suit us very well.'

The postman, still standing on the path holding an ankle in each hand, felt increasingly uncomfortable with the whole situation. He was trying to work out how he'd managed to become an accomplice to murder by just propping someone up a bit, and he certainly didn't like the way the lady kept saying, "we'll" and "us" all the time. But the longer he just stood there, holding the feet of a frozen dead guy, the more he felt like an accomplice. So there he remained, following this demented lady's insane instructions, like an evil henchman looking to please his new master.

Cate marched back to the torso and heaved it up again.

'OK,' she said, breathing hard, 'we'll stick his legs in first, and the rest should follow.' Obediently the postman lifted the feet up and dropped them straight into the bin.

Having successfully posted something into a hole he felt much better - more like a postman again, and less like an evil henchman - so he continued to help the lady shove the rest of the body in. Then he closed the lid and stood gazing at the man-sized wheelie bin before asking, absently, 'Shall I take it out for you?'

'If you could, yes, thank you. Oh, and by the way, did you have any post for me?'

He did, so he reached down to pick out the correct bundle from his bag. Then he eased the bin onto its wheels and rolled it out onto the quiet, still dark suburban street.

'Right! Bye then,' he called out, trying hard to regain some semblance of normality.

'Yes, and thanks again!' Cate called back, waving the retrieved murder weapon at him, before hurrying inside with her post.

She shut the front door, dumped the letters on to the cabinet under the hall mirror and went through to the kitchen, where she dropped the leg of lamb into the sink. She then gave her hands a quick wash, popped the kettle on and hurried upstairs to fetch her smartphone.

Opening up her Facebook page she typed, "Barry didn't come home last night. I know we've had our differences but I still love him. I hope he's OK!"

Then she made her way back down to the kitchen to make herself a coffee, before returning upstairs to bed.

I'll wait till Thursday before I call the police, she decided. *That would probably be about the right sort of time to wait,* and she snuggled down to chat with those Facebook friends who'd already seen her post and were now diligently responding with the usual sympathetic comments of support and mutual condemnation for the male population in general.

Act 1, Scene 2

Avec une certaine réserve
With some reservation

"These words are razors to my wounded heart."
Titus Andronicus, Act I Scene I

AFTER SOME MUESLI and another coffee, and having put on the thickest, warmest jumper she could find, Cate made her way out of the house, humming the theme tune to *Poldark* as she went. She had a meeting with her literary agent at half past ten that morning and had to drive from her home in Portsmouth to his office in Southampton, a journey she knew all too well as it was very similar to her normal term-time commute.

Treading carefully down the icy porch steps, she noticed that her General Waste wheelie bin was still out, awaiting collection along with all the others down the street. She'd never understood the council's refuse timetable; it seemed to differ each week, but the bin men were supposed to make their rounds that morning and she hoped that they would. She really didn't want her husband to be hanging around for another seven days. She was keen to move on with her life, and anyway, she'd need the bin space for when she started to throw out all his clothes.

Putting her late husband out of her mind once again, she climbed into the car and began to think about more important things, and in particular her forthcoming meeting. Although a well-respected university lecturer, her main aim in life was to become a successful author, something she hadn't quite achieved yet. Yes, she was an author, and yes, she was even published, but her one and only book had been a commercial disaster. She had just submitted the proposal for her second one, and her agent had called her in for a chat. In the early days these meetings had been joyous affairs, but they'd become less so as each zero book sales day had passed, and the way he'd sounded on the phone, she'd been left with the distinct impression that this meeting wouldn't be much better. However, she was still hopeful. She'd had some really good ideas since submitting her proposal and was confident that these would help turn things around.

After a thirty-minute drive, and leaving her car in the Ocean Marina Village car park, she made her way towards the high-rise building that over-looked Southampton Marina. The agency's office was on the ninth floor, and she gazed up at its windows as she pressed the labelled bell.

'Hello, Fairdown & Herbert,' came the metallic-sounding voice over the intercom.

'Oh, hello, it's Cate Jakebury to see Mr Herbert.'

'Hi, Cate, I'll buzz you up.'

She pushed the door open, and walked over to the elevators. As the lift carried her upwards she hummed the theme tune to *Poldark* to herself, just to help pass the time.

A minute or two later the doors opened straight out into her agent's reception area where Liz, the receptionist, gave her a welcoming smile.

'Hello, Cate. You can go straight in if you like, Peter's all ready for you.'

Suddenly feeling rather nervous, Cate did her best to return the smile and made her way over to the door that bore the name 'Peter Herbert' on an engraved plaque. She knocked, heard a muffled, 'Come in!' and walked in to a large, opulent room with huge windows that gave a panoramic view of the harbour.

Peter stood up from behind his desk.

'Ah, Cate, there you are! So good of you to come.'

'Hello, Peter.'

He ushered her over to the small meeting area in the corner of the room. 'Do, please, sit down.'

'Thank you.'

'How's your husband?'

'Oh, working all the hours God sends, as usual.'

Even though he was dead, she still hadn't forgiven him.

'Can I get you something to drink, a coffee perhaps?'

'A coffee would be great.'

Turning back, he called, 'Liz, could you bring us two coffees please? Thanks!'

Closing the door he returned to his desk, where he picked up a file from the top of a big pile of similar files and came to sit down opposite her. 'So, Cate, I received your new book proposal.' He crossed his legs. 'Now, I see where you're trying to go with it, but I do have some reservations.'

'Yes, I understand, Peter, but I've had some new ideas since sending it over.'

'Oh, good! Do tell.'

'Well, for example, instead of having the protagonist shipwrecked off the coast of Borneo, I thought it would be better if her ship went down off the coast of Madagascar.'

'I see. And that's better...because?'

'Because of the cartoon, and the BBC documentary. Madagascar's very well-known now, but I doubt if anyone's even heard of Borneo.'

Peter nodded, though he'd actually heard of both of them. 'Any other ideas?' he asked, without much hope.

'Yes! Instead of her being washed ashore on a desert island where she meets Kevin the Pirate King, who's also been marooned there, I thought she could be fished out of the sea by him from his pirate boat as she just happened to drift past.'

Peter put his reading glasses on and started leafing through the twenty page synopsis that had accompanied her proposal.

'So... if they don't then meet at the island, then at what point would they be captured by its native inhabitants, roasted over an open fire, escape using a raft whittled from driftwood and coconuts before being rescued by the Royal Navy who make your Pirate King, Kevin, walk the plank, the Captain marries your protagonist, they have children together and all live happily ever-after?'

'Oh, I thought I'd skip all that.'

'Look, Cate, it all sounds like great fun and everything but I really think it needs more thought. It's just all a bit...half-baked.'

Cate couldn't help but be offended. Since finishing her first novel, another Elizabethan naval romance, she'd spent months thinking up this story as its sequel.

'And the title,' he continued. 'Again, it needs more thought. At the moment you have it down as being called, what was it now...oh yes, here it is. *Blown Away.*'

'Yes, that's right.'

'But why?'

'Because she's *Blown Away* by her love for Kevin the Pirate King, and also because of the wind, and because the story is set on the high seas where everyone is blown about, on boats.'

'But don't you think that the title *Blown Away* has more in common with a man being shot with a very large gun, than with a woman falling in love with a pirate king called Kevin?'

The question was left hanging in the air as he continued to flick through her synopsis. Eventually he gave up, took his reading glasses off, looked at her with a frown and asked, 'As I assume this is another historical romance, can't you think up a title with less…ambiguity?'

Cate was becoming increasingly upset, but more so now that he'd just used the fingers of both hands to accentuate the words, "historical romance".

'Well, what would you suggest then?' she asked, unable to hide her rising anger.

'It's not for me to think up a name for your book, Cate. Don't you have any other ideas?'

She thought for a moment. '*The Wind and the War?*'

'Is it about a war?' he asked, replacing his glasses to re-study the proposal.

It wasn't. '*The Wind and the Warlock?*'

'Is there a Warlock in it?'

'Okay, how about, *A Winter's Wind*?'

'But it's set in the tropics, isn't it? I'm not sure they have a winter season there.'

'Alright, what about, *A Westerly Wind* then?'

'But what's that got to do with an Elizabethan love story?'

'*The Wind of my Heart Goes on Forever and Ever*?' she finally said, gazing up at the ceiling, lost in the creative moment.

'No!' Peter was losing his patience. 'Look, Cate, it's not just the title, it's the whole thing. We took you on because we specialise in books about the sea, and we thought your idea of a historical navy-themed romance fitted well within our portfolio, but it's becoming increasingly clear to us that you don't know anything about ships, the sea or even the basic rudiments of sailing. For example,' he re-opened the file to find his own notes, 'in your first proposed chapter which you've called, Your Wind Fills Up My Sails,' he glanced back up at her, frowned, and then returned to his notes, 'you refer to a ship's galley as the kitchen, a cabin as the bedroom, the head as the loo, the deck as the floor, portholes as windows and the poop deck as the upstairs landing. And the 104-gun first-rate ship of the line that you called HMS Celebration, and which I can only assume is a thinly disguised HMS Victory, you describe as being, "a really big boat with a large wooden steering wheel".'

Cate's teeth locked together as she glared at him.

'And I'm not even particularly impressed with your knowledge of the Elizabethan Age. You refer to the Battle of Trafalgar and how Queen Elizabeth the

First,' he checked his notes again for accuracy, '"was distraught with mournful sorrow over her noble Nelson's death"; but she'd already died herself, two hundred years earlier, in 1603. And I found another paragraph where you say that the ship's captain,' again he read from his notes, '"had a good wash, a close shave and then brushed his teeth with Colgate". I'm fairly sure Colgate didn't make toothpaste during the latter part of the sixteenth century. I'm not even sure they'd invented toothpaste by then!'

Cate had had enough.

'How dare you! I've got an "A" level in History and I lecture in Classical English Literature at Solent University. I doubt there's anyone who's ever sat in this chair who knows more about the Elizabethan Age than I do, thank you very much!'

'Yes, well, that's as maybe, but you really don't know much about sailing though, do you?'

He had her there. She didn't. She'd never even been in a rowing boat, let alone one with sails, but she wrote historic love stories, not sailing anthologies, and really didn't see that it mattered.

'So? What's there to know? The wind blows and the boat moves around a bit. It's a very simple concept.'

It was now Peter's turn to stare at her.

'Unfortunately, Cate, there is just a little more to it than that, especially when talking about an Elizabethan flagship such as the Ark Royal.'

Cate had never heard of a boat called the Ark Royal. She hadn't even heard the term "flagship" before, and was now trying to work out why anyone would need a boat that was covered in flags, but then realised that it must be for the transportation of them, and not their display.

Peter, on the other hand, knew everything about boats from Viking Longships all the way through to the aircraft carriers of the modern age.

'Anyway, Cate, we've decided that we're going to have to terminate this relationship. I'm really sorry to be the bearer of such bad news but we need to be working with authors who share our passion for the sea.'

She was expecting that; but just then she had an idea, and suddenly exclaimed, 'I've bought a boat!'

'I'm sorry, what did you say?'

'I said I've bought a boat.'

There was a pause in the conversation before Peter asked, with some reservation, 'What sort of "boat" is it?'

'I don't know, but it's parked out there,' and she gestured towards the marina which the office overlooked.

Peter still didn't look convinced and just continued to stare at her, so she added, 'You can probably see it from here,' and got up, walked over to the window, opened it and leaned out.

'Yes, you can, just. It's over there. The big white one.'

Unable to contain his excitement at the possibility that one of his clients had actually gone and bought a sailing yacht, he leapt up from his chair and headed for the window to take a look for himself, and as he leaned out he asked, 'Where? Which one?'

'You can see it, around the corner of the building. If you lean out just a little more...'

And as he did so she gave him a hearty shove and listened to him saying "Aaaggghhh" for rather a long time before splatting into the pavement.

'NOBODY SPEAKS TO ME LIKE THAT!' she shouted down at what was Peter Herbert, but now looked more like a half-eaten water melon.

Realising what she'd just done, she was forced to make a few rather hasty decisions, the first being to close the window, as it was still very cold. Then she headed over to his desk and rummaged around to find a pen and some paper. With her left hand she wrote, "I can't take it anymore!" which was probably more how she felt about their conversation than how Peter was feeling about his life in general, but anyway, she thought it would do the job and left it at that.

Keeping the pen, she picked up her proposal and headed out of the room, being sure to close the door behind her.

As she approached the reception desk, Liz looked up.

'Oh, sorry, I'd completely forgotten to make you a coffee.'

'Don't worry, I've got to be off anyway, but could you maybe look in on Peter at some point? He didn't look very happy when I left. I've no idea why, but you may want to pop in, just to make sure he's OK.'

Liz's face creased in concern. 'Oh dear, yes of course. I wonder what's up with him? I'll just send this email and then I'd better make him that coffee. Would you like one yourself?'

'Er, no, sorry, I've really got to get back. Anyway, see you soon.'

'Oh yes, see you, Cate. Take care.'

Cate gave her a little wave, and an even smaller smile before pressing the button for the elevator. And as she stood there, watching the light count up from the ground floor, she began to think. Unfortunately Peter was right. She was going to have to get some sort of experience out at sea before writing her next book. She was also going to have to find a new agent, but as a published author who'd only lost her current one due to a rather sudden and unexpected suicide, she didn't foresee that as being a problem.

Act 1, Scene 3
Le corps dans la poubelle
The body in the bin

"Suspicion always haunts the guilty mind."
King Henry IV, Part III, Act V, Scene VI

A S PETER HERBERT was making a rather rapid descent towards the pavement outside his office in Southampton, Police Inspector Capstan and Sergeant Dewbush were making a much slower ascent of the hill leading up towards Belmont Road in Portsmouth.

Only half an hour earlier they'd received word of a body being discovered in a wheelie bin outside someone's house, and as it wasn't very often a body was found anywhere in the City, unless it was lying outside a night club, they were driving as fast as the traffic would allow to reach the scene of what they were hoping was a very serious crime. However, traffic is traffic, and there was a large amount of it, and their progress was being further hindered by people's stock reaction to seeing an unmarked police car directly behind them with its lights flashing and its siren on full blast, which was to stop exactly where they were, grab hold of the steering wheel and hope to God that it wasn't them they were after. Of course this sort of behaviour was to be expected, but it was all rather annoying and made the idea of speeding towards the scene of a possible murder virtually impossible.

With Dewbush left to fight his way through the cars that had all stopped dead in the middle of the road, Capstan had a chance to do some thinking, which, at that moment, involved him contemplating just exactly how both he and his terminally stupid Sergeant had ended up working for the Solent Police.

After what the media had termed "The Battle of Bath", and his visit to Number 10 in August the previous year, he'd received three letters in the post that all stood out for different reasons. The first was from the Prime Minister, thanking him for his many services to the City of Bath and the country as a whole, and informing him that he could look forward to receiving a generous salary increase in the very near future. The second was from Her Royal Highness, Queen Elizabeth II, which said that he was going to be included in the New Year's Honours list with a view to being awarded an O.B.E. The last letter was from his boss, telling him that he was fired, well, from Bath City Police at least, and that he was going to be transferred down to the South Coast.

What Capstan didn't know at that time was that Dewbush had also received a couple of unusual items; the first being a box stacked to the brim with Spank n' Wank magazines along with a free, life-time subscription, and the second a letter from his boss, telling him that he, too, had been fired and was to be found a job down on the coast somewhere.

Having finally returned from his somewhat extended sailing holiday, their former Chief Inspector was keen to be shot of the both of them and, thinking that they were clearly as bad as each other, that it would be a shame to have them separated. So he'd made a personal request to have them both transferred down to Portsmouth, while making sure that neither of them knew about the other's fate.

So, after spending six weeks re-locating themselves, Capstan and Dewbush were just a little surprised to find themselves staring at each other on a Monday morning in October, while being introduced to their new boss, a Chief Inspector Morose. But neither was particularly unhappy with the situation. Starting a new job, in a new city, with a new boss, was always a nerve-racking experience, and having a familiar face to stare at did make the transition easier, for both of them.

Arriving at the turning into Belmont Road, Dewbush turned off the siren and crept along as they stared out of the windows, looking for the right house.

'What number was it again?' asked Capstan.

'142.'

'Well it must be up the other end; I've got 7 on this side.'

'Hold on Sir, I've got 386, so it must be half-way up.'

Several minutes later, having managed to identify the correct house by the clever use of door numbers, and after Dewbush had seen the council's refuse truck parked directly outside along with a group of men, all taking pictures of what seemed to be just an ordinary black, General Waste wheelie bin, Capstan said, 'Give them a quick blast of the siren, will you please, Dewbush? I don't fancy going through all the formal introduction stuff.'

Pulling up to the curb, and having turned on the siren for just two seconds, they stepped out, Capstan taking a little longer than his colleague as he still depended on a stick to walk. His doctor had told him that he'd probably need the aid of one for the remainder of his life. His encounter with Rebecca of Bath and her Roman Army the previous summer had left many lasting impressions on him, but the most obvious was a pronounced limp and a somewhat crooked jaw.

Hobbling up to the group of refuse collectors, Capstan asked, 'We understand that someone's found a body?'

Having spent the last half hour taking photographs, calling up their wives and girlfriends, and generally having a jolly good laugh about the whole thing, the group of men all began to look somewhat disconcerted. Few people enjoyed being in such close proximity to the police, as just about everyone had done something during their lives that they'd rather not be known to the Law, and so they all decided to clam-up, apart from the oldest who must have been their foreman, or something.

'Yeah, that's right. It's in the bin. Right there, in the fuck'n bin! We've ne'er seen any 'fin like it. A real-life fuck'n body, in a real-life fuck'n bin. And it's a fuck'n wheelie bin as well! A real-life fuck'n body in a real-life fuck'n wheelie bin!'

And just in case there was any question as to where the body was, he pointed at it before taking another picture.

Dewbush pulled out his notebook and carefully wrote, "The body is in the bin," and then looked up, ready to take down the next important clue.

Meanwhile, Capstan lifted the lid of the bin under discussion, glanced inside and closed it again.

'And what's your name?' he asked the speaker.

'Dan. I'm the driver.'

Dewbush returned to his notebook and wrote down, "Driver Dan," and then looked up again.

Capstan continued his investigations. 'Did you see anyone near the bin when you arrived?'

After looking around at his cohort of chums, who were all clearly unwilling to admit to anything at all, not without having seen a lawyer first, the driver was forced to continue acting as their spokesman.

'Not that you'd notice. Just the normal really.'

'I don't suppose you know who lives here?'

None of them had a clue, and unless the home owner was a buxom blonde who made a habit of standing naked in the doorway, waving to them as they emptied her bins, it was unlikely that they would have done.

'And when did you realise there was a body in it? Don't you just empty them straight out?'

'Well, yes, normally that's what we do, but cus it's so fuck'n cold we have to check that the lids ain't frozen on first.'

'And what do you do if the lids are frozen on?'

He was asking more out of personal curiosity. It hadn't happened to his bins before, but it had been colder than normal recently.

'We av't leave a note on it saying that we can't empty ya fuck'n bin today cus its fuck'n lid is fuck'n frozen.'

Assuming that such a note wouldn't actually say, "Sorry, but we've been unable to empty your fucking bin today because the fucking lid is fucking frozen," Capstan moved on. 'And who was it who discovered the body?'

'Percy did,' the driver said, now pointing at one of the refuse collectors who gave Capstan a wide, innocent grin, but was unwilling to offer a verbal response, still happy to let his boss continue speaking on his behalf.

'He saw some'n strange and called us over to take a butchers.'

Dewbush wrote down, "Saw something strange, taken to butchers," and looked up again.

'So, anyways, he was fuck'n dead alright, so I called the police.'

'And how did you know he was dead?' asked Capstan.

'How'd mean?'

'Well, he might have still been alive.'

'Oh no, I've seen fuck'n dead people before, and that'n was one of 'um.'

'Really?' asked Capstan, eager to learn exactly how this man had been able to gain such intimate knowledge of what dead people looked like.

'Yeah, dead people aren't like regular people, ya' know.'

'Oh! And how's that then?'

'Cus they're dead.'

Capstan made a mental note to make sure Dewbush took down the man's name, address, national insurance number, driver's licence and passport details, and to collect a DNA sample before letting him go – and then to make sure he was followed. He knew far too much about dead people to be left wandering the streets of Portsmouth without someone keeping an eye on him.

Just then a car pulled up and began reversing into the drive.

Leaning over to Dewbush, Capstan whispered, 'Take down all their details before you let them go, and make sure we know exactly where *that* man lives,' and indicated with his eyes that he was referring to the driver, who he now considered to be his prime suspect.

'Yes, Sir!'

Capstan then observed what looked to be a vaguely attractive young lady climbing out of the now parked car and walking over towards them.

'Is everything alright?' she asked. 'The lid's not frozen on again, is it?'

'No, miss,' said the driver, 'there's a dea…'

'Thank you!' Capstan butted in. 'We'll take it from here.'

Pulling out his police identification, he made a formal introduction.

'I'm Inspector Capstan and this is my colleague, Sergeant Dewbush, Solent Police. And you are?'

'Who, me?'

'Yes, you, Miss. Your name is...?'

'Oh, Cate. Cate Jakebury. That's my bin!'

'And you live here, do you?'

'No, I just own the bin.'

Looking a little confused, Capstan glanced over at Dewbush who was carefully writing, "Cate Jakebury, bin owner."

'Of course I live here!' she said, and under her breath muttered, '*moron*,' but too quietly for Capstan to hear, and Dewbush wasn't paying attention as he was too busy rubbing out, "Bin owner" to replace it with, "Home owner".

'And do you live here on your own, Miss Jakebury?'

'No, I live here with my husband. Why? What's all this about? Is there something wrong with my bin?'

'And where is your husband now, Mrs Jakebury?'

'I've no idea. He didn't come home last night.'

'Is that normal?'

'What, that he didn't come home? No, not really, but he's been working late a lot recently.'

As she talked, Capstan observed her face for signs of undue stress, but none were obvious. She simply looked like an almost attractive young lady. There *was* something unusual about her eyes that he couldn't quite make out, but it was nothing suspicious. They just made him feel uneasy, somehow. They didn't give him the impression that she was lying, they just looked odd. And as she seemed to be completely in the dark about what might be in the bin, and the possible whereabouts of her husband, he said, 'Now, Mrs Jakebury, I want you to prepare yourself for a shock.'

Taking half a step back she gave him a worried look before asking, 'You're not a strip-o-gram are you?'

Dewbush snorted.

'No, of course I'm not!' said Capstan, as he narrowed his eyes at his Sergeant. 'It's about your husband.'

'What about him?'

'Well, it would seem that a body of a man has been discovered in your bin this morning, and if you say that your husband didn't come home last night, it may well be that it's him.'

'What is?' she asked.

'The body, in the bin.'

'Really? What on Earth is my husband doing in the bin?' and she pushed past him, marched over to it, pulled opened the lid and peered inside before exclaiming, 'That's not my husband!'

Somewhat surprised, Capstan asked, 'Are you sure, Miss?'

'Yes, of course I'm sure. My husband's got dark hair. That man's got white hair, and it's all sparkly.'

'But, Miss, you hardly looked at...'

'Are you suggesting that I don't know what my husband looks like?' and she dropped the lid back down and gave Capstan a peculiar glare.

'Well, no, of course not, but maybe if you could have another look, just to make sure.'

For a few moments she continued to stare at him, without blinking, almost as if she'd slipped into a coma, but after two or three seconds her face brightened and she smiled a sweet, home-baked sort of a smile.

'Yes, of course I can.'

She opened the lid again, reached in with a hand, prodded the body a bit and then turned back to look at Capstan.

'So?' he asked. 'Is it your husband?'

'Nope!'

'Then who the hell is it?'

'WELL, I DON'T BLOODY KNOW!'

They stared at each other for a moment before Cate asked, 'May I go in now? It is just a little bit too cold to be standing around chatting about some dead guy that neither one of us seems to know.'

'Well, I suppose so, but we're going to have to seal off your bin, at least until forensics arrive.'

'Fine, but can you please find me another one? I'm planning on throwing out some old clothes today. Oh, and whilst you're there, can someone please keep a look out for my husband? He really should be home by now and I'm becoming rather worried.'

'When did you last see him?'

'When he went to work, yesterday morning.'

'I'm very sorry, Mrs Jakebury, but we can't file a missing person's report until forty-eight hours have elapsed.'

'Yes, that's what I thought. Oh, well - but if you can't find my husband, can you at least find me a bin?'

She opened the front door and stepped inside before adding, 'And preferably one that's empty. I've got a huge amount of stuff to throw out. Thank you.'

And with that she disappeared inside and closed the door.

Act 1, Scene 4
Vente porte à porte
Selling, door-to-door

"Can one desire too much of a good thing?"
As You Like It, Act IV, Scene I

'STRANGE woman,' muttered Capstan.

'Do you think she's lying, Sir?'

'About what?'

'About the bin, Sir.'

'Oh no, I'm sure it's hers alright. It's even got her house number painted on it.'

'I meant not knowing about the body, Sir.'

'I don't see why. If it's not her husband, then it's not her husband! And I can't see why on earth she'd kill a complete stranger and then dump the body in her General Waste bin, only to leave it directly outside her house. If she had decided to murder someone on her driveway, she'd at least have had the sense to leave the body in the neighbour's bin. I said she was strange, not completely stupid.'

'No, Sir, of course, Sir.'

'It's much more likely to be the driver of the refuse truck. What was his name again?'

Dewbush looked back down at his notes.

'Dan, Sir.'

'Yes, that's the one.'

'But why would he have left a body in a bin outside someone's house?'

For about the twelve-millionth time, Capstan found himself questioning his Sergeant's IQ level and just exactly how he'd managed to pass the police entrance exam. But as he was in a surprisingly good mood, probably because he actually had a decent case to work on, and wasn't having to deal with some sad domestic dispute, or a fight over some girl outside a pub, he went easy on his subordinate.

'Honestly, Dewbush, if you ever want to become a police inspector like me, you're going to have to put your brain into gear occasionally. The driver, Dan, knew he was going to pick the body up when he did his rounds. He also knew that once dumped into the back of that refuse truck, there was no way it would have been discovered. But he slipped up!'

'What, on the ice, Sir?'

'No, you moronic, half-brained, dim-witted twat! He slipped up by forgetting that it was winter, and that someone would have to check that the lid wasn't frozen on before tipping it out. But as you'll learn, well, at least I hope you do at some point between now and the end of time, criminals *always* make some sort of mistake.'

Dewbush was becoming more than just a little pissed-off with his boss's seemingly continuous sarcastic attitude towards him, let alone the verbal abuse. He knew he didn't have Capstan's natural mental aptitude for the job, but wished he didn't have to be reminded of the fact quite so obviously, and quite so often. But just then he had what he honestly thought was a good idea.

'Do you think we should talk to the neighbours? Maybe they killed the man and did what you just suggested; left the body in the bin next door.'

'That's more like it, Dewbush. Well done! Tell you what, I'll see if they're in, and while I'm doing that, you can head over there and take down the details of the bin men; especially the driver, and the other guy, the one who found the body.'

'Yes, Sir,' came Dewbush's upbeat response, and as he crossed to where the refuse collectors were still hanging about, Capstan headed over to the house opposite.

When he'd finally managed to make his way up the path to the neighbour's house, he rang the bell and waited. There was no reply, so he rang again, and was about to give up when he heard someone shuffling around inside.

Eventually a thin, frail voice came from behind the still closed door.

'Yes? Is somebody there?'

'It's the police. Could you possibly open up?'

'Not today, thank you.'

'I just have a few questions…'

'I said, not today, thank you very much.'

'Madam, I just…'

'I'm not a madam, I'm a mister!'

'Oh, er, sorry, mister, I'm Inspector Capstan, from the police. I just have a few…'

'Whatever it is that you're selling, I don't want it!'

'I'm not trying to sell you anything, I just want to ask you a few questions.'

'That's what they all say. Now bugger off before I call the police.'

'But I *am* the police!'

'If you're the police, then why are you standing outside my front door trying to sell me something?'

'But I'm not!'

'Of course you're not. You just get paid to knock on people's doors to engage in polite conversations. Now I mean it. If you don't go away, I'm dialling 999.'

Capstan was almost tempted to let him call the police, but then realised that they'd just have to go through the whole thing again, with no guarantee of a more successful outcome, so he gave up.

'Sorry to have taken up your time. I'm leaving now.'

'Good! And make sure you don't come back. I've had just about enough of door-to-door sales people coming round here all the bloody time!'

As Capstan turned away, questioning society's obsession with keeping old people alive for as long as possible for no obvious reason, he saw a white police van make its way slowly up the road. He watched as it pulled up to the curb, the doors opened and a number of people, all dressed head to foot in white overalls, hopped out like giant earless bunnies.

His phone rang.

'It's all go,' he said to himself with a rare smile, and as he limped towards the Forensics team, he pulled the phone from his jacket pocket and pressed it to his ear.

'Capstan here!'

There were a few moments of quiet as he listened to the caller before he responded with, 'Right! We'll be on our way,' and ended the call. He headed straight over to the man he assumed must be David Planklock, the Solent Police's Chief Forensics Officer. All the members of the police Forensics department looked virtually identical whenever they were out in the field, but he could always make Planklock out as he was the only one who ever had a clipboard.

'Morning, Planklock.'

'Oh, morning, Capstan,' Planklock replied, pulling down his white mask to aid inter-personnel communication. 'What's been going on here then?'

'There's a body of a white male in that General Waste wheelie bin,' Capstan responded, pointing.

'Right you are. Any clues?'

'Not really. The woman who lives here told us that although her husband didn't come home last night, the body isn't him, so we need a formal ID and a cause of death. For all we know, it could be some homeless guy who just climbed into it when looking for something to eat, and couldn't get out again.'

'Yes, very possibly,' said Planklock, rubbing his chin as he reflected back over his many years of professional experience. 'It wouldn't have been the first time, and it's hardly the sort of weather you'd want to end up stuck inside a wheelie bin.'

'Quite!' replied Capstan. 'Anyway, I've got to head up to Southampton. There's been another body reported there, lying on the pavement outside an office block. That one does sound more like a suicide, but you may be called up to take a look yourself at some point.'

'Ah, okay. We'll push on here with this one then. If it is some homeless chap, then it won't take long to wrap up.'

Looking over towards Dewbush, Capstan called out, 'Are you done yet?'

Dewbush strode over to him as he finished off his notes.

'Yes, Sir. Just about. '

'Good. We need to head up to Southampton. Another body's been found!'

'Another one! Really?'

'Yes, another one!'

'That's great Sir.'

'Yes! Feels good to be busy, for a change,' and they climbed back into their car and left the scene with the obligatory wheel spin and an acrid smell of burnt rubber.

Act 1, Scene 5

Rien à voir ici

Nothing to see here

"If you prick us, do we not bleed?"
The Merchant of Venice, Act III, Scene I

ARRIVING AT Ocean Marina Village in Southampton, they had no need to look out for door numbers this time, as a large crowd had already gathered around where the second body of the day had been discovered. There was also an ambulance at the scene, along with three police cars, and various constables, who'd already closed the area off with the traditional blue and white "POLICE DO NOT CROSS" tape.

As they approached, Dewbush gave a quick blast of their siren, and the entire crowd looked up at them, so making them feel very important.

'Where shall I park, Sir?'

'I really don't think it matters, Dewbush. Here will probably do.'

'Right you are, Sir.' Dewbush stopped the car, double-checked that the siren was definitely off, and then stepped out to wait for his boss, who'd had a real struggle getting in and out of cars ever since he'd been stampeded over by a horse, two chariots and a couple of thousand Roman centurions the previous year.

As they headed towards the crowd, a police constable walked over to them.

'Morning, Inspector. It's a bit of a mess, I'm afraid, Sir, but looks like a bog-standard suicide.'

'Okay, we'd better take a look,' and as the three of them made their way towards what must have been over a hundred people, all standing on their toes taking pictures and videos, Capstan asked, 'Isn't there some way you can get the people back? We're not exactly giving a free street performance.'

'Well, Sir, we've told them all that there's nothing to see, but unfortunately they can all see that there is most definitely something to see, especially as he's splatted out all over the pavement.'

'Oh, very well.' As they pushed their way through the throng of general public, it became abundantly clear what the police constable was referring to. The body had split, right down the middle, and bits that were supposed to be inside him were now outside, and had pebble-dashed the wall of the office block and two cars parked next to him.

Dewbush gagged at first sight. He'd never seen anything quite like it before, and now wished he hadn't.

Capstan didn't much like the look of it either, but had at least seen numerous pictures of dead people during his Fast-Track Graduate Police Training Programme, and so was a little more prepared.

Stepping away, Capstan looked up to try and see which window he would have fallen from, asking the constable, who seemed unfazed by the whole affair, 'Any idea who he is?'

'Yes, Sir,' and pulled out his own little black book. 'It's Peter Herbert, a literary agent and partner of the firm Fairdown & Herbert. They have an office on the ninth floor, second from the top.'

Capstan imagined someone falling all the way down and shuddered.

'Were there any witnesses?'

'None that have stepped forward Sir, but their receptionist is over there by the ambulance. Liz Brook-Miller, Sir. Mild shock, nothing serious.'

'Right, we'd better start with her then. Thank you, Constable. If you could just try and keep everyone back as best you can, that would be helpful.'

'Yes Sir. I'll have another go at telling them that there's nothing to see, Sir.'

Capstan glanced over at Dewbush, who still looked a little peaky.

'Are you alright to continue?'

'Yes, Sir. I just wasn't expecting it to be quite so…graphic.'

'You'll get used to it. Come on, we'll go and have a chat to that girl. That will help take your mind off it.'

They made their way over to the ambulance as the police constable they'd just been talking to started calling out behind them, 'There's nothing to see here, please move along. Nothing to see, really, no, there isn't,' but he wasn't sounding particularly convinced himself.

Sitting on the back of the open ambulance was a pretty girl with a red blanket over her shoulders holding a smouldering cigarette as she stared out into space.

Pulling out his formal ID, Capstan introduced himself.

'Good morning, Miss. I'm Police Inspector Capstan and this is Sergeant Dewbush. Is it alright if we ask you a few questions?'

'He was in his office,' she said, still with a vacant look about her. 'He seemed quite happy. He even said I looked nice!'

'Right, but is it okay if we ask you a couple of questions?'

'Maybe he did it because I forgot to make him a coffee. I should have made him that coffee. That was stupid of me. I'll remember next time.'

'Hello! Miss! We're from the police! We'd just like to ask you a couple of questions.'

'Oh, but there won't be a next time will there; because he's dead. He's just dead! Just completely dead! Absolutely and completely dead! Just totally, absolutely and completely dead!'

Capstan glanced over at Dewbush, who just shrugged back at him, and as they both looked down at the girl, she turned her head to stare wistfully towards where her boss lay. 'And he won't be coming back,' and with a sagacious look added, 'At least I hope he won't, not looking like that at any rate.' Then she took a pull on her cigarette and returned to just staring out at nothing.

Capstan was about to have another go at talking to her when she started up again.

'And now I'm going to have to cancel all his meetings, and Sir Benjamin Duberforce is due in this afternoon, back from circumnavigating his grandson's Optimist dinghy around the Isle of Wight, single-handed. He wants to write a book about it and we were going to agree on a title. My favourite was *Crampt At Sea*, but Peter preferred *Voyage of the Damned*, as he thought it sounded more dramatic, and also because Sir Benjamin had just said, "Damn!" all the way round. But Peter is dead now, so I suppose his opinion doesn't really matter. If only I'd made him that coffee!'

'I am very sorry, Miss, truly I am,' said Capstan.

She finally looked up at him; and as he seemed to have engaged her attention, he continued, 'But you really shouldn't blame yourself. I'm sure he wouldn't have killed himself just because you forgot to make him a coffee.'

'Yes, I suppose you're right. I'm sorry, but who are you again?'

'Police Inspector Capstan, Miss, and this is Sergeant Dewbush. Is it alright if we ask you a few questions?'

'Oh, yes, of course. Sorry, I was miles away.'

Before she fazed out again, Capstan thought he'd better push on.

'Do you know if he was worried about anything in particular; marriage, relationships, money?'

'No, not that I know of.'

'How about the business; was that okay?'

'As far as I know, yes. Peter always seemed so happy, like he never had a care in the world, and was the last person I'd have thought to have done... *that* to himself.'

'What about his business partner?'

'Who? Oh, you mean Frank Fairdown. No, he disappeared a few years back now; trying to sail to the Caribbean from Land's End in a Mirror dinghy he bought off Ebay. He never came back. We just continued to run the business with his name, sort of in memory of him, but nobody could really see the point of changing it.'

'Would you mind if we took a look at his office?'

She looked up and smiled.

'Yes, of course. I'll take you up myself. I need to get back to work anyway. Follow me!'

Dropping her cigarette on the floor she took the blanket off her shoulders, stood up, made a point of stepping on the discarded cigarette, and began walking around the crowd towards the front of the building, with Capstan and Dewbush following behind.

On the ninth floor, the elevator doors opened and she led the way in. 'It's just through here.'

She opened her deceased boss's office door and ushered them inside.

'Nice view!' said Dewbush.

Nobody responded.

'So, is this exactly how it was when he, um, went out the, er…?' asked Capstan, not sure if it was too early to use either the words "window" or "jumped" quite so soon after the event.

'Yes, just as it was. I haven't touched a thing. I only popped my head in after going round the back to make him a coffee, as Cate had suggested. She said that he didn't seem very happy, but when I looked in, he wasn't here. I couldn't find him anywhere! I just assumed that he must have slipped past my desk to go to the loo when I was putting the kettle on. So I thought I'd pop outside for a cigarette, and that's when I saw…' and she slipped back into her former trance-like state.

'So which, er, window did he, um…from?'

'I've really no idea.'

'But wasn't there a window open when you came in?'

'Oh no. It was exactly like it is now. As I said, I haven't touched a thing.'

Dewbush, who'd been having a look over Mr Herbert's desk, suddenly called out, 'Sir, there's something here,' and picked up a piece of paper. 'Looks like a suicide note, Sir,' and before anyone had a chance to stop him, he read it out.

'"I can't take it anymore!"'

There was a stunned silence, so Dewbush added, 'That's what it says, Sir.'

'Thank you, Dewbush, but would you mind not picking up what could quite possibly be a key piece of evidence at what is now the scene of a murder investigation?'

There was an audible gasp from the receptionist, who'd covered her mouth with her hands as she stared, wide-eyed at Capstan.

'How do you mean, Sir? I thought he just jumped out the window?'

Capstan took a deep breath. 'Yes, thank you again, Dewbush, but as I fail to understand how someone would be able to close the very window that they'd just jumped out from, I think it's safe to assume that he was pushed out. Call Forensics will you? This is now an official crime scene!'

'Yes, Sir, right away, Sir!'

'And put down the bloody note, you muppet-brained moron!'

Dewbush looked back at the piece of paper he still held in his hands and slowly placed it down on the desk, spending several moments making sure that it was in exactly the same place as it was before he'd picked it up.

'Just leave it alone, for Christ's sake, Dewbush!'

'Yes, Sir, of course, Sir. Sorry, Sir,' and he changed the angle ever so slightly, before pulling both hands away.

'Now, Miss,' Capstan said, looking back at the receptionist, who still had her eyes wide open and her hands covering her mouth. 'Who did you say was here before, the one who said that he didn't seem very happy?'

'Oh, that was Cate.'

'Cate..?'

'Cate Jakebury. She's one of our clients.'

It was now Capstan's turn to stare at her.

'I'm sorry, but what did you say her name was again?'

'Cate Jakebury.'

Without taking his eyes off the receptionist, Capstan called back to Dewbush. 'What was the name of that girl we met earlier Dewbush; the one with the bin, and the body?'

Dewbush opened up his notebook.

'Cate Jakebury, Sir. Do you think it's the same girl?'

Capstan sighed. 'No, Dewbush, I think it's a completely different girl who just happens to have exactly the same name and has a body of another dead man stuffed inside her General Waste wheelie bin that she left right outside her very own house.'

'Really, Sir? So you think there are two of them?'

'NO, OF COURSE I DON'T THINK THERE ARE TWO OF THEM, YOU STUPID, MORONIC, HALF-BRAINED FUCK-WIT!'

'I'm sorry, Sir. I thought you were being serious.'

Capstan took a long, deep breath. 'Look, just give Planklock a call, will you? I'm going to pop down and get some more of that blue police tape. Looks like we're going to have to get this whole floor sealed off, and then I suggest we go back to have a chat with our Mrs Cate Jakebury!'

Act 1, Scene 6

Pouviez-vous enlever vos chaussures s'il vous plaît?
Could you take your shoes off please?

"The first thing we do, let's kill all the lawyers."
King Henry the Sixth, Part Two, Act IV, Scene II

BACK IN Portsmouth, they pulled up quietly outside Mrs Jakebury's house, made their way up to her front door and rang the bell.

After only a few moments, a rather flustered looking Cate pulled it open, stared out and said, 'Yes? Oh, it's you two again. Good timing! Here, can you take these out for me?'

A rather surprised Capstan looked down at two large black bin bags and, not knowing what else to do, took one from her and said, 'Er, well I suppose we could. Where do you want them?'

'Oh, just around the side please. And by the way, they've still not found me another bin, so maybe one of you can sort that out whilst you're here?'

'Tell you what,' said Capstan, looking over at Dewbush, 'I'll take these two and you go around and get next door's bin. I'm sure they won't mind if we borrow it for a while.'

'Yes, Sir.'

But then Capstan remembered his leg, and changed his mind.

Hold on, Dewbush, you'd better take these and I'll get the bin. It's my leg, I'm afraid. I just can't carry them.'

Dewbush took one of the bags from his boss, and the other from Cate, and then attempted to lift them both up.

'Crikey, Mrs Jakebury, what've you got in these?'

'Oh, just some old clothes. Thanks, you two. Come in when you're done and I'll make you something hot to drink.'

Trying to work out why they were helping their brand new prime suspect to throw away some old clothes, Capstan limped his way over the shared drive towards next-door's bin and, with one hand, tipped it onto its wheels and rumbled it over. He then opened the lid and Dewbush hefted both bags inside before they both returned to the front door.

Seeing that it had been left ajar, Capstan pushed it open to hear Mrs Jakebury call out from the kitchen at the back of the house.

'Thanks again! That was very kind of you. If you can just take your shoes off, you can come in.'

'Right you are,' he called out, and slowly bent down, still holding on to his stick, to remove his shoes. He then glanced up at his Sergeant. 'Well, Dewbush, take your shoes off!'

'Do I have to, Sir?'

'Yes, of course you have to!'

While Dewbush reluctantly removed his footwear, Capstan made his way towards the kitchen.

'Tea or coffee?' Cate asked.

'Tea, please. Milk, one sugar; and my colleague will have the same.'

Cate smiled at him and opened up the cupboard above where the kettle sat.

'So anyway,' she said, 'what have you come to talk to me about? You haven't found my husband, have you?'

'Er, no, not yet Mrs Jakebury, it's, er…'

But now that it was time to start questioning her about how, and why, she'd murdered Peter Herbert, her literary agent, Capstan felt a little odd; probably because he'd just helped her throw some old clothes away, was standing in her kitchen without any shoes on, and was now being made a nice cup of tea. It just didn't feel like the right time to start interrogating someone who, earlier that day, may have purposefully shoved someone out of a ninth storey office window.

'It's about Peter Herbert, Mrs Jakebury.'

'Oh, really? Do you know him? Don't tell me you're writing a book!'

'Er, no, Mrs Jakebury.'

She pulled out three mugs from the cupboard, and looked around for some tea bags, asking with a pre-occupied tone, 'What's it about?'

'Er,' he answered.

'Have you finished it yet?'

'Um, no, Mrs Jakebury, I haven't actually…'

The kettle was boiling furiously, and she opened a drawer near the sink to rummage around for a tea spoon.

'Do you have a title for it? That's the most important thing. That and the cover.'

'Er…'

Finding a teaspoon, she looked back at him and smiled.

'If you need a book cover designer I know just the girl. She did my first one. It was a masterpiece. Remind me to give you her email.'

Dewbush joined them, and to prove he'd been following their conversation from out in the hall, said, 'I didn't know you were writing a book, Sir!'

Capstan looked at him with narrowing eyes.

'As I said, I'm *not* writing a book!'

Cate finished pouring the boiled water into the three mugs, looked up at Capstan and said, 'Oh, sorry, I thought you said you were.'

'No, Mrs Jakebury. I just said that we're here about Peter Herbert.'

'Yes, that's right. Sorry, I just assumed you'd been talking to him about a book you were writing. Do you know that he's my book agent?'

'We are aware of that Mrs Jakebury, yes.'

'So you know that I'm a published author then?'

'Yes, Mrs Jakebury, we do.'

'That's great! You know, I hate having to tell people all the time. It's much easier if they find out from someone else. Let me fetch you a copy of my novel,' and she pushed past them both, and headed for the dining room from where she called out, *'Do you both want one?'*

Capstan looked at Dewbush and grimaced. He didn't even know how to answer her.

'Er, no, Mrs Jakebury. Just the one book would be fine.'

There was a slight pause in the conversation before they heard her ask, 'Who should I say it's for?'

Capstan pushed past Dewbush and followed on after her. He'd never told anyone at work his first name before, and the whole situation was becoming rather awkward.

As he entered, he saw her leaning over a hard-backed copy of an immense book, poised with a fountain pen, ready to write something on the inside cover.

'Oh, um, if you could just say it's for Andrew,' he whispered.

She smiled and wrote, "For Andrew. May all your wind be fair!"

Then she closed it up and gave it to him along with a huge smile.

'Oh,' he said, taking it from her. 'Thank you very much.'

Pushing past him again she asked, 'Did you say you wanted milk and sugar?'

Embarrassed and confused, Capstan looked down at the cover and called out, 'Yes, please. Milk and one sugar, for both of us, thank you!'

Then he read the title of the book out to himself.

'*A Strong Wind Blew Over My Bows.*'

He raised an eyebrow, and then peeked inside to see what she'd written.

Moments later, Cate reappeared with two mugs, and Dewbush followed behind, carrying his own.

'Come through to the sitting room,' and as they followed her through the adjoining door, she said, 'I must admit, Andrew, I didn't have you pegged for someone who'd be interested in Elizabethan naval romance.'

Again, he didn't know how to respond, and for want of anything better to say, responded with, 'It's a new interest I seem to be developing.'

'Well, you'll enjoy that one. I'll let you know when I've finished my next. Now, do sit down, please, both of you, and I'll tell you what it's about.'

Realising that they could end up being there all day, without ever having the chance to ask her a single pertinent question relating to the murder of Peter Herbert, Capstan sat down, took a deep breath and said, 'I regret to inform you, Mrs Jakebury, that Mr Herbert's been found dead outside his office in Southampton.'

Perching on the edge of one of her floral armchairs, Cate looked at him with her mouth half open.

'Really!' she exclaimed, and then took a sip from her tea.

'I'm afraid so. And we understand that you had a meeting with him this morning.'

'Yes, that's right, I did. How awful! Do you know how it happened?'

'I was going to ask you that very same question, Mrs Jakebury,' and both Capstan and Dewbush stared at her.

'Well, he was fine when I left him. He did seem a little depressed about something, but I've been told that's quite normal. Apparently, he's never got over the shock of losing his business partner. Did you hear about what happened to him? Imagine trying to sail all the way to the Caribbean in a tiny boat made of plywood!'

Ignoring what he saw as a poor attempt at changing the subject, Capstan continued by asking, 'Can you tell me what the meeting was about?'

'Oh, yes, of course! He was very keen to help me publish my second book and we were just chatting about it.'

'Well, it would seem that he somehow "fell" out of his office window.'

Cate took another sip from her tea and said, 'Oh dear, how dreadful!'

'We did find a note,' added Capstan, and found himself suppressing a grin. He'd just realised that by signing her book, she'd inadvertently given him a sample of her handwriting that they could use for analysis against the alleged suicide note.

'Oh dear,' she said again. 'Well, I did tell Liz that he didn't seem very happy when I left. He must have been having one of his "dark" days.'

'The problem is,' Capstan continued, 'that when we had a look around his office, we couldn't find an open window.'

She took another sip from her tea, paused, and then asked, 'Sorry, why is that a problem? Are you not allowed to keep office windows closed anymore? Is there some sort of new "fresh air" bill that's been passed that I've not heard about?'

'No, Mrs Jakebury. It's just that we've never heard of anyone killing themselves by leaping from an office window who closed it behind them, just before jumping.'

'Clearly you don't know Peter very well!' she said. 'He was always going on about energy saving. It was one of the reasons why he liked sailing so much, because the boats are powered by the natural force of the wind. He'd never have left a window open, not on such a bitterly cold day.'

'So, you're suggesting that he would have climbed out of his window, closed it, and then jumped?'

'Well, yes! It does sound like the sort of thing he would have done.'

Capstan glanced over at Dewbush before saying, 'But there wasn't even a ledge for him to stand on to close it!'

'I promise you, Peter would never have left his office window open during the middle of winter. He'd have found some way to close it before jumping. Now, can I get anyone some more tea?'

Realising that his only reason for assuming that Peter Herbert had been murdered was that he'd never thought someone would take the time to close the window before leaping out, Capstan was beginning to feel rather stupid, and was only pleased that he wasn't having this suggested to him by a defence lawyer during a public murder trial.

He took a sip from what was now a lukewarm mug of tea and said, 'Thank you for your time, Mrs Jakebury, but we'd better be off.'

'Oh, it's been my pleasure.'

As all three of them stood up, Capstan said, 'And thank you for the book. That was very kind of you.'

She smiled at him.

'Let me show you out.'

Leading them into the hall, she added, 'Do pop by again when my next book is finished, and I'll give you another signed copy.'

Watching them as they began putting their shoes back on, she asked, 'Should I phone you tomorrow, if my husband still hasn't shown up? Would that have been forty-eight hours since he went missing?'

Capstan sighed, and with his shoes back in place, searched his pockets for one of the rarely-used business cards that bore both his mobile number and email address.

'Here you are, Mrs Jakebury. Just call me on that number tomorrow and we'll start an official enquiry into the whereabouts of your husband, but I'm sure he'll turn up somewhere. He probably stayed over at a friend's house, and forgot to tell you.'

'Oh, well, I do hope so. Now, take care down the steps. They're probably still a little icy.'

As she watched them make their way down the path, and with Capstan's business card in her hand, she waved goodbye to them from her doorway before shuddering, closing the door and heading back inside to turn the heating up.

Act 1, Scene 7
Savez-vous grand-chose à l'informatique?
Do you know anything about computers?

"Some rise by sin, and some by virtue fall."
Measure for Measure, Act II, Scene I

P ASSING CHIEF INSPECTOR Morose's office, as they always had to in order to get to their own, they heard him call out, 'Capstan, Dewbush, can you come in here for a moment, please?'

Cringing, Capstan said, 'Bugger,' to himself and pivoted around on his stick to head back the other way.

'C'mon Dewbush, I suppose we'd better see what he wants.'

As they entered, they saw him sitting behind his desk wearing formal evening attire and bashing away at his laptop's keyboard, as if it were an innovative new percussion instrument that he was using to perform Alexander Tcherepnin's Second Symphony.

'Damn, bloody, stupid, fucking, bloody, machine!' Morose exclaimed, in perfect rhythm to the thrashing he was giving it. He then hit the ENTER key a few more times as a finale, before pushing it away from him and asking, 'I don't suppose either of you knows anything about computers?'

'I'm afraid not, Sir,' answered Capstan.

'Me neither, Sir. Sorry, Sir,' added Dewbush.

'No? Oh well, never mind,' and he started leafing through a file that sat open on his desk.

'Was that it, Sir?' asked Capstan.

Morose looked up and asked, 'Was what it?'

'Can we go now, Sir?'

'No, of course you can't bloody go!'

'Sorry, Sir, I thought you asked us in to help fix your computer.'

'Why the hell would I ask you in to fix my computer? You don't know anything about the damned things!'

'No, Sir. Sorry, Sir.'

Morose gave Capstan a sideways glare. 'So, anyway. How're those two murder cases coming along? I haven't seen any reports yet.'

'No, Sir. Well, we only found out about them this morning,' replied Capstan, 'and we're not even sure they are in fact murder cases at this stage, Sir.'

'How'd you mean? I've been told that someone was found dead in a bin and someone else had been thrown out of a ninth storey window. How can they possibly not be murder cases?'

'Well Sir, it would be easier to explain after we've written up our reports, Sir.'

'You can give me the basics now, can't you?'

Capstan hated having to talk to his new boss. Morose by name and morose by nature, the guy was just a miserable fat old bald-headed git, who'd apparently only been able to get the position by going to Oxford University, and then joining the Freemasons. With those two credentials on his CV he could have had any job he wanted, in the UK at least, but had asked to become a police chief inspector because he was very keen to spend the rest of his life shouting at people with minimal risk of being killed in the process, which of course ruled out the military. And he'd chosen the Solent Police as he was one of those weird sailing types who thought that sitting on a large plastic boat with lots of ropes to pull that floated around at a maximum speed of ten miles an hour, on a good day, and which always left you feeling both sick and wet, usually at the same time, was fun! And as Southampton was the mecca for British yachting types, the Solent Police had been an obvious choice.

As Capstan found himself wondering how someone quite so fat could ever possibly get onto a boat without it sinking, Morose waited patiently for him to answer, but eventually gave up. 'You *can* hear me Capstan, can't you? You're not deaf or something, or should I be using a megaphone?'

'No, Sir, sorry, Sir. I was just taking a moment to formulate my answer.'

'Well, can you hurry up please? Unlike you, I haven't got all bloody day. I've a dinner engagement this evening, I've got a stack of emails to get through and my sodding computer never does what I tell it!'

'Yes, Sir, of course, Sir.' He made an effort to change the subject. 'May I enquire as to who you're dining with?'

'None of your bloody business! Now are you going to tell me why a body found in a bin and a man who's been pushed out of a ninth storey window isn't murder, or am I going to have to get someone up here to beat it out of you?'

'Well, Sir, it's like this…'

Morose sat back in his black leather executive's chair and attempted to fold his arms over his enormous stomach.

Capstan took a deep breath.

'Planklock thinks that the body in the bin may have been a homeless person who climbed in last night looking for food, and then couldn't get out, and so he froze to death; and there really isn't any evidence to suggest that the man *was* pushed out of the window, and that it's more likely he jumped out because he wanted to, Sir.'

Morose leaned back even further in his chair and Capstan was beginning to hope that it might just collapse under his immense weight, causing him to have a massive heart attack, but it didn't; it just squeaked a bit.

There was a moment's pause, as Morose digested this information along with his lunch, and the four pints of Portsmouth Pride he'd had with it. Supressing a belch, he asked, 'Have you ever heard of a homeless person climbing into someone's bin, looking for food and then getting stuck?'

'No, Sir, but Planklock seems to think that it's the most likely explanation, Sir.'

'Yes, well, Planklock's an idiot! Did you talk to the bin owner?'

'Yes, we did, Sir, but she didn't seem to know anything about it, Sir.'

'Well, it won't be her, will it? Nobody's stupid enough to kill someone and then dump the body in their own bin! But did she see anyone suspicious hanging around it?'

Apart from the bin men, who all fitted that description perfectly - especially the driver - Capstan doubted it, but as he hadn't actually asked her, and wasn't prepared to admit that he'd forgotten to, he simply answered, 'No, Sir.'

There was a pause in the conversation, which gave Capstan time to remember just how much he hated having to say "Sir" all the bloody time; but unfortunately it was one of the very first lessons he'd been taught during his Fast Track Police Graduate Training Programme – that he was never, under any circumstances, to forget to say "Sir" at the beginning and end of each sentence when talking to a Chief Inspector, especially if it was a really fat miserable one with a bald head and who went by the name of Morose.

'How about the neighbour?'

'Yes, Sir. I did speak to the man who lived next door, but he wasn't very co-operative and wouldn't give me the chance to talk to him, Sir.'

'Well, it's probably him then. I suggest you head back down there, arrest him on suspicion of murder and bring him back for questioning.'

'Yes, Sir, but I, er, really don't think…'

'I don't give a shit what you *think*, Capstan. I expect you to *do*, not *think*!'

'Yes, Sir. Of course, Sir. Right away, Sir.'

But as Capstan and Dewbush started to edge backwards towards the door, Morose asked, 'And where the hell do you think you're going?'

Through gritted teeth, Capstan answered, 'To arrest the neighbour, Sir.'

'But you haven't explained to me why you think that the man who was pushed out of a ninth storey window wasn't murdered. I spoke to Planklock on his mobile and he said that none of the windows had been left open - is that correct?'

'Well, yes, Sir.'

'Then it's a murder investigation!'

'Possibly, Sir, yes, but we've just come back from interviewing the person who saw the, er, victim last, and she explained to us that he was particularly conscious about the environment, and would never have left a window open during the middle of winter, Sir.'

'Is that it?'

'There was also a suicide note, and he was into sailing, Sir.'

'Oh well, fair enough. At least we can put that "body in the bin" case down as a murder. If we don't get some more decent crime going on down here, I'm never going to get enough funding for next year, and these computers we've got are worse than useless.'

'Yes, Sir.'

'Well, off you pop then, and let me know when that man's confessed. I don't want any fuck-ups with this one. I want a signed confession and I really don't care how you go about getting it.'

'Yes, Sir, right away, Sir.'

'Good. I'd better be off. Call me on my mobile the moment he's admitted to it, and I'll let the press know we've been able to solve a murder in just a single day. That will get the attention of Head Office!'

'Yes, Sir. Right away, Sir.'

And as Morose used all his strength to push himself out of his chair, Capstan and Dewbush used their advanced knowledge of stealth tactics to slip out the door before their boss had a chance to order them down to the nearest old people's home, collect up all the residents and have them beaten up in a large holding cell, so that they could announce to the press that they'd miraculously been able to find the culprits to every major crime that had remained un-solved since 1931, and subsequently secure enough funding to buy some more up-to-date office equipment.

Act 2, Scene 1

Cinquante livres et une boîte de Ferrero Rocher

Fifty pounds and a box of Ferrero Rocher

"That it should come to this!"
Hamlet, Act I, Scene II

CATE JAKEBURY stood behind her lectern, waiting. She'd just asked her assembled audience of ninety-seven students a question, and was curious to know how long it would take before one of them came up with an answer.

'Anyone?' she prompted.

Seeing a solitary hand being slowly raised from the middle left hand side of the auditorium, she asked, 'Yes?'

The good-looking young man, who the hand belonged to, looked up from his copy of *War and Peace*, and then glanced behind him, to make sure she wasn't referring to somebody else.

'Yes, you!' she exclaimed again, and pointed directly at him.

'Who, me?'

She sighed.

'Well, you're the only person who seems to have their hand up.'

'Oh, er…right, of course, yes, sorry. I was just wondering which page we were on?'

Cate really wasn't cut out for this. She'd become a university lecturer for two main reasons, the first being that she was keen to have a dynamic engagement with highly intelligent young adults, all keen to learn about some of the greatest authors to have ever picked up a pen but who had, regretfully, passed away, like William Shakespeare, Charles Dickens, Jane Austen and Barbara Cartland; but all she ever seemed to get, year on year, was a bunch of brainless Neanderthal types who only seemed to be there because either their parents had insisted, or because they were wannabe authors, looking for inspiration, and an idea as to how to correctly structure a sentence. However, it was her final lecture on the very last day of the summer term, and she had nearly three months of holiday to look forward to; and that was the other reason she'd decided to become a lecturer. The long holidays gave her uninterrupted time to write, and with her late husband unable to be late ever again, and annoy her in the process, she was looking forward to finally having a chance to start her second book.

There was a knock at the door, and the University's Principal's secretary pushed her head in.

'Professor Dobbins would like to have a word with you, Cate.'

She rolled her eyes. This was hardly the first time she'd been summoned to see the University's Principal halfway through a lecture. She made her way over to the door and said in a low voice, 'I'm in the middle of a lecture, Mary, could I not drop by afterwards?'

'I'm sorry, Cate, but he wants to leave early to start his holidays.'

Cate looked back at her students, who seemed to have slipped into a mass coma, so in a bid to snap them out of it she called out, 'I just need to pop out for a moment. Whilst I'm gone, if you could all read page one thousand, four hundred and sixty seven. I think you'll find the answer there.'

She waited for a response, but there was none, so she added, 'I won't be long,' and then left them to it to chase after Mary, who was already halfway down the corridor.

Reaching the Professor's door, his secretary knocked and pushed it open.

'Cate Jakebury to see you, Professor.'

'Thank you, Mary. Cate, do come in.'

She entered the dark wood-panelled room that had been filled with old leather-bound books, two mannequins displaying highly polished suits of armour, and, above the unused fireplace, a shield that had a single sword slotted behind it. The other matching sword was being polished by the Professor as he sat behind his opulent antique desk.

Cate loved his office. It was just a shame that the person who occupied it was such a twat.

'Sit down, will you please?' Dobbins asked, without bothering to look up.

She fetched the chair that had been left in front of the fireplace when he climbed up to take the sword down from the wall.

Professor Dobbins carefully propped his sword up against the desk and, for the first time since she'd walked in, looked up at her.

'How are you?' he asked.

'Very well, thank you.'

'That's nice,' he said, and gave her a thin smile. 'I'm afraid I have some rather disappointing news for you.'

'Oh, really, what's that?'

He looked down at the single piece of paper that rested on his desk and said, 'It would seem that the Government is, once again, cutting back on their higher education spending next year, and the Board has therefore decided to close down our English Literature Department.'

'That's my department!'

'Yes, that's right.'

'And I'm the only one in it.'

'Correct again.'

'So, basically, you're firing me.'

'Yes.'

Cate then just sat there, and stared at him.

'If you could make this your last day, that would be great.'

She didn't respond, so he added, 'And I'll make sure you're paid up until the beginning of the next academic year.'

She continued to stare at him.

Professor Dobbins started to feel uncomfortable. He was used to firing people, and the emotional outburst that normally followed, but her response was highly irregular. So he decided that he'd better go into a little more depth as to why such a decision had been made.

'You see, Cate, it's just that you haven't been yourself lately, not since your husband, er...'

She still just sat there.

'And the results from your students this year have all been well below our expected average.'

Still nothing.

Dobbins shifted in his chair.

'Look, Cate, I can see that this has been a bit of a shock, but the decision's been made and it's completely out of my hands.'

Her eyes began to glaze over, and he was beginning to wonder if she'd managed to pass out without actually falling off her chair, but wasn't sure that was possible, so he carried on.

'It may have been different, if things had worked out between us.'

That caught her attention, and as her eyes refocussed on him, she blinked.

'I am still officially married, Professor Dobbins.'

'Yes, well…'

'And quite frankly, even if I wasn't, and you were the last male of the Homo Sapiens species left roaming Planet Earth whose bits were still fully functional, there's just no way I'd ever go to bed with you, despite your generous offer of fifty quid and a box of Ferrero Rocher.'

'But that was your decision, Cate, not mine.'

There was another pause in the conversation.

'So that's it then?' she asked.

'I'm afraid so.'

'I'm fired?'

'Made redundant would be the correct term, but yes, you are. Sorry.'

She shrugged her shoulders and sighed.

'Oh well, I suppose it just gives me more time to write. Did I ever tell you that I was a published author?'

She knew she'd never mentioned it. She hadn't told anyone at the university; after all, her book was hardly academic in content and she really didn't care for having her fellow lecturers laughing at her behind her back for writing what they'd probably all consider to be childish romantic nonsense. But it hardly seemed to matter now, so she thought she may as well start telling everyone in the vague hope that one of them might show an interest and actually buy a copy.

'No, I didn't know that, Cate. What do you write about?'

But now that she was being asked, she still found herself reluctant to talk about it, so she just said, 'Oh, historical fiction, mainly.'

Professor Dobbins gave her a condescending smile but failed to make any further enquiries about her writing.

'You know, Professor,' Cate said using a pleasant, conversational tone, 'I've always loved your office, especially your collection of weapons,' and she turned to have a look around.

Surprised by the fact that someone was finally showing an interest in his obsession with swords, knights, castles, damsels-in-distress, and huge great fiery dragons, the Professor sat up and said, 'Oh, thank you very much.'

'Are they real, those suits of armour?'

'They most certainly are! 16th Century!'

'And that sword,' she said, pointing at the one he'd been polishing. 'Is that real as well?'

'Absolutely! It's actually called a Cutlass. 18th Century,' and he stood up, took hold of the hilt and held it out to show her.

'Is it dangerous?'

'How do you mean?'

'Could it kill someone?'

He chuckled to himself.

'My dear, they were designed for just that purpose, so yes, in the right hands, it could most definitely kill someone.'

'May I hold it?'

'Of course! Here, take it by the hilt, and please, don't drop it. It's worth over £20,000.'

'Really!'

'Yes, indeed. I had this one and the one on the wall valued last year, for insurance purposes. As a pair they're worth at least £50,000! They're highly collectable.'

'Wow! And it's much heavier than you'd expect. So, is it sharp enough to go right through a man?'

'Of course!'

'Let's have a go,' she said, and ran him all the way through with it, and then let go, so that the hilt stuck to his suit jacket like an over-sized brooch.

Taken completely by surprise, the Professor stared down at his new fashion accessory, and just as it dawned on him that he had, indeed, been run through with his very own sword, there was a knock at the door and his secretary came in.

'Professor Dobbins, your wife's on line one.'

The Professor looked up at Mary, back down at the sword's hilt and then up at her again.

Mary looked surprised as well, and asked, 'Professor, what on Earth have you got stuck to your chest?'

Unable to speak, he looked at Cate, hoping she may be able to answer on his behalf.

'It's a sword Mary, haven't you seen one before?'

Cate then took hold of the hilt again, and pulled it all the way out from the Professor's chest, which acted as a cue for him to keel over and die.

Mary was trying to work out how the trick had been done, thinking that it must have had some kind of clever retractable blade, until she saw the blood dripping off its end. Then her eyes rolled back into her head, and she collapsed onto the floor.

'Shit,' said Cate. She really should have thought this through a little more. There was no way she'd be able to make this one look like a suicide, and the nearest wheelie bin was out in the carpark. There was also Mary to contend with. She had no intention of murdering her as well, even if she did wear too much makeup, but it wouldn't be long before she came round and started screaming, and Cate was going to need a fair amount of time to exit the building, and, at the rate she was going, possibly even the country. She looked around for something to use to tie her up. The curtains caught her eye and, in particular, the two cords that were used to hook them open.

'Perfect,' she said, and carefully propped the sword back up against the desk, took both curtain cords off, and knotted one round Mary's ankles, and the other round her hands, securing them behind her back. Then she had a look around for something to tape up her mouth. Seeing some Sellotape on the Professor's desk, she stripped off a piece and attempted to flatten it over Mary's lips, but it just kept coming off. The girl really did have far too much make up on.

'Shit,' she said again, and scanned the room for an alternative.

Seeing one of the suits of armour standing in the corner, she had an idea. She removed its helmet, carried it over to Mary and wedged her head inside it. It wouldn't shut her up, but would at least help to muffle her screams, and hopefully give Cate long enough to come up with some sort of a "Stay Out Of Jail" plan.

Retrieving the murder weapon, she left the office, making sure that the door was firmly closed behind her, and worked her way back towards her lecture hall, leaving a thin trail of blood behind her as it dripped from the end of the sword.

Back in the lecture room, ninety-seven pairs of eyes looked up from their tablets, laptops or smartphones. She gazed straight back at them and said, 'Right, I suppose you can all head off home.'

The room erupted with a cacophony of noise, forcing Cate to raise her voice to finish what she was about to say.

'Have a good holiday everyone, and do please try to finish reading *War and Peace*, if you can.'

As her students began their mass exodus, those who noticed what she held in her right hand all said, 'Nice sword, Miss!' as they filed past her on their way out.

Last to leave was the good-looking young man who'd had his hand up earlier. He'd had a crush on her since the beginning of the year, which had only intensified when he'd found out that her husband had disappeared. He knew this would be his very last chance to ask her out, so he edged his way up to the lectern where she now stood, cleared his throat and said, 'Excuse me, Cate, but I don't suppose you'd um, like to come to a party with me tonight, would you?'

She looked up at him, totally lost in thought and said, 'Huh?'

'Tonight. I don't suppose you'd like to come out with me? There's an end of year party going on at the Badger and Hamster in town.'

He then handed her a flyer, which she took off him and read the title out.

'"Party Like A Pirate!"?'

The young man looked a little embarrassed. 'Yes, well, it's one of our Pirate Parties, where we all dress up as, er, Pirates. We've had quite a few of them. Anyway, it's only £2 a pint, and I see you've already got the sword for it. Why don't you come? I could meet you outside at, say, eight o'clock?' He winced, waiting to be turned down flat.

She looked back down at the flyer, then at the sword, then at the flyer and finally back at him.

'Fuck it,' she said, 'why not?' and gave him a flirtatious smile.

He beamed back. 'That's great! That's really great! So, I'll see you outside the pub at eight then?'

'Absolutely!' she answered, and then thought to ask, 'Er, sorry, but where is the Badger and Hamster?'

'Oh, it's the pub right opposite HMS Victory, along the quayside. You can't miss it.'

'Sorry again, but I'm really not very good with names. You are..?'

'Peter!' he replied.

'That's right, of course, yes, Peter. Well, Peter, I suppose I'll see you there at eight then.'

He bounced backwards towards the door, grinning like a love-struck chimpanzee. 'Yes! See you then!' he called out and gave her a sort of half-wave before opening the door and disappearing around the corner.

Placing the flyer on top of her notes, she picked up the pile with her left hand, stuffed it into her bag and made her way out to the carpark.

When she reached her car she threw both the bag and the sword into its boot, slammed it shut, headed around to the driver's side, climbed in, and drove home, deep in thought. She could certainly do with a good night-out, and maybe one of her students might know someone who had a boat. She doubted she could stick around where she was for very much longer, and she still desperately needed some experience out at sea for her book research, and now was probably a highly opportune time to try and get it.

Act 2, Scene 2
Une autre bonne idée
Another good idea

"As good luck would have it."
The Merry Wives of Windsor, Act III, Scene V

'IS THERE REALLY nothing better for us to do than sit outside bloody YouGet for hours on end, in the vague hope that someone might rob the place?' moaned Capstan.

Dewbush didn't reply.

There followed a long pause, which was just one of many they'd experienced since starting what was basically a high street store stakeout that they'd been stuck on for over six and a half hours.

'What are we doing here anyway, Sir?' asked Dewbush.

Capstan stared over at his Sergeant, sitting in the driver's seat opposite him, unsure as to why it had taken him quite so long to ask.

'Weren't you at the briefing this morning?'

'Yes, Sir, I was. I just had something else on my mind at the time.'

Questioning whether it was possible for Dewbush to have anything on his mind at all, Capstan decided that that was probably the problem. So, with nothing much else to do, he thought he may as well explain it all to him again.

'As Morose said, YouGet is being targeted by people who seem to think that they can waltz in, any time they like, buy a kitchen utensil and then use it in a threatening manner to upgrade for something more valuable.'

'Oh!' came Dewbush's reply. 'But I thought they'd managed to stop all that when they removed kitchen knives from their catalogue last year?'

'Well, it doesn't seem to have worked. Apparently someone stole a seventy-two inch widescreen TV from their Manchester store yesterday, armed only with a hand-whisk.'

'Really?'

'So they say.'

There was another long pause before Capstan sighed and said, 'Look Dewbush, why don't you jump out and find us a cup of tea from somewhere, and maybe pick up another paper?'

'Yes, Sir. Good idea, Sir.'

Capstan was becoming more than a little irritated by being told that half the things he said were good ideas, but he had to keep reminding himself that Dewbush probably did genuinely think that his suggestions were, indeed, good, being that the man had a brain similar in size and functionality to that of a gerbil who'd been dead for two weeks.

Realising that Dewbush had yet to move, Capstan gave him a prompt.

'Are you going or not?'

'What, now, Sir?'

'No, later on tonight, just before the pubs close.'

Dewbush gave Capstan an all too familiar look of bewilderment.

'Yes, now, please, Dewbush, for Christ's sake!'

'Oh, right you are then,' and Dewbush stepped out, leaving Capstan free to gaze over at the YouGet store without having to engage in any more suicide-inducing conversation.

About twenty minutes later, the door opened and Dewbush passed Capstan a Coffeebean tea and a copy of The Portsmouth Evening Standard, hot off the press.

'There's news on that trial, Sir.'

'Which one?'

'The Belmont Body-in-the-Bin Murder, Sir.'

Capstan remembered it well. A few weeks earlier, Morose had forced him to appear as a witness at the trial of the old man who lived next door to Cate Jakebury. Capstan had to testify to the man's reluctance to open his front door, despite making it abundantly clear to him that he was from the police. It turned out to be a pivotal moment in the trial as that was when it emerged that the man sitting in the dock, a Mr. Martin Counterfoil, a retired banker who'd lost all his money gambling, had a strong dislike for salespeople, male ones in particular. They'd therefore been able to establish that it must have been one of them he'd killed on his doorstep, before dumping the body in his neighbour's bin. Unfortunately they'd never been able to identify just exactly who the body was, as it didn't have any ID on it, and neither its fingerprints, dental records nor DNA samples had come up on the police database.

Capstan took the paper off Dewbush and unfolded it to reveal the headline.

'BELMONT BODY-IN-THE-BIN MURDERER FOUND GUILTY!' he read. 'Well, there's a turn up for the books. Looks like Morose was right after all!'

His mobile started to ring, so he gave the paper back to Dewbush, and dug out his phone from inside his suit jacket.

'Capstan here!'

Dewbush sat quietly, trying to hear what the caller was saying, but it wasn't long before his boss exclaimed, 'We're on our way!' and ended the call.

'We've been saved, Dewbush. No more stakeout duty. Another body's been found, and this one definitely looks like it's been murdered.'

'That's great news, Sir,' said Dewbush, who threw the newspaper onto the back seat to join all the others they'd read that day. He then carefully placed his coffee in the car's cup-holder, started the engine and asked, 'Where to, Sir?'

'Solent University. It's in Southampton, but I've no idea where. Just start heading up that way and they'll probably text me the postcode at some point.

Act 2, Scene 3
Comment pousse votre jardin?
How does your garden grow?

"Though this be madness, yet there is method in't."
Hamlet, Act II, Scene II

SOLENT UNIVERSITY was very quiet. Apart from an ambulance, three police cars, a Volvo Estate, a Skoda, and four mopeds, the huge carpark was deserted, and as Capstan and Dewbush made their way into the building, the halls rang out with their lonely footsteps.

After wasting some time exploring different corridors, Capstan eventually asked, 'Where the hell are we?'

'I'm not exactly sure, Sir. That last cleaner said it was just down here on the left.'

'Well, there's bugger all down here on the left. She must have meant the right. Look, there's another cleaner. Let's ask her,' and they set off towards an old lady who was facing them, swinging a large mop from side-to-side as she slowly made her way backwards down the corridor.

'Excuse me!' Capstan called out.

The cleaner looked up, saw two men wearing dark suits heading her way, and started moving her mop, and herself, just a little faster down the hall away from them.

'We'd better show her our I.D.s,' said Capstan, and as he picked up his pace he called out, 'Madam! Excuse me!' and reached inside his suit jacket pocket.

The old woman's eyes widened, and she changed up a gear.

'Oh, for God's sake,' muttered Capstan, and with his hand still inside his jacket pocket, he upped his own pace, and Dewbush hurried along after him. But seeing them increase their speed only caused the cleaner to increase her own, and her mop started to whip back and forth at quite a pace.

'Fuck it,' said Capstan, and broke into the best jog he could manage with his dodgy leg, at which point the old lady dropped her mop, threw her hands in the air and began screaming, 'QING BUYAO SHA WO, NO KIRRY, PREASE NO KIRRY, WO HUI ZUO RENHE NI SHUO, DAN QING NI BUYAO SHA WO,' and fell to her knees wailing like a Banshee left jilted at the altar.

Assuming that they must have frightened the life out of her in some way, Capstan and Dewbush stopped dead in their tracks.

'We're not after you, Madam,' called Capstan, in an effort to placate the poor woman. 'We're just looking for directions.'

But it made no difference, and she continued to sob, 'QING BUYAO SHA WO, NO KIRRY, PREASE NO KIRRY, DAN QING NI BUYAO SHA WO!'

'Shall I have a go, Sir?' asked Dewbush.

Having deduced that the woman must be deranged, Capstan said, 'Help yourself!'

Easing himself over towards her, and when he was just a couple of meters away, Dewbush crouched down on his knees and said, very quietly, 'We no hurty you. We looky for dead man.' But she clearly couldn't understand what he was going on about, so he started to act out the scene of someone being murdered, by lifting his right hand and stabbing violently at the air whilst saying, 'Killy, killy, man been killyed!'

The old lady covered her face with her hands and let out a terrifying, blood-curdling scream that was loud enough to wake the dead from the local cemetery. Then she passed out and keeled over.

'For fuck's sake, Dewbush, what did you do that for?'

'I thought it might help, Sir.'

'Evidently not!'

Giving her a prod with his foot, Capstan said, 'Well, I suggest we leave her here and see if we can find someone with a slightly more developed knowledge of the English language.

'What about the old woman, Sir?'

'Don't worry. We'll send a paramedic back for her when we find them.'

'*If* we find them, Sir.'

Capstan ignored the remark, but Dewbush did have a point. The place was a vast labyrinth of corridors that all looked identical, in every way, apart from the one they were in, which at least now had a sprawled-out old woman and a mop to act as a marker for them.

Stepping over her body, they continued down the hall in their search for the office where, apparently, there lay a brutally murdered man who was waiting patiently for his somewhat earlier-than-expected demise to be expertly investigated.

Half an hour later, having caught up with a slightly less paranoid cleaner, who also had the good fortune to own an English to Chinese phrasebook, they were finally able to solve the case of the missing office, although helped to a large extent by spotting the all too familiar police tape that had been blue-tacked across the very corridor they'd been looking for.

'Oh, hello again, Sir,' said a familiar looking police constable. 'The body's in there. Looks like he's been run through with something rather sharp, Sir.'

'Okay, thank you,' acknowledged Capstan. 'We'd better take a look,' and Dewbush and he stepped into the dark, wood-panelled office where, on an old Persian-style rug, lay the body of a scrawny, middle-aged man in a brown suit, a yellow tie, and a pool of dark red blood.

'Do we know who he is yet?' asked Capstan, glancing up at the constable.

'Yes, Sir. It's a Professor Dobbins. He is, or at least he was, the Principal of the University, Sir.'

'I don't suppose there were any witnesses?'

'Yes, Sir. His secretary, Sir. She's next door, being taken care of, but she's in a bit of a state. She was found lying next to the body with her hands and feet tied up and wearing an old helmet, Sir.'

'You mean like a crash helmet?'

'No, Sir. An armour type one. It's there, on the desk, Sir.'

Capstan stepped over to examine it, but was careful not to breathe on it, just in case he contaminated what could be a vital piece of evidence.

'I think it came from that set behind you, Sir,' and his attention was directed towards the armoured mannequin, the one without the helmet.

Capstan then crouched down beside the Professor's body as he asked, 'Who raised the alarm?'

'A cleaner, Sir. She heard strange noises coming from inside the office, and when she came in, she found the body as you see it, and the secretary tied up next to it, with the helmet on, Sir.'

'And where is the cleaner now?'

'She wanted to get back to work, probably to take her mind off it, so we said she could, as long as she didn't leave just yet. She's very old, and has a large mop.'

Capstan frowned at Dewbush, and said to the constable, 'Oh, by the way, there is in fact an old lady down the corridor who may need some medical attention. She fainted when we asked her for directions. I've really no idea why,' and gave Dewbush a hard stare.

'Oh, okay, Sir, I'll send someone down to take a look.'

'Thank you, Constable. Right then, where's this secretary of yours?'

'Just through here, Sir,' and Capstan and Dewbush were shown into the office next door, where there sat a lady who wore a generous amount of makeup that had been smudged all over her face, so that she looked like The Joker who'd just returned from a good night out with Batman.

As Capstan approached, the paramedic who was kneeling down beside her mouthed the words, 'Be very gentle, please.'

Nodding, Capstan crouched down and looked into the secretary's blood-shot, mascara-smudged eyes. He attempted a smile and said with a low, calm voice, 'Hello, my name's Police Inspector Capstan. May I ask what your name is?'

The lady looked at him and said, 'Mary,' but so softly, Capstan could barely hear her.

'Hello, Mary,' he replied, trying to keep his voice as quiet as hers. 'I understand you had the misfortune to see what happened to the, er, Professor. Is that right?'

Still staring at him, she put her lips together, thought for a moment, and then whispered, 'Mary,' again.

'Yes, that's right. Your name is Mary, but did you see what happened to the Professor?'

Gazing up at the ceiling, she gave the question some considerable thought before looking back down and answering, 'Yes.'

'So, what happen to him then?'

With a very serious look she answered.

'Murdered!'

Capstan's heart picked up a beat. He could sense he was very close to finding out who did it.

'Great, right. Now Mary, did you see who it was who murdered him?'

She nodded, slowly.

'Good. Who was it?'

A look of terror crept over her face and slowly, ever so slowly, she glanced over both shoulders before turning back to face Capstan again. Then she gesticulated for him to come closer, so that she could whisper something into his ear.

Becoming a little perturbed himself, he looked back to make sure his Sergeant was still behind him, then he leaned in towards the woman, who whispered, oh so quietly, 'Mary,' again.

Capstan lost his patience, grabbed hold of both her shoulders and shook her violently, shouting, 'TELL ME WHO MURDERED THE PROFESSOR, YOU STUPID BLOODY WOMAN!'

Mary immediately shouted back, 'MARY, MARY, QUITE CONTRARY, HOW DOES MY GARDEN GROW?' Then she stood up and started dancing around the room to continue with her impromptu poetry recital. 'WITH SILVER BELLS AND COCKLE SHELLS AND PRETTY MAIDS ALL IN A ROW!' and ended by cackling like an insane witch who'd just read a high quality joke from out of a Waitrose Christmas Cracker.

The paramedic shoved Capstan aside.

'I said be gentle, you fucking moron. She's completely lost it now.'

'I'm – I'm sorry,' he replied. 'I just lost my temper.'

And as Mary started to endlessly repeat the poem whilst twirling and laughing like a four year-old doing her Grade One ballet exam, the paramedic said, 'Well, you'll be lucky if you get anything out of her now,' and added, 'twat,' for good measure, as he dug inside his medical bag to find her another sedative.

Capstan stood up, looked at Dewbush and shrugged, and then headed back out into the corridor. It was then that he noticed a trail of blood leading out from the Professor's office. He called Dewbush over, gave him a nudge and without saying anything, used his eyes to signal the thin red line that, although it had clearly been walked over a few hundred times, was still obvious enough.

'Good job the cleaners haven't been down this way yet,' he said to Dewbush. 'C'mon! Let's see where it leads.'

After about five minutes, they'd followed the smeared blood line to a door marked Lecture Hall F. Capstan pushed it open and stepped into a large auditorium, where the line of blood led up to the lectern and stopped.

'Looks like it ends there, Sir.'

'Yes, I can see that, thank you, Dewbush.'

Looking around, Capstan couldn't see any more clues, so he said, 'We need to find out who used this room last. That's our first job!'

'Right, Sir.'

'Then we need to get that secretary in to see a shrink. She must have seen who killed the Professor, else I can't see why she'd have been tied up. That's our second job!'

'Yes, Sir.'

'And then we need to make sure Forensics can come up with something useful for us, for a change. That's our third job!'

He looked around at Dewbush, who was just standing with his hands in his pockets, gazing up at all the seats.

'Didn't you write all those down?'

'Oh, er, no. Sorry, Sir,' and searched around for his little black notebook and pen. He was just about to start taking notes when he paused, put his pen to his mouth and asked, 'Sorry, Sir, what was the first one again?'

Capstan growled at him, but he couldn't remember what it was either so, not keen to make himself out to be as stupid as his subordinate, who *was* stupid, he stalled for time and said, 'Let's just head back to the office and we can sort out a plan of action from there.'

He looked at Dewbush again, who was now frantically taking notes.

'What on earth are you writing down now?'

'I'm just making a note that we need to head back to the office so that we can sort out a plan of action from there, Sir.'

If Capstan had been carrying a gun, he'd have used it to end his professional relationship with his Sergeant, once and for all, either by killing the man or himself, or both, one after the other. But he wasn't, so instead he let out a heavy sigh and said, 'C'mon then, let's just get back.'

Act 2, Scene 4
Un bateau, un bateau. Quelqu'un at-il un bateau?
A boat, a boat. Does anyone have a boat?

"Love looks not with the eyes, but with the mind,
and therefore is winged Cupid painted blind."
A Midsummer Night's Dream, Act I, Scene I

CATE WAS a little early. Since her arrival home from the university, she'd been expecting the police to knock on her door at any minute, so had wasted no time in getting ready for the Pirate Party whilst also packing a large silver suitcase, along with her passport, for what she expected to be a lengthy leave of absence from the country of her birth; but hopefully only until things calmed down and she could learn to control her temper a little more.

Fortunately though, she didn't need to go shopping for a pirate costume. Pirate Parties were nothing new. She'd been to plenty of them herself as an under-graduate. She also had a naturally high metabolism, which meant that she was still the exact same size as she was back then. So her brown leather basque that laced up at the front, the matching mini skirt, low neck white blouse and black leather belt with the obligatory skull and crossbones on the buckle still all fitted her perfectly. She'd even bought a pair of knee-high leather boots a few weeks earlier that were ideal for the occasion. But her new sword, which she'd taken the time to wipe clean, was the pièce de résistance, and when she'd finished her make-up, she picked it up and admired herself in her full length bedroom mirror. She did look good! The belt buckle may have been a bit tacky, but apart from that, she really did look like a real-life 18th Century pirate!

After some thought, she decided to leave the car and take the bus into town. It was a bit of a pain, having to trundle a large suitcase behind her with a sword shoved through her belt, but she knew there'd be nowhere to park down by Portsmouth Docks and certainly not for the long duration she intended, not without picking up a stack of parking tickets and drawing unnecessary attention. She might as well leave the car outside her house where it would be safe. Her only concern was that people might look at her a little oddly, seeing that she'd be dressed as a pirate while waiting for a bus, with a large suitcase, and a sword; but when the time came, no one gave her so much as a second glance. The sight of pirates walking around Portsmouth, with or without suitcases, was common-place. Someone was even kind enough to help her get the case down off the bus.

And so there she was, strolling along Portsmouth Docks dressed as a pirate, using one hand to trundle a generously-proportioned silver suitcase behind her, and the other to try to control the 18th Century sword that kept bashing her thigh, hitting the suitcase and clanking against every lamppost and bollard she happened to pass.

She saw HMS Victory long before she saw the Badger and Hamster pub which, as Peter had said, was directly opposite; and then she spotted him standing outside wearing a black waistcoat over a white office shirt, a dark red bandana wrapped around his head, jeans, and a plastic sword pushed through his own obligatory pirate-buckled belt.

'Cate! Over here!'

'Oh, hello, Peter,' she said, and trundled her way over to him.

'Cate, you look amazing! Just like a real pirate!'

'Thank you,' she said with a flirtatious smile. 'I must admit that I have actually been to one of these parties before, when I was a student, so I already had the outfit.'

'Well, you look great!'

They smiled at each other before Peter noticed the suitcase.

'Are you going somewhere afterwards?' he asked, hoping that she'd packed with the intention of staying the night at his place, although she did seem to have rather a lot of stuff for a one-night stand, even by a girl's standards.

'Hopefully, yes!'

'I'd better buy you a drink then!' he said, with a presumptuous grin. 'Let me help you with your case. Most people are already here. You'll recognise a lot of them from our year,' and Peter took the case from her and began wheeling it inside the pub, leaving Cate to follow along behind.

Just inside, Peter stopped and called out, 'HEY GUYS, CATE JAKEBURY'S HERE!'

David Blake

The place exploded with rapturous applause, catcalls and wolf-whistles. Everyone in Peter's year liked Cate. From a student's perspective, what wasn't to like? She was their youngest lecturer by far, she had a good body, was vaguely attractive and had seriously weird eyes, and the fact that she'd just rocked up to one of their Pirate Parties, looking like the best girl-pirate ever, sent them into a state of orgasmic overload.

Then, one of the more inebriated pointed at her and shouted, 'LOOK! SHE'S GOT A SWORD! IT'S A REAL-LIFE FUCKING SWORD!'

On hearing the news, the hundred or so young patrons flocked to the front of the pub to take a look at their very own lecturer, Mrs Cate Jakebury, dressed up as a pirate and with a "real-life fucking sword".

Another pirate asked, 'Hey, Cate, can I buy you a drink?'

With a sudden surge of jealousy, the pirate next to him said, 'No, Cate, can *I* buy you a drink?'

'Sod off! I asked her first!'

'I thought of it first!'

Then a tall pirate, standing directly behind the two now arguing, piped up, 'Ignore these two, Cate, they're drunk! Can I buy you a drink?'

'Oi! We asked her first!'

'No, you didn't!'

'Yes, we did!'

'Oh, no, you didn't!'

'Oh, yes, we did!'

'OH, NO, YOU BLOODY DIDN'T!'

'OH, YES, WE FUCKING DID!'

Beginning to think that she'd just walked into an evening dress-rehearsal for a new adult pantomime that was possibly going to be called, "The Pirates of Penelope's Pants", or something similar, Cate thought she'd better end the argument before a massive fist-fight broke out.

'ALRIGHT, EVERYONE! SHUT THE FUCK UP!' she shouted, and in a very similar way that she always had to during the first few lectures of each new academic year, when the students had a tendency to be a little over-enthusiastic.

As the drunken pirate rabble began to quieten down, she continued, 'Peter's already said he'd buy me one, thank you.'

'OH, THAT'S JUST SO NOT FAIR!'

'WHY'S PETER ALLOWED TO BUY YOU ONE?'

'YEAH. WHY PETER? WHAT'S SO SPECIAL ABOUT HIM?'

'Okay, okay, SHUT UP AGAIN, FOR FUCK'S SAKE!'

She gave them a few moments to stop bitching, and then answered, 'Because he invited me. Now sod off please and let him buy me a bloody drink!'

'It's still not fair,' moaned the pirate who'd started the whole thing off, as they all drifted back to where they'd come from.

'Sorry about that,' said Peter. 'I think they were just a little excited to see you. They said you'd never show up! So anyway, what would you like to drink?'

'I'll have a Bloody Mary, thank you.'

'Sure, no problem.' He caught the barman's eye and shouted, 'ONE BLOODY MARY AND A PINT OF PORTSMOUTH PRIDE, PLEASE!'

He then turned back to Cate and said, 'I've thought of a pirate name for you.'

'Oh, really?'

'Yes! I thought you could be called Cutlass Cate, because of your sword.'

She gave him a sweet smile.

'That's nice, but I think I prefer the pirate name I had when I was at university.'

As he reached over to pick up her Bloody Mary from the bar, he asked, 'What was that, then?'

'Cut-Throat Cate!'

He turned and stared at her, as he handed over her deep red cocktail.

'My God, that name really suits you!'

He wasn't just saying that - it did! It was her eyes. There'd always been something strange about them, almost as if she could happily slice open someone's throat mid-way through dicing a carrot.

He picked up his pint. 'Is there a story behind that name?'

'Not that I can remember. It's just what they used to call me.'

She omitted to mention that it was what she'd always been known as, ever since she'd started going to school.

'Well, Cut-Throat Cate it is then! Cheers!'

They both took a generous sip before Cate asked, 'So what's yours then?'

Peter wiped the beer's froth from his upper lip. 'What's my what?'

'Your pirate name?'

'Oh, nothing very original I'm afraid. Unfortunately, if you're called Peter, then there really is only one pirate name you're ever going to be given.'

'Pirate Pete?'

'Yes! No prizes for that one, I'm afraid.'

'Well, maybe you can help me, Pirate Pete. I don't suppose you know anyone who's got a boat?'

'A boat?'

'Yes, you know, it's that thing that floats on water.'

'Oh, you mean a boat!'

She took another sip from her drink to stop herself asking him which one he was - deaf or stupid - before putting her sword to work again.

'Yes, that's right, a boat,' she said, with a steadying breath.

'No, sorry. Why? Do you need one?'

'It's for my book.'

'Why do you need a boat to read a book?'

'No, it's to help me research it.'

'So, you need to do some research about a boat? I thought you taught English?'

She took another sip from her drink, along with another calming breath.

'I need a boat to help me research my new book!'

'Are you writing a book?'

'I am, yes. It's actually my second. I'm a published author!'

'I'd no idea!'

'Well, I don't like to tell too many people.'

'So, what's the book about?'

'Oh, historical fiction, with a naval theme, which is why I need to find someone who's got a boat. My agent says that my books are very good, but I need to get some experience out at sea, to help make them more true-to-life.'

'So, you need a boat for research?'

'Yes, that's right.'

'I see,' and he scratched his head whilst gazing up at the ceiling. 'I can't think of anyone who's got a boat.' Then he added, 'Loads of *that lot* have a stack of sailing experience though,' he said, pointing at his friends. 'They do the Tall Ships Race every summer.'

'What's the Tall Ships Race?'

'It's when they go out on those massive old fashioned sailing boats; you know, the ones with the big square sails, like that one out the front.'

'Not you?' she asked.

'Oh, no. I don't mind dressing up as a pirate occasionally, but I get sea sick, even on the cross-channel ferry.' He noticed her glass was empty. 'Can I get you another drink?'

'My round,' she said. 'Same again?'

'Yes, another Portsmouth Pride. Thank you.'

A few minutes later, when they both had their drinks, Peter said, 'C'mon, we'll go over and ask that lot and see if anyone knows someone with a boat,' and then began to weave their way through the pirate throng towards a particular group who were obviously, totally and completely drunk.

'OI, WILL!' Pete called out.

'THAT'S WELL-HARD WILL TO YOU, MY YOUNG SCALLY-WAG.'

'Cate's looking for someone who's got a boat. Do you know anyone?'

'WHAT, LIKE A SAILING TYPE ONE?'

'Yes, one of those.'

'WELL, I CAN'T SAY THAT I DO. LET ME ASK THE MEN,' and he turned round and bellowed, 'OI, LADS! DOES ANY OF YOUS LOT KNOW ANYONE WHOSE GOT ONE OF THEY SAILING TYPE BOAT THINGS?'

The crowd picked up the call and they all started asking each other the same thing.

'NO-ONE HERE, WELL-HARD. WE'RE ALL JUST TOO SKINT!'

'AI, THAT IT BE! THAT IT BE! SORRY ME-LADDY BOY, BUT WE'RE JUST ALL TOO SKINT TO HAVE ONE OF THEM SAILING BOAT THINGS.'

But then someone shouted out from the back, 'HOW ABOUT THE ONE OUT THE FRONT?'

'WHICH ONE BE THAT?'

'THE VICTORY, YOU KNOB!'

'ARRRRR, NOW THAT BE A SPLENDID VESSEL! THE HMS VICTORY. NO FINER BOAT BE THERE THAN LORD NELSON'S OLD GIRL!' and raised his pint to call out, 'TO HMS VICTORY!'

'TO HMS VICTORY!' everyone shouted, as they all swung their flagons in unison before gulping down half the contents.

'Do they always talk with such thick Somerset accents?' asked Cate.

'Only when they're drunk, and dressed up like pirates. Didn't they do that when you were at uni?'

'Not that I recall, no.'

'Anyway, can I get you another drink?'

'Sure!' she answered, and they wove their way back towards the bar.

Act 2, Scene 5
Posez ce navire!
Put that ship down!

"Why, then the world's mine oyster."
The Merry Wives of Windsor, Act II, Scene II

THREE HOURS AND a pub-full of grog later, the bell for closing time rang out for the very last time, and the barman shouted, 'DRINK UP, PLEASE, C'MON, FINISH UP NOW!'

As they all spilled out onto the pavement, they collected themselves together and wondered what to do next.

'OI, LADS,' Well-Hard shouted, 'LET'S TAKE A LOOK AT THE VICTORY!'

They'd seen her loads of times before, of course, but seeing that they were dressed as pirates, it was an obvious choice. They staggered over to where the mighty flagship lay in its dry dock, as it had done since the early part of the 20th Century, a testament to the glory days when Britain ruled the waves and sank anything that dared suggest otherwise. Even to Cate's drunken untrained eye, she was a sight to behold. With over a hundred guns and weighing in at around three thousand five hundred tonnes, HMS Victory was a first-rate Ship of the Line. Launched in 1765, she'd served under Admiral Augustus Keppel during the

Battle of Ushant in 1778, Admiral Richard Howe during the Battle of Cape Spartel in 1782, and, most famously, under Lord Horatio Nelson during the Battle of Trafalgar in 1805. And despite being critically damaged during that fierce engagement, she'd undergone extensive repairs and went on to serve in numerous campaigns afterwards, right up until 7th November, 1812, when she was moored up in Portsmouth for the very last time.

'IS THIS WHAT YOU HAD IN MIND, CATE?' Well-Hard shouted over.

'Oh, yes. This is just amazing!' she replied as she staggered over with Peter towards the Victory's main gangplank. 'Does it still work?'

'You mean, could she still sail? Of course! She remains an official part of the Royal Navy's surface fleet and is the world's oldest commissioned navy ship.'

'Wow! Does that mean we can take her for a spin?'

'I'm 'fraid not. She's dry docked. Has been for years.'

Visibly sagging with depression, Cate propped herself up against Peter. She still hadn't found a boat and was far too drunk now to do much about it.

Over-hearing their conversation, one of Will's chums wove his way through the crowd to join them.

'You could, you know,' he said, as he steadied himself against a bollard.

'You could what?' asked Will.

'Take her for a spin. She's not chained up with a giant padlock or anything. She's in a dry dock, and it's not half as large as some. It works like a canal lock with the gates at the back. You open the gates, the water comes in, you untie the warps and then just sail her straight out.'

'You know what, Barnacle?'

'What?'

'Sometimes you really do talk bollocks!'

'Fuck you, Will. I'll show you!'

And Bill, currently known as Barnacle, led them to the ship's stern and pointed down at two colossal black steel half-gates that sat at an angle to each other pointing out into the Solent, the river estuary that feeds directly into the English Channel.

'Well, crack Jenny's teacup, if he ain't tell'n the truth!'

'They're actually called Miter gates, invented by Leonardo da Vinci.'

'That's why we call him Barnacle,' Will said to Cate. 'Useless information sticks to him like a stick insect does to a stick.'

'Can we take her out then?' she asked, cherishing a little hope.

'If you got those gates open you could, in theory at least,' Barnacle continued, surprisingly lucid despite having drunk six pints of Portsmouth Pride. 'There are two winding mechanisms on either side that are linked by a balance beam, so you'd need two people on each winder to stand any sort of a chance.'

'C'mon, me hearties,' Will said, 'let's give it a go!'

He turned around to face the hundred or so of his drunken pirate chums, who were all milling about on the starboard side of The Victory.

'OI, CANNONBALL, DEADWEIGHT! GET YOUR ARSES OVER 'ERE!'

Cannonball Jim and Deadweight John were the two props for the university's rugby team. They were also the grinders for whenever they took part in the Tall Ships Race. With each standing at six foot seven, and about four feet wide, they were by far the biggest pirates in town.

As they ambled over, Will called out to them, 'We're going to get these gates open and take The Victory for a spin.'

They both beamed, and excited chatter broke out amongst the pirate crowd who surged forward to see what was going on.

'Cannonball, you have a go at the winding gear on the other side. Barnacle, you go with 'em. Deadweight, you stay here and try to open this 'n.'

'Bloody good idea Will,' said Cannonball as he looked down at the gates. 'I've always wanted to take The Victory out. No point keeping her locked up here. She's a Ship of the Line, not a bloody museum!'

The gathering crowd mumbled their agreement, and as he jogged around to the other side, a group of onlookers went with him, closely followed by Barnacle who'd already started to sober up and was beginning to wonder what he'd got himself into.

Watching their progress, Will asked Deadweight, 'Do you think you can do it?'

'I'll give it a go,' Jim answered, and positioned himself beside the winding handle and waited for his friend to make it around to the other side.

When both men were in position, Will called out, 'ARE YOU READY?'

Cannonball shouted back, 'READY!'

'RIGHT, HEAVE AWAY ME'ARTIES, HEAVE AWAY!'

And like two fully stoked steam-powered locomotive engines, the giant men began grinding the handles with their natural God-given strength.

'Smooth as butter,' Deadweight said, looking up at Will as his face darkened in the yellow street light. It was clearly a massive effort, but he wasn't going to let on that he was struggling. However, the gates were beginning to creep open and sea water started to seep in.

Excitement began coursing its way through the spectators, as the gap between the gates widened, and they all started to follow the water, right down to the ship's bow where it flowed into the corners of the dry dock, collected and then started to rise.

As more of the Solent poured through the gates, Peter said to Will, 'Christ, we're really doing this!'

'Looks like it!' replied Will, whose body thumped with adrenaline. 'Even the tide's in our favour. It should take us straight out.'

They stood still and tried to take in what was very quickly becoming an historic event of national importance. After a few more turns of the winch handles, the gates were fully open, and the sea water thundered its way in.

With the dry dock now filling up fast, the mighty Victory let out an age-old groaning shudder.

'SHE'S LIFTING! SHE'S FUCKING LIFTING!' Will shouted, unable to contain his excitement. 'Right, we've got work to do. Cate, tell everyone to get on board. Peter, you pick some men and start casting off the lines. Then get on the ship as fast as you can.

We're going to have to do some serious fending off if we're to get her out in one piece.'

But Peter and Cate were just staring up, transfixed by the majesty of HMS Victory as it continued to creak and groan.

'NOW, PEOPLE!' bellowed Will.

There really was no time to lose.

Cate turned to the assembled masses, who were all standing, just as she herself had been, mouths agog, with none of them quite able to believe what was happening.

'EVERYONE ON BOARD, QUICK AS YOU CAN!' she shouted.

Will joined in the call for action.

'USE THE MAIN GANGPLANK. C'MON ME'HEARTIES, SHIFT YOURSELVES!'

As most of the assembled pirate mass began charging up the walkway, Will shouted up at them, 'AND WHEN YOU'RE UP ON THE DECK, FIND WHAT YOU CAN TO FEND OFF.'

Having caught his breath, Deadweight made his way over, followed by Cannonball and Barnacle, who'd jogged around from the other side.

'Okay you's lot,' Will continued. 'We need the warps taken off and heaved aboard. She's shifting already, so we have to be quick!'

They made their way over to the giant steel bollards and began casting off the warps. As each one came off, they called up to the quarterdeck, 'HEAVE'EM UP, HEAVE 'EM UP!

As Cate and Peter finished lifting a heavy rope off a bollard towards the starboard bow of the ship, they heard footsteps and voices making rapid progress towards them.

'HEY! YOU!' and three security guards came pelting around the corner.

'WHAT THE FUCK DO YOU THINK YOU'RE DOING?' asked the one leading the charge, in complete shock at seeing his beloved HMS Victory being nicked before his very eyes.

'STOP WHERE YOU ARE. GET YOUR HANDS UP, AND PUT THAT BOAT DOWN!'

Cate and Peter instinctively raised their hands, but then Cate said, 'Fuck-this,' pulled out her sword and screamed, 'WHY DON'T YOU TRY AND STOP US!' with an intense look of drunken demonic possession.

The three guards stopped dead in their tracks and just stared into her eyes, before one of them said, 'Sarge, it's not a real sword. They're just students, dressed up as pirates.'

Hearing what he'd said, Cate replied, 'You're right, it's just plastic, from YouGet,' and she dragged the tip of it along the concrete so that sparks danced along the ground behind it.

Will, Cannonball and Deadweight fell in behind Cate and Peter, and now that the three guards were confronted by the strangest and most dangerous-looking group of people they'd ever seen in their entire lives, their Sergeant said, 'Now look, we don't want no trouble, but - but that's HMS Victory! You can't just sail her out to sea, you dumb fucking students.'

'Why not?' asked Cate. 'It's a ship, and I'm told it's a pretty good one at that.'

Will backed her up.

'HMS Victory is a fine sailing vessel, possibly the finest ever built. It's not right for her to be kept ashore like this. She needs the sea and we're taking her a-sailing!'

There was a noise of wood being torn apart from behind them as the huge fixed gangplank was ripped off its hinges from the quarterdeck.

Barnacle shouted down at them from on board.

'HURRY UP, FOR FUCK'S SAKE, SHE'S HEAD'IN OUT!'

The security guard at the front took a tentative step towards them.

Cate did likewise, and as she did she held up her sword and whispered, 'One more move and I'll open up your throats and leave you for the foxes.'

'She's bluffing,' said the security guard behind his Sergeant's left shoulder.

There was a brief pause.

'I really don't think she is,' replied the Sergeant.

'No, you're probably right.'

Having reached that collective agreement, the three of them began to edge away from this psychotic girl-pirate who looked like she'd just been employed by the devil and was keen to get busy.

As they inched backwards, their sergeant said, 'You'll never get away with this,' with little conviction, and only because he thought he should say something, given the circumstances.

With the stand-off settled, Will called out, 'C'MON, ME'HEARTIES, LET'S GET ONBOARD HER SHARPISH, BEFORE THE GANGPLANK GOES.'

The five of them turned and ran to the base of the walkway and launched themselves up just in the nick of time as HMS Victory lifted and surged backwards, ripping the gangplank from its hinges, leaving it to fall into the dock's black water below.

As Will scrambled on board he cried out, 'ALL HANDS ON DECK! GRAB ANY BOAT HOOK YOU CAN FIND AND FEND OFF, ME'HEARTIES, FEND OFF!'

Then he ran backwards towards the ship's great steering wheel and tried to pull it around to port, but it wouldn't turn.

'CANNONBALL! DEADWEIGHT!' he called out again. 'Give me a hand with this wheel. It won't budge.'

Under their combined strength and weight, the wheel came over to port and the finest vessel ever to have set sail from British waters continued to drift backwards, out of the dry dock where it had been held captive since January, 1922.

The three security guards just stood there transfixed, aghast at what they were witnessing; and as HMS Victory slowly disappeared from view the Sergeant said, 'They're never going to believe this one down the pub.'

'What - what should we do, Sir?'

'Do? Do? What the fuck do you think we should do? Call everyone, and I mean EVERYONE!'

And with that at the forefront of their minds they sprinted back to their hut where, only ten minutes before, they'd been engrossed in a tense game of Battleship.

Act 2, Scene 6
Une différence d'opinions
A difference of opinion

"The robbed that smiles steals
something from the thief."
Othello, Act I, Scene III

EARLY THE NEXT morning the Solent's Police
Briefing Room bustled with activity as Chief
Inspector Morose waddled his way to the front with a
couple of newspapers wedged under his huge fat arm.

As the collected assortment of inspectors and
constables bemoaned the fact that they'd had to come
to work slightly earlier than usual, Morose raised a
hand for silence, and began to address the room.

'Thank you all for coming in so early.'

A number of those present shifted themselves in
their chairs, thinking that a pay rise would have been
more appreciated, but at least the man had the decency
to acknowledge their effort.

'I assume you all know why you're here?'

A solitary hand went up from the middle of the
room.

It was Sergeant Dewbush.

'Is it because a wide screen TV was stolen from
YouGet, Sir?'

'No, a TV has not been stolen from YouGet, not since the day before yesterday at any rate; but thank you, er, Bushdew isn't it?'

Another hand went up.

Although Morose hadn't expected to field answers to his question, now that he'd taken one he felt obliged to answer the next.

'Yes, you at the back.'

'Was it a fridge freezer, Sir?'

'Again, no. A fridge freezer hasn't been stolen.'

'Was it a dining room table?'

'A sofa?'

'A three piece suite?'

'A double bed?'

'A wardrobe?'

'A garden shed?'

'Another washing machine?'

'NO!' Morose shouted. 'NOTHING'S BEEN STOLEN FROM YOUGET!'

The room fell into an awkward silence.

'Doesn't anyone know what *was* taken? Yesterday evening, at around 11:30pm?'

A plastic clock ticked against the wall of silence.

'Does nobody watch the bloody news around here?'

Just about everyone in the room began to stare down at their feet.

'HMS VICTORY WAS STOLEN LAST NIGHT, FOR FUCK'S SAKE!'

'I was just about to say that,' said a young constable at the front.

Morose took a deep breath.

'Now, as we all know,' he continued, casting his fat little eyes over his men, 'the Victory is nothing less than a national treasure, and the Commissioner is absolutely furious.'

Half the congregation shrugged. As far as they were concerned it was just a stupid old boat that should have been turned into an adventure playground a long time ago, and shortly after the Portsmouth Parent Squad had led a massive march through town with a petition for such.

Another hand went up from the middle left, holding a newspaper.

'Ah, I see someone here at least has taken the time to stop by the newsagents. Yes, Inspector Chupples, you have a question?'

'Thank you, Sir. I picked up a copy of The Guardian, and they seem to think that it's a good thing, Sir.'

'They seem to think that what's a good thing, Chupples?'

'That HMS Victory has been taken out to sea again, Sir.'

'Well, it really doesn't matter what the British Press says about the matter.'

Chupples carried on regardless.

'They have the headline, "HMS VICTORY SAILS AGAIN", and they go on to say that it's about time that it did, Sir.'

'As I just said, Chupples, it really doesn't matter what The Guardian says. This is about what is right and wrong, and this clearly falls into the "wrong" category, being that it's an incident of grand larceny. Those responsible need to be brought to justice, and it's our job to do it.'

Ignoring his Chief Inspector, Chupples continued, 'The Telegraph said pretty much the same thing, Sir, as did the Observer, The Times, The Express, The Mirror, The Sun and the F.T.'

'WELL, THE PORTSMOUTH POST DIDN'T!' Morose shouted. 'Their headline was, and I quote,' he went on, taking both newspapers out from under his arm, '"VICTORY STOLEN"! And whilst I'm here, The Solent Salute went with, "HMS NICKED"! Both these headlines I wholeheartedly agree with. Now sit down, Chupples and shut the fuck up!'

Chupples, a keen sailor himself, did what he was told and sat down to continue reading his own paper.

'The Commissioner,' continued Morose, 'has put every single constabulary that boarders the British coastline on high alert. He wants those responsible under lock and key before the end of the day, and I for one am going to do all that I can to make sure that happens.'

There were no further comments, so Morose ploughed on.

'Unfortunately we don't have many boats to start a pursuit, and we're also short of staff with the correct experience to drive them.'

It was Capstan's turn to raise his hand.

'Yes, Capstan?'

'Isn't that the Coastguard's job, Sir. To go after them, I mean, Sir?'

'It would seem that they're not allowed to. They can only go to the assistance of vessels that are in trouble, and would therefore have to wait until they received an S.O.S. from the ship.'

'What about the Navy, Sir?' suggested Capstan again, hoping to find some way for the police to duck the responsibility.

'They've said that they're more than happy to keep an eye out for it, but any more than that would detract from their main job of defending our coastline.'

A few murmurs could be heard coming from the direction of Chupples, who couldn't help but agree with both the Coastguard and the Royal Navy. He also knew that the National Boating Association, the entire Royal Family, and just about everyone up and down the country who'd the slightest interest in sailing was of a similar opinion; that HMS Victory was a seafaring vessel and should therefore be at sea, and not propped up in Portsmouth Docks to be gawped at by millions of stupid tourists who probably didn't even realise that it was a ship.

'How many boats do we actually have at our disposal, Sir?' Capstan asked, simply curious. Until then, he'd no idea they had any at all.

'Only two motor launches, although Thames Valley Police said they may be able to lend us another one. So at this stage, what we need to know is, who here has any decent experience of being out at sea?'

Two hands went straight up: Dewbush's and Chupples'.

'You, Bushdew, what experience do you have?'

'I've sailed to Calais and back, Sir.'

Morose was both surprised and impressed. 'That's great! And what type of boat did you sail in?'

'It was the ferry, Sir. From Dover to Calais.'

Morose sighed. He should have known better.

'How about you, Chupples?'

'I've been sailing since I was five, Sir. I was the World's Inland Optimist Dinghy Champion in 1987 and have since taken part in numerous races out at sea including the Fastnet, in which we won "Best in Class". I'm also a powerboat instructor at my local sailing club and a regular volunteer for the RNLI, Sir.'

Now that was more like it!

'Right, well, there we have it,' said Morose. 'Chupples, you go out in the first boat with your sergeant and Capstan, you take the second with Bushdew.'

'BUT SIR!' Capstan objected.

'NO BUTS, CAPSTAN! And I'm not changing my mind! Now the Duty Sergeant has the keys for both boats. You can pick them up from him. And I don't want either of you back here until you've found the ship and arrested all those responsible for taking it. DO I MAKE MYSELF CLEAR?'

Silence fell over the room.

'Right, dismissed! And I look forward to seeing The Victory back in her dock by tea time.'

Act 2, Scene 7

Vous avez le corps d'un chien et le QI d'un enfant de cinq ans

You have the body of a dog and the IQ of a five year old

Or...

Amene ta mere pour que je te refasse

Bring your mother so I can stuff you back up her

"I like this place and willingly could waste my time in it."
As You Like It, Act II, Scene IV

CATE WOKE with a start. She was in some sort of open-coffin box, heavily lined with an off-white floral patterned cloth. Freaking out, she sat bolt upright and stared around the room, feeling very much like Dracula's Bride, late for her own wedding.

The room was resplendent with wood-panelled walls, highly-polished antique furniture, a beamed ceiling and some cute lead-lined windows, but it did two things that she'd never known a room to do before. Firstly it undulated in the most peculiar way, and secondly, it creaked and groaned each time it did so.

It was only then that she remembered.

We didn't?

Clambering out of her cot-bed coffin thing, she hit her head on an insanely low wooden beamed ceiling. Cursing loudly, she ducked and made her way over to the nearest window, making a mental note of how the floor seemed unable to stay still. She didn't need to study the view for very long to get the picture. She was out at sea, and unless she was very much mistaken, standing on board HMS Victory!

Nauseous, she staggered over to an ornate door on the opposite side and walked straight out on to The Victory's quarterdeck, where Peter, Will, John and Jim all stood, clinging onto the ship's huge double-barrelled wheel and looking very serious about it.

'Morning Cate!' said Peter, without taking his eyes off the starboard side compass that sat in a pristine antique glass-panelled box directly in front of him. 'We're heading south-by-south-east, looking for some breakfast.'

'I see that we did take HMS Victory out after all. I thought for a minute there I might have just imagined the whole thing.'

'Damned right we did!' Will called over. 'And she's a-lov'n it!'

After spending a few moments becoming familiar with her radically different surroundings, she asked, 'So, where exactly are we?'

'We're heading south, following the coast of France.'

'I see you've managed to get some sails up.'

'Just a couple on the fore and mizzen masts, for now,' continued Will. 'Enough to give us steerage way at least. There's only a slight breeze and the sea state's flat, so we'll probably have a go at getting some up on the main mast after we've found something to eat.'

Cate began to study the horizon. There was nothing there at all, just blueness that seemed to go on forever.

'Are there any other boats or are we alone out here?'

'Oh, no! There are loads of boats out there - you just can't see them. The horizon's only three miles away, so they'll all be just out of sight. Mainly tankers and container ships, though.'

She stared around again, and as she tried to get used to the way the ship moved she began to feel hungry.

'How are we going to find breakfast out here?'

'We're looking for a vessel small enough to approach without being run over. A fishing boat perhaps, or maybe a yacht. Hopefully they'll have some tins of something to help keep us going.'

'We've got some bottled water if you want some,' said Peter. 'Here, have a drink.'

'Thanks!'

She took a few generous swigs before remembering, 'Shit, I forgot my bloody suitcase!'

'Well it wasn't exactly a planned trip,' said Peter. 'Don't worry. I'm sure the Badger and Hamster pub will look after it for you.'

'And how are you doing, Pirate Pete? I thought you said that you get sick at sea?'

'Yes, I know! I seem to be OK though. Being up on an open deck seems to be helping, and the sea is very calm.' He gave her the briefest of smiles before returning to gaze back out over the ship's great bow.

'Does it really need the four of you on the wheel?' she asked.

'Six, normally,' answered Will, but was then distracted by an echoing cry that came drifting down to them from the top of the main mast.

'SHIP AHOY! SHIP AHOY! JUST OFF THE PORT BOW.'

Will cupped his hands together and called up, 'WHAT IS IT?'

'FISHING BOAT, I THINK!'

It was only then that Cate realised that there were loads of other students up on deck, and she watched them all scramble over to the left hand side of the ship.

'I can see her,' said Cannonball John, whose height gave him a distinct viewing advantage.'

Deadweight Jim also caught a glimpse and confirmed. 'Yes, she's on the horizon, port bow.'

'Right, well, we really need to take a break from helming. I'll get six others to take over and we can head up to the forecastle and take a look from there.' He cupped his hands again and bellowed, 'ANDREW, JAKE, LEWIS, CARL, BILL, JASPER. GET YOUR ARSES UP HERE, IT'S YOUR TURN TO HELM!'

When the change-over was complete and the Victory had been brought around to port slightly and was now heading towards what looked to be a decent-sized fishing vessel, Cate, Peter, Will, Cannonball and Deadweight all made their way along the quarterdeck and then up again onto the forecastle, near the front of the ship. There they watched and waited, as the trawler slowly grew bigger.

As they approached they could see the small crew, all decked out in blood-splattered, chest-high, braced up yellow oilskins, staring back at them with eyes wide and mouths open at what was possibly the most famous ship ever built, bearing down on them with a substantial crew of misfit pirates who were all lining the entire length of its port side.

'Excuse me!' Cate called out. 'I don't suppose you could spare us something to eat, and possibly some water as well, if you have it?'

There was no response. The seven fishermen just continued to gawp up at the immense black wooden hull, the giant-sized set of double fore-anchors and its unmistakable three tiers of guns embedded within its striking yellow borders.

'Maybe they're not English,' suggested Peter.

'FOODEZ AND WATEREZ HAVE YOU?' asked Cate again.

Finally one of the fisherman, who had a dead fish in one hand and a bloodied knife in the other, turned to his shipmates and said, 'Sacré bleu! N'est-il pas l'HMS Victory?'

'They're French!' said Peter.

Cate turned to look down the length of the ship where everyone, except the six still at the wheel, had gathered.

'DOES ANYONE HERE SPEAK FRENCH?'

A tentative hand went up and a skinny young man wearing thick black-rimmed glasses that didn't go at all with his pirate costume poked his head out.

'Yes, you!' and Cate gestured for him to come over.

He was clearly shy but slunk his way down past all his pirate chums.

'What's your name?' she asked.

'Crispin, Miss,' he said, staring down at the deck.

'So, you can speak French then, Crispin?'

'Sort of, Miss. My cousins live there and they've taught me a few phrases.'

'Do you know any that are about food? We need to ask them if they can spare us something to eat and drink.'

'Yes, I think so.'

'Well, have a go then, and see how you get on.'

He didn't look like he wanted to, but as he was now being stared at by the entire crew of both boats, he thought he'd better try. So he cleared his throat, looked down at the fishing boat that they were rapidly closing in on and called out, 'Vous êtes une pomme de terre avec le visage d'un cochon d'inde!'

However, Crispin's cousins had done him a disservice and he'd no idea that he'd just said, 'You are a potato with the face of a guinea pig'

'Mon Dieu!' came the immediate response. The man with the dead fish looked around at his fellow crew members before shouting back, 'Vous avez le corps d'un chien et le QI d'un enfant de cinq ans!'

Cate looked at Crispin. 'Did you understand that?'

He shrugged. 'No, sorry.'

'Okay. Try another foody type one and see if that works any better.'

So again he coughed a little, leaned over the side and shouted, 'Vous sentez comme le boeuf et le fromage!'

That particular phrase meant, 'You smell like beef and cheese.'

The French crew began to become just a little agitated and huddled together to confer before the one with the dead fish shouted back, 'Amene ta mere pour que je te refasse!' prompting them to all fall about laughing.

'That seemed to work a little better,' said Cate. 'I don't suppose you know what he said?'

'Not a clue, sorry.'

'Well look, try one more, and if that doesn't work, we'll have to think of something else.'

Crispin took a deep breath, leaned back over and shouted, 'Vous avez le cerveau d'un sandwich au fromage!' which roughly translated meant, 'You have the brain of a cheese sandwich.'

All the French fisherman stopped laughing, looked around the deck of the trawler, picked up whatever they could find that was both heavy and sharp, and hurled the objects at the Victory, along with what must have been some rather abusive words, judging by the looks on their faces.

'My God!' said Will. 'They're throwing things at us, and it's not food!'

As a boat-hook shot straight past his head, missing him by just a few inches, he exclaimed, 'Fuck me!' ducked, and said, 'I'm not having this,' before joining his friends who'd all instinctively taken cover behind the ship's side. Looking over at Cannonball and Deadweight he nodded at them and then, without warning, stood up, pulled his plastic sword out of his belt and screamed, 'ATTACK!' and then threw the sword at them.

Seeing this, the entire hundred-strong crew of the Victory did the same, and the fishing boat came under a heavy barrage of plastic swords.

But as soon as the fishermen realised they were only made of plastic, they came out from their various hiding places and started pelting the Victory with their latest catch which, being half-frozen, were even more dangerous than the boathooks. One particular fish slapped Deadweight right across the face. 'RIGHT, THAT'S IT!' he shouted, and with a malevolent look, stormed over to the base of the forecastle where there were dozens of huge cannonballs, neatly stacked in a series of pyramids. He heaved the closest one from the top of its stack and lumbered it back to the Victory's port side.

'TAKE THAT, YOU FISH-BRAINED FRENCHIE SCUM!' he cried, and hurled it down at them.

It missed all the men, fortunately, but crashed straight through the deck of the trawler and disappeared.

'Why didn't I think of that?' Cannonball asked himself. 'Come on Lads, let's all grab one!'

Seeing the damage that just one of the solid cast-iron balls had done to his trawler, the fisherman who'd been holding the dead fish, and who was also the Captain, said, 'Sacré bleu!' and raced off to start the engine to get the hell out of there. He only just made it up the steps of the wheelhouse when the first of over a hundred cannonballs began descending down onto his boat, all of which just disappeared. It was only then that he realised where they'd all gone: straight out through the bottom. He knew this because his fishing boat began to sink, and before he could say "Sacré bleu!" again, the entire stern of the boat was under water and his crew of six were already up to their knees in it. So the Captain gave up any idea of making a run for it and shouted, 'ABANDONNEZ LE NAVIRE! ABANDONNEZ LE NAVIRE!' before throwing himself overboard.

The remaining crew members looked around at each other, and at the water that was now up to their hips, and followed their captain. But like most people who spend their lives working at sea, none of them could swim particularly well, and within just a few moments they all started gasping for breath and murbelling, 'Au secours! Sauvez-nous! Nous coulons!' between gulps of air.

Having had their morning exercise, the crew of HMS Victory caught their breath by resting their elbows on the ship's side as they watched the fishing boat disappear beneath the water, while trying to work out what the Frenchies were going on about. Eventually Crispin looked at Cate and said, 'I think they're asking for help. It doesn't look like any of them can swim.'

Cate just shrugged and carried on watching them. It was Will who eventually felt it necessary to take some sort of benevolent action.

'C'mon lads, we'd better get them out before they all drown,' and he climbed up onto the side and dived in, closely followed by a number of other obliging crew members, all of whom had parents intelligent enough to make sure they'd learnt to swim before the age of ten.

Act 2, Scene 8

À quoi est-ce que ça ressemble ?
What does it look like?

"Will all great Neptune s ocean wash this blood clean from my hand? No, this my hand will rather the multitudinous seas incarnadine, making the green one red."
Macbeth, Act II, Scene II

'DO YOU HAVE *any* idea what you're doing, Dewbush?' asked Capstan, as he threw his stick down into the police boat's small cabin, grateful at least that he didn't have to walk anywhere for a while.

'I think so, Sir. It's a bit like driving a car. The steering wheel makes it go left and right and this hand-throttle thing makes it go forwards.'

'So why are we going backwards then?'

'I'm just trying to turn it around, Sir.'

'Well, hurry up! Chupples and his minion are already half way out of the harbour and we can't let that twat beat us!'

'Beat us at what, Sir?'

'At cricket,' Capstan said with a heavy sigh.

'But…we're…When are we playing cricket, Sir?'

'BEAT US TO THE VICTORY, YOU MUPPET-BRAINED KNOB-HEAD!'

'Oh yes, of course, Sir.'

'Chupples' head is quite big enough already. If he finds that ship before we do he'll probably have a statue made of himself and stick it next to Nelson's bloody Column.'

'Yes, but then we could all call it "Chupples' Knob", Sir!'

Dewbush had made a joke.

Although not officially laid down in the Police Best Practice Hand Book, it was common knowledge that jokes were not allowed to be made to superior officers during the course of active duty, not on purpose at any rate.

'Are you trying to be funny, Dewbush?'

Dewbush was treading on very thin ice and so with unusual foresight, turned the joke into a statement of personal opinion by saying, 'Not at all, Sir, I just think that "Chupples' Knob" would make a very good name for a statue of him standing on top of a hundred foot pillar, directly opposite Nelson's Column, Sir.'

'Well, it wouldn't, Dewbush! In fact it's probably the most stupid name for anything I've ever heard in my entire life. Now, will you please watch where you're going! There's a boat right there!'

'Where, Sir?' asked Dewbush, looking behind him.

'There! Right there! IN FRONT OF YOU, FOR FUCK'S SAKE!!!'

As Dewbush hauled the boat somewhat dramatically over to one side, and Capstan was sent flying over to the other, the sergeant apologised.

'Sorry about that, Sir, I thought you meant that there was something behind us.'

'But why…' Capstan was about to ask as he hauled himself back into a standing position, but he decided

that it wasn't worth investigating the reason for
Dewbush thinking that the order, "Watch where
you're going!" actually meant, "Look behind you!" The
mental anguish involved would be far too painful; so
instead he said, 'No, that's fine, Dewbush. No need to
apologise. But if you do it again I'll have to beat you to
a pulp with my stick!'

'Yes, Sir, of course, Sir, sorry, Sir.'

There was a long silence before Dewbush dared
speak again.

'We're just coming out of the harbour now, Sir.'

They spent several minutes just gazing around. The
place was cluttered with a huge variety of boats, from
giant-sized container ships that could probably be seen
from space, to boats so small they could float in a
puddle.

'Where do you think we should go, Sir?'

'To be honest, Dewbush, I'm not exactly sure.'

There was another long pause before Capstan
asked, 'Can you see the Victory anywhere?'

'Not yet, Sir.'

'No, neither can I; at least I don't think I can.'

Capstan rotated himself around a full three hundred
and sixty degrees before asking Dewbush, 'Do we even
know what it looks like?'

'Oh, hold on, Sir. They gave me a picture of it
before we left,' and Dewbush produced a printout that
someone had pulled off the internet. He leant forward
and gave it to Capstan, who snatched it from him with
the hand that wasn't holding onto the top of the
windscreen. Just as he was about to unfold the A4
piece of paper, the boat ploughed straight into the base
of what was to turn out to be an endless number of

really annoying waves, which hadn't been there when they were in the harbour. As Capstan was sent flying forwards he was forced to let go of the picture of HMS Victory to prevent himself from being plunged head-first down into the boat's tiny cabin.

'CAN YOU PLEASE BE CAREFUL, DEWBUSH, FOR GOD'S SAKE! You just made me drop the one thing we had that may have helped us to find what we're supposed to be looking for!'

'Sorry, Sir. I wasn't expecting the boat to go up and down quite so much, Sir,' and they watched as the piece of paper danced away on the wind before dropping behind a wave and disappearing.

'Well, that's that!' said Capstan. 'I don't suppose you could describe it?'

'Yes, Sir. It was white and had a picture of HMS Victory on it, Sir.'

'Surprisingly I didn't mean the piece of paper. For some unknown reason I meant the boat, Dewbush, THE BOAT!'

'Oh, that! Er, yes, I think so, Sir. Now let me think. It's quite big, it's made of wood, painted black, has yellow stripes down the sides, lots of cannons, and some really big wooden posts that stick up in the middle, Sir.'

Capstan had another good look around. 'I can't see anything that looks like that.'

As their boat continued to plod out of the Solent and into the English Channel, Capstan had an idea.

'Tell you what, let's just follow Chupples. At least he seems to know where he's going. Hopefully we'll see it before he does, then we can race him to it and arrest them all before he has a chance to.'

'Good idea, Sir!' and Capstan and Dewbush settled themselves down to the age old method used by racing yachts throughout the world: if you don't have a clue where you're going, just follow the guy out in front.

Act 2, Scene 9

Es-tu fou?

Are you insane?

"All the world's a stage, and all the men and women
merely players. They have their exits and their
entrances; And one man in his time plays many parts."
As You Like It, Act II, Scene VII

'QU'EST-CE QUE vous faites? Otez vos mains de moi! Vous avez coulé mon bateau et mes poissons! Vous aurez payer pour cela, vous chiens de porcs anglais. Vous ne pouvez pas faire le tour de couler le bateau des autres, parce qu'ils vous jettent quelques poissons morts! Maintenant, nous allons tous ou j'appelerai la police!'

'Don't French people ever stop talking?' asked Cate.

'I've no idea,' replied Crispin.

'I thought you said you'd been there?'

'No. My cousins just taught me some phrases. I've never actually been to France.'

Having been hauled out of the English Channel using a subtle blend of thick rope and boat hooks, the French fishermen now stood huddled together in the middle of HMS Victory's quarterdeck. With a large puddle expanding around their feet, they resembled a freshly caught school of halibut who'd spent so much time swimming around the coast of France that they'd become fluent in the language, and were now keen to try out their new-found linguistic skills.

Cate and Crispin stood there and listened to them go on for another couple of minutes before she asked, 'Any idea what they're saying?'

'Not a clue, sorry, but they don't look very happy.'

'Well, we can't listen to them all bloody day. It's not good for the ship's morale. And besides, they smell! They're not even attractive. I thought French men were supposed to be good-looking?'

Crispin just shrugged.

'Anyway,' she looked over at Will before continuing. 'Can you please take them somewhere where I can't see them, hear them or smell them? They're making me feel sick.'

'No problem, Cate. Shall we tie them up as well?'

'Yes, I really think you should. And maybe stick something over their heads.'

'I suppose we could just hang them from the yard arm?' he suggested, beginning to regret having fished them out in the first place.

'No, better not. I think it's just that they're French, so it's probably not their fault.'

As the fishermen were escorted down into the depths of the ship to be tied up before having bags put over their heads, another call came down from the top of the main mast.

'SHIP AHOY! STARBOARD BOW!'

In Will's absence, Cate called up, 'WHAT IS IT?'

'MOTOR BOAT, WHITE, PROBABLY PLASTIC!'

She called over to the six pirates manning the wheel.

'Can you take us over to that boat, please?'

'Aye, aye, Captain!'

A moment later the call came. 'STANDBY TO WEAR SHIP!'

A period of intense activity followed. Cate watched various people pull on numerous lengths of rope as the Victory came through the breeze that Cate could feel blowing from behind them. Within just a few moments there was a brief spasm of sails, ropes, pulleys and people, all doing different things, and the great ship slowly began heading up towards the white plastic boat that seemed stationary out on the horizon.

Cate joined the crew as they all made their way up onto the forecastle, where she took her place beside Peter to watch the other boat as they started to make headway towards it.

'I hope they're not French,' she said.

'Me too,' Peter agreed.

Crispin, who was standing next to them, nodded. He'd had quite enough of speaking French for one day.

Cate squinted out at the distant boat. 'I'm surprised they even let French people go sailing out here. Isn't there some sort of law that says you can't go out on the English Channel unless you can speak the language?'

'There must be,' Peter said.

'I think there is,' Crispin added. 'It's just too dangerous otherwise.'

'Well, let's hope this lot aren't, and that they've got something for us to eat. I'm starving!'

Will, Cannonball and Deadweight came back onto the quarterdeck, and when Will saw that everyone was peering out at something, he ran onto the forecastle to stand behind Cate.

'Another boat?' he asked, a little out of breath.

'Yes, a white one.'

'Well, I hope they're not French!'

Cate, Peter and Crispin all nodded in agreement.

Unfortunately it wasn't long before they could see the Tricolor flag fluttering out over its glamorous-looking bathing platform. It also had a very French sounding name, La Vierge de la Cupidité. And although tiny compared to the Victory, it would have probably been described as a Gin Palace by your average yachtie type, as it had three levels with a fly-bridge at the top and a Jacuzzi that bubbled away towards the stern.

After a few more minutes they could make out various items on the good-sized teak table near the Jacuzzi; a bottle of something, possibly champagne, four or five tall elegant glasses, two cigars left smouldering in an ash tray, a half-opened brown package that looked like a behind-the-counter bag of flour, a knife, some biro pens, and a mirror. But despite all that, they couldn't see any signs of life.

'Maybe they're asleep?' suggested Cate.

'Maybe,' said Will. 'Let's find out.' He pushed himself between Cate and Peter, climbed up on the side, and with one hand holding on to a shroud and the other cupped around his mouth he hollered, 'LA VIERGE DE LA CUPIDITE, THIS IS HMS VICTORY. IS THERE ANYONE ON BOARD?'

A long silence followed as The Victory edged ever closer.

'I thought I saw something move inside,' said Cate. 'Look, there! That window just slid open.'

Will didn't see it, so he called out again, 'LA VIERGE DE LA CUPIDITE, IS ANYONE THERE?'

'Another window's opened,' said Peter. 'And I'm sure I saw something being poked out of it. I don't like the look of this. There's definitely someone on board!'

'I'll try once more,' said Will, who again called out, 'LA VIERGE DE LA CUPIDITE, THIS IS HMS VICTORY. WE NEED FOOD AND WATER. CAN YOU HELP US?'

Out of nowhere something whistled past his ear, followed by the clattering of what could only have been automatic gunfire.

'JESUS CHRIST! GET DOWN EVERYONE! THEY'RE SHOOTING AT US!'

As just about the entire crew of HMS Victory, including those at the wheel, but excluding the poor chap still stuck at the top of the main mast, dived for cover, more bullets sang through the air with some thudding into the ship's side.

'WHAT THE FUCK?' cried John.

'IS EVERYONE ALRIGHT?' asked Will.

'I've…I've been hit!' said Crispin, clutching at his arm.

Cate took a quick look at him and then up at Will. 'I think they've shot Crispin!'

'The bastards!'

Will turned to Peter, Cannonball and Deadweight who, like just about everyone else, were splayed out on the deck with their hands covering their heads. 'Oi, you lot! They've gone and shot Crispin!'

'You're joking!' Cannonball said.

'I'm not joking. They've shot him in the arm!'

'The bastards!'

'Are you alright, Crispin?' asked Peter.

'Y-yes. Sort of,' he replied, trying hard not to cry.

Another round of bullets thundered into the side of the ship, throwing up splinters of wood and bringing everyone's heads back down to the deck.

'They must be insane!' said Deadweight.

'They must be drug dealers,' concluded Cannonball.

Will got back onto his feet, but kept his head well below the ship's side. 'Well, sod this for a game of soldiers. Cannonball, Deadweight, follow me!'

'Where are you off to?' asked Cate.

'We're not on the finest man-of-war ever to have set sail from our fair land to be shot at by a bunch of fucking French drug dealers, not when we've got a hundred and four cannons to play with.'

The three of them began crawling their way down to the gun decks beneath them, keeping their heads just as low as possible.

'How're you doing there, Crispin?' asked Peter.

'Okay. I think it just grazed me.'

He took his hand away for Peter to look more closely. There was a fair amount of blood, but it did look like it had only caught the back of his arm.

'Looks like you'll be alright. But still, we need to get you cleaned up. Keep pressure on it, that will help stop the bleeding, and I'll see if I can find some water, and something to use as a bandage.'

Meanwhile Cate kept watch over the side. There hadn't been any more shots fired for a while, but she still couldn't see anyone on board. The two windows remained open but nothing was sticking out of them, not that she could spot, at any rate. With nobody at the wheel, the Victory was beginning to drift off her original course and away from the other boat. Keeping her head as low as possible, she made her way along the entire length of the starboard side, stopping every now and again to make sure that everyone else was okay, and when she eventually reached the other end, she carefully lifted her head up again to take a look at the other boat.

A huge explosion made her nearly jump out of her skin, as a giant plume of smoke billowed out from the Victory's side, right beneath her feet. She instinctively ducked down and asked the pirate closest, 'What the fuck was that?'

'I think it was a cannon, Captain.'

'Bloody hell! That must have done some damage.'

She looked over the side again as a strong smell of sulphur and cordite filled the air; but when she saw that the only result of such a huge explosion was a tiny splash about a hundred feet beyond the other boat, she said, 'Well that was a complete waste of time,' to nobody in particular, and made her way over to the ship's wheel. There she found the six pirates who were all supposed to be helming, but were very sensibly taking cover behind the stairs that led up to the poop deck.

She crouched down beside one of them and whispered, 'Do you think it's possible to get us a bit closer to the other boat?'

'You want to get closer?'

'Yes, I want to board her.'

'You want to board her?'

'Well, we can't hang about here all day being shot at.'

There was a moment's pause before the pirate asked, 'Are you some sort of deranged psycho nut-job?'

She'd never thought about it before, but having killed three people that year, which was probably more than average, she answered, 'Possibly, but that's not important right now. Can you get me closer?'

The pirate she was talking to looked at the sails, and at the White Ensign flag on top of the main mast, and then took a very quick peek over at the other boat.

'If you *really* want to, then yes, we can.'

She nodded. 'Yes, I *really* want to!'

He could tell by the look in her eyes that she did, so he leaned over to his pirate helming chums and said, 'Chaps, we're going to try and get her a little closer.'

'Closer to what?'

'The other boat.'

'The other boat?'

'Yes, I know, but our Captain here seems very keen to board her.'

The nearest helm pirate took one look at Cate and said, 'Fair enough. C'mon lads, let's bring her round again!'

As they all started to heave the great wheel over, Cate made her way back to the starboard side, and all the way to the front of the quarterdeck where Peter was still taking care of Crispin.

She approached him with a wide grin and said, 'I'm going to board her,' and pulled out her sword in readiness.

Peter had always known that she was a bit mad, but this was on a whole new level.

'Are you completely insane?'

'Well, I wouldn't have to if they could shoot that bloody cannon straight! Anyway, I'm hungry, and I'm sure they'll have something to eat.'

Peter didn't know quite what to say, so he just continued to stare at her.

'Wish me luck!' and with one last peek to see that they were now virtually on top of the other boat, she leaped up on to the side like a feral cat, balanced for a moment, and then jumped.

Act 3, Scene 1

Meurtre, Mort, Tuer
Murder, Death, Kill

"Neither a borrower nor a lender be."
Hamlet, Act I, Scene III

IF CAPSTAN and Cate had been busy, the British Prime Minister, Robert Bridlestock, had been rushed off his feet, and for almost the entire morning.

Since news of the theft of HMS Victory had broken, he'd had numerous people on the phone to him. First up was the Home Secretary, Harold Percy-Blakemore, apologising for the occurrence and assuring the PM that he already had his very best man on the job. That call was followed by the person who *was* the Home Secretary's "very best man", Police Commissioner, Brian Buggerington, who also apologised for the occurrence and went on to say that he too had his "very best man" on the job. Buggerington then asked if it was at all possible for the Royal Navy to lend them a couple of boats to chase after the criminals, to which the PM said that he had no idea, and that he'd have to ask the Royal Navy. So Robert was then forced to phone the First Lord of the Admiralty, Sir Reginald Anthem. He'd already heard about HMS Victory being taken, but didn't seem to mind too much, as long as those responsible were careful not to do anything silly with it. However, he was unable to lend the Police any boats as, unfortunately, the smallest one they had in the immediate vicinity was the aircraft carrier HMS Platonic, which was moored up in Portsmouth Docks having its communication systems upgraded to include Sky Movies Premier.

As soon as he'd ended the call with Sir Reginald Anthem, the PM then had the Chairmen of Her Majesty's Coastguard on the phone, keen to find out if the thieves were wearing life jackets. And finally, he'd had The Sun's Editor-in-Chief calling to say that the country was fully behind his decision to let the Victory sail again, and that it was about time!

After spending another ten minutes explaining to the Sun's Editor-in-Chief that HMS Victory had been stolen, and that he had absolutely nothing to do with it, Robert was exhausted. And he'd only just managed to put his feet up on his desk and pick up that month's issue of Golf Club Owners magazine, when his Private Secretary, Fredrick Overtoun, knocked on the door and barged straight in for what must have been the twelfth time that morning.

'Excuse me, Prime Minister, but Sir Ronold Macdonold is here to see you.'

'Who?'

'The Chairman of MDK Industries, Prime Minister.'

'Oh, yes, of course, sorry. I forgot. But for God's sake, Freddy, this is the last meeting of the day. I'm supposed to be teeing off at three and haven't even had my lunch yet.'

'Yes, of course, Prime Minister. Sorry. I'll show him straight in for you.'

A few moments later, Fredrick returned with Sir Ronold Macdonold, a morbid-looking chap who was barely able to manage a smile.

'Good of you to see me, Prime Minister.'

'Not at all Ron. Do please have a seat.'

'May I get either of you something to drink?' asked Fredrick. 'A cup of tea or a coffee perhaps?'

'No, I'm fine, thank you,' replied Ronold.

'We're both fine, thank you, Freddy. Now bugger off, there's a good chap.'

'Very well, Prime Minister,' and the Private Secretary slunk out of the room before securing the door behind him.

'Right then, what is it that I can do for you, Ron?' asked Robert, as he sat himself down opposite his guest in the corner of the office that he always used for his more private meetings.

'I'm sure you've heard, Prime Minister, that I've recently been voted in as Chairman of MDK Industries after the sudden death of Sir Gordon Boltestrode.'

'Yes, I was very sorry to hear that. I hear it was accidental.'

'I'm afraid so. He stepped on our very latest landmine, the Shadow-Maker 4000 Mark 3, during its press launch, Prime Minister.'

'Oh, dear. Well, never mind. Do please continue.'

'Thank you, Prime Minister. As you know, we're Britain's largest manufacturer and supplier of advanced weapons.'

'I didn't know that, but again, do carry on,' he said, and purposefully looked at his watch.

'Right, yes, well, of course. So, anyway, it seems that we've been having a few difficult years recently, financially speaking, and we're, um, going to have to ask for the Government's help.'

'What, you need money?'

'Oh, no, Prime Minister, we'd never ask the Government for money. You wouldn't have enough! No, Prime Minister, we need a war, and a good-sized one at that.'

'But didn't we only just invade Iraq? Wasn't that enough?'

'Yes, of course, and we were certainly very grateful. But unfortunately that was back in 2003, twelve years ago. In order to stay afloat we really need a decent war to take place at least once every ten years.'

'How about that other one going on in the Middle East?'

'What, Syria?'

'Yes, that one.'

'Well, that certainly has helped, but unfortunately it's nowhere near enough.'

'I see.' Robert leaned back in his chair, crossed his legs and knotted his fingers together. Unlike the majority of his predecessors, he had little interest in showing the world how important he was by flexing his political muscles. His only interests in life were golf and money, in that order, and since being elected he'd done all that he could to get hold of as much cash as possible whilst spending as much time on the golf course as the job would allow. Becoming embroiled in the machinations of international disputes only seemed to serve as annoying and unnecessary distractions, as did all those endless domestic problems he seemed permanently inundated with by both his Cabinet and Private Secretary.

'Well, I'm awfully sorry, Ron, but I really don't see how I can help. If there's nothing going on that could lead to a war, then there's really not much I can do about it.'

'But Prime Minister, with all due respect, there's never been anything going on in the world that could lead to a war, not since Hitler invaded France that is. They've always had to be, one might say…encouraged.'

'Well, that may be so, but I've no personal desire to go around encouraging a war just for the hell of it. I've got far more important things to do, thank you very much.'

'I appreciate that, Prime Minister, really I do, but then again, you don't seem to understand the adverse effect that long term peace has on the British economy.'

'I've always been given the impression that wars are rather expensive and should be avoided at all costs.'

'Quite the opposite, I'm afraid, Prime Minister. Of course we don't want them to be too big, or drag on for too long, but the occasional one is absolutely essential for the economic stability of our country.'

'I'm sorry, I don't follow you.'

'What I mean to say is that yes, they are hugely expensive, as are bridges, nuclear power-plants, cross-channel tunnels, peculiar-shaped domes constructed in the middle of nowhere, and hosting the Olympic Games, but you can't make an omelette without breaking a few eggs. Business just doesn't work like that. We need to keep spending money in order to maintain a vibrant economy. That's why the American government built the Hoover Dam in the middle of the Arizona Desert. It was an insanely stupid idea and cost them an absolute fortune, but it provided many thousands of jobs and gave the American manufacturing industry a huge shot in the arm. It was the same story with the Golden Gate Bridge built that same year, and those were just two of many capital projects that helped bring them out of the Great Depression. But dams and bridges aside, what we've learnt since then is that a decent war is by far the quickest way to inject money into the capital economy. But it also goes one step further by encouraging people to live in a state of perpetual fear, so they're more likely to keep working hard to ensure that they've plenty of money at all times, so keeping their ongoing sense of deep-rooted psychological insecurity at bay, but only just.'

Robert was beginning to wonder whether the man sitting opposite him wasn't the most intelligent person he'd ever met in his entire life, but he hadn't finished.

'If we don't have a decent war soon, and I do mean soon, MDK will have no choice but to fold. If that does happen, and God forbid it does, I suspect our current losses of £940 billion would be enough to crash the market, again, and I know for a fact that the Bank of England is in no position to weather another storm like the last one. So if we go, then the banks go, and if the banks go, then you go, along with Great Britain as we know it today!'

Without his realising it, Robert's heart had dramatically increased its tempo and now pounded hard inside his chest. The idea of losing all his money, his job and his new golf course, in quick succession, was inducing his own state of deep-rooted psychological insecurity.

'This is serious, isn't it?'

'Yes, Prime Minister, I'm afraid so. We need a war and we need one soon. I'd say MDK has six months at best.'

Robert stood up from his chair and started pacing the room in an effort to calm himself down.

'Right then!' he said. 'I don't suppose you've any suggestions as to who we can start one with?'

'Not really, Prime Minister. To be honest, we've never been in this situation before. All your predecessors seem to have been champing at the bit to start a fight with someone! As long as it's far enough away to minimize British civilian casualties, it doesn't really matter. The financial markets don't like it when too many of our own people start getting killed on home ground. The odd one here and there's fine, but when it starts to run into the hundreds they do seem to get a little jittery.'

'Do you think we should have a go at bombing Iraq again?'

'I'd suggest that maybe it's a little too soon to start there. You don't want to keep bombing the same ground too often. It's a bit like farming. You need to give the land time to recover, re-plant and grow before you can have a good harvest, otherwise it becomes counter-productive.'

'Where would you suggest then?'

'Well, let's take a look, shall we?' and he reached down to extract something from his laptop bag. 'I brought my iPad with me. Perhaps we could have a look at Google Maps?'

'Oh, okay!' said Robert, not too sure what that was, so he returned to his chair to watch Sir Ronold Macdonold set his iPad down on the coffee table and wake it up, before tapping on the icon labelled "Maps".

'Right, if I just zoom out like this…we can take a look at a map of the world.'

'This is great!' said Robert. He really wasn't into technology and was still trying to get used to his new smartphone. 'What's it called again?'

'What, Google Maps?'

'Yes, that's the one. Can I get it on this?' and he pulled out his phone to show Sir Ronold.

'Oh, yes, I'm sure you can.'

They stared down at the illuminated map of the world.

'Where's Iraq?' asked Robert, out of curiosity.

Ron gave him a quick glance to see if he was joking, but he didn't look like he was. 'It's right here, Prime Minister, next to Iran.'

'Oh, yes, and look, there's Syria!'

'That's right,' and couldn't help but give the PM another questioning look. 'So, anyway. Lots to choose from, as you can see.'

'How about Saudi Arabia?'

'Maybe not, Prime Minister. We've just too many investors out there.'

'Oh, okay. What about Egypt then, or Libya, or Algeria?'

'Yes, well, I'd say they're all possibilities, Prime Minister, but may I be so bold as to suggest Tunisia?' It was evident that the PM didn't have a clue where that was, so Sir Ronold Macdonold pointed at it. 'It's just here.'

'Oh, yes, so it is.'

'As you can see, they're close enough to Europe to be considered a possible threat, were they to have any WMDs, but far enough away not to be, if you see what I mean.'

'And do they have any WMDs?'

'God, no! But that's really not important. Anyway, it's also quite small, so hardly anyone is going to have heard of it, and it's not part of NATO, which will prove useful if you decide to try and get them on your side, this time around.'

He glanced up at the Prime Minister, who just looked very confused, so he suggested, 'Maybe you should talk to your Defence Minister, and see what he thinks?'

'Yes, good idea. Hold on, let me just take a few notes.' Robert stood up and went over to his desk to find a pen and wrote "Tunisia" on the back of his golf magazine.

Sir Ronold Macdonold picked up his iPad, put it back into his computer's padded bag, and stood up, delighted with how the meeting had gone.

'Thank you once again for taking the time to see me, Prime Minister. I really do appreciate how busy you are.'

'Not at all, not at all. Let me just call Freddy and he'll show you out.'

As he underlined Tunisia and then put a big question mark after it, he picked up his desk phone and asked his Private Secretary to come in to see Sir Ronold safely out.

Act 3, Scene 2

Ils m'abattus, les salauds!
They shot me, the bastards!

"Off with his head!"
King Richard III, Act III, Scene IV

CATE MADE an elegant landing on the plastic boat's fly-bridge with her sword in her hand and a steely grin on her face. Apart from the now familiar creaking of HMS Victory as it continued to slip past, she couldn't hear anything, so she crept over towards the steps that led down to the next level.

A call came from above - 'Look out below!' - and Will leapt down to join her, closely followed by Cannonball and Deadweight, all three of them landing on the padded fly-bridge seats, which was handy, otherwise they'd have made a hell of a noise.

'I thought you were still playing with that cannon,' she said.

'This looked like more fun,' said Will, and gave Cate his own deranged sort of a grin. 'So, what's the plan, Captain?'

'Oh, was I supposed to have a plan? I was just going to pop downstairs, find the one who shot Crispin and then stick this in him until he apologised, or died. Either one really, but that's about as far as I'd got.'

'You do know they've got machine guns, don't you?'

'Yes, thank you! And I've got an 18th Century cutlass, and I bet my sword's seen more action than their guns, in the last few days, at least. Anyway, how about you? What's that you've got?'

The three men each held up a short length of solid-looking rope.

'They're called Starters,' explained Will. 'They're what ships' officers used to "start" the crew with.'

'You do know they've got machine guns, don't you?'

'Tell you what,' said Will. 'Let's see which works better, your sword or our Starters.'

'Deal!' she said, and peered down over the fly-bridge to see if the coast was clear. There was nobody around, so she made her way down the plastic steps to the next level, where she crouched low to the deck and waited to be joined by the other three. Then she led the way over to another set of white moulded steps and peeked over the side again, before continuing down.

Grouping at the base, Cate pointed inside at what must be the main cabin.

'*This is where the windows were opened,*' she whispered. '*They must be in there.*'

Using her hand to indicate that they needed to stay down, she raised her head to steal a glance through the window directly above her.

'*I can see two of them, both with guns and both on the left side, below the windows, next to a door. And there's another door on the right, opposite.*'

Ducking back down, she thought for a moment. *'If I distract them by going in through the left-hand door, then you can come in through the right, and we can meet in the middle. Agreed?'*

The three pirates gave her a thumbs up.

'Okay, let's go, but keep it real quiet.'

Cate began to slink around to the port side of the cabin, making sure that her head was well below the level of the windows, and as she did that, her pirate chums crept around to starboard.

Reaching the door she waited a few moments to collect her thoughts, and to give Will, Cannonball and Deadweight time to get into position. Then she counted to three in her head, stood up and walked straight in, sword in hand, and glared at the two suspected drug dealers, saying, 'Hello, boys. Nice day for it.'

They fell over in surprise, dropping their guns in the process. And as they scrabbled around on the floor to retrieve them, the other members of HMS Victory's boarding party burst in through the opposite door and descended upon them to begin a practical demonstration of how Starters would have been put to good use on a couple of lowly, obstinate and lackadaisical members of the Victory's crew, back in the day.

'No time for that, men,' said Cate, mindful that there could be others on board. 'Deadweight, sit on them for a while and make sure they don't go anywhere. Will, Cannonball, pick up their guns and follow me.'

As Deadweight made himself comfortable, the remaining three headed over towards a narrow staircase that led down to another cabin below.

'We've lost the element of surprise,' Cate whispered. *'If there are more down there, they're going to be expecting us, so I suggest Will goes first.'*

'Huh?' said Will.

'Just kidding! I'll go, but you need to follow straight after.'

She craned her head down the steps, but couldn't see anyone, so she looked back at her men and said, *'We're going to have to move fast, and I'm not taking prisoners - got it?'*

They nodded.

'Okay. On three. And one, and two and THREE!' She sprang down the stairs to be met with a hail of gunfire coming from behind a drinks bar towards the back end of the cabin. In no mood to stand around to be shot at, she let out a terrifying scream and charged straight at them.

Somewhat surprised to see a demented, sword wielding girl-pirate heading their way, the two Frenchies stood up from behind the bar and hesitated for a moment before firing again; but that was all Cate needed, and she jumped over the bar, took one of their heads clean off and sliced open the other's throat before crashing down on top of the two now gurgling bodies.

Breathing hard, she stood up and grinned over at Will and Cannonball, who'd only just made it down the stairs, but who now found themselves transfixed by the head of a suspected drug-dealing Frenchie that had landed in a large bowl of peanuts, right on top of the bar.

Cate glanced at the severed head and said, 'Bon appétit!' before looking down at the floor to admire her handiwork.

'I-is he alright?' asked Cannonball. He'd never seen someone decapitated before.

'I hope not!' replied Cate. 'But hold on, let me ask him.'

She lowered herself down to be level with the head and asked, 'Excuse me, but are you okay?'

There was no answer, so she looked back at Cannonball and said, 'I suspect that he might be dead, same as the other one. Hey-ho! Anyway, the bar's open. What d'ya fancy?' and she reached over to grab a handful of peanuts before realising that she must have been hit somewhere, as her arm wasn't working. Then one of her legs gave way.

'Fuck it, they shot me, the bastards!' and she grabbed the bar-top with her good arm to stop herself falling back down onto the two blood-soaked bodies.

Will and Cannonball ran over to help.

'Christ, Cate, you really are a complete psycho, you do know that, don't you?'

Assuming Cannonball's question to be rhetorical, she didn't answer, but just let them scoop her up.

Will said, 'Let's take her over to that settee.'

'Hold on, fellas!' Cate said, and grabbed the handful of blood-splattered peanuts she'd meant to take before. Cramming them into her mouth, she reached over to the drinks cabinet on the wall and helped herself to a bottle of rum.

'Okay, you can go now!'

They eased her down onto the settee.

'Unscrew that for me, Will? I don't seem to be able to do it with one hand.'

As he helped her with the bottle, he said to Cannonball, 'Stay with her. I'm going back to the ship to see if anyone's got some decent first aid experience.'

'But what if there are some more drug dealers down here?'

'Good question. Tell you what, if you see any, just shoot them.'

'Oh, okay,' he said, but didn't look convinced and stared down at the cold black metal semi-automatic machine gun he cradled in his hands with a concerned look.

'If you prefer, you can always run them through with Cate's sword,' suggested Will.

'Er, no, it's okay. I think I'll stick with the gun, thank you.'

'Good job. Right, look after Cate,' and Will headed for the base of the stairs but there he stopped, dead in his tracks. He thought he heard something move behind the bar, and lifted an index finger to his lips as he looked over his shoulder at Cannonball and Cate. With the same hand he then pointed towards where he thought he'd heard the noise coming from and began creeping towards it. Reluctantly, Cannonball got up as quietly as possible and followed suit.

They approached the bar from opposite ends, and after Will mouthed a count to three, they sprang around the sides, with their guns pointing downwards. But there was nothing there except the two bodies, one with a head and the other without. Then Will noticed that one of the arms looked out of place. The material of the suit it wore was a different colour from the rest, light blue instead of plain black. Will leaned over, grabbed hold of the odd-looking arm and pulled on it to reveal another body, that of a small, well-groomed man in a shiny suit, wearing a Rolex.

'Is he dead as well?' asked Cannonball.

'No. He's moving a bit. He must be semi-conscious. Right, I'd better take him upstairs with me.' He pulled the man clear of the other two, and then slid him over the highly-polished wooden floor to the base of the stairs. He looked over at Cannonball, who was making his way back towards Cate, and said, 'Back in a mo,' before heading up the stairs, pulling the shiny-suited man behind him as he went.

Act 3, Scene 3

Les Drogues, l'Argent et l'Or
Drugs, Cash and Gold

"Cry 'Havoc,' and let slip the dogs of war."
Julius Caesar, Act III, Scene I

CANNONBALL had to go to the loo. He'd needed to go before he jumped onto the fly-bridge, and now he was desperate, but the potential risk of lurking drug dealers, or gangsters, or whatever they were, wasn't conducive to leaving the relative safety of his current position. However, his need had reached the point where either he wet himself, or found a toilet. He looked down at the gun that still rested in his lap, and with the knowledge gained from hours playing Call of Duty, he lifted it into a firing position and placed his finger on the trigger. It felt alright, not too heavy, and his bladder wasn't giving him much choice, so he said to Cate, 'I'm just going to find a toilet. You'll be okay, won't you?'

'I'll be just fine,' she replied, taking yet another swig from her bottle of rum. 'You go. Have a great time, and maybe find me another bottle whilst you're there.'

She really was getting quite drunk; either that or the loss of blood was taking its toll on the normal functionality of her brain. Either way, Cannonball had to go, so he got to his feet and crept towards a wooden door in the bulkhead near the front. Reaching it, he listened, but couldn't hear anything, so he took a deep breath and pulled it open, hiding behind it as he did so. No gunfire ensued, so he peered around.

There was nothing there except an empty cabin way and multiple doors leading off it. *This could take a while,* he thought, so, doing his best to control his desperation to do a wee, he stepped into the corridor and approached the first door on the port side. He did exactly the same with that one, pulling it open and hiding behind it, but again there was no gunfire. He was in luck! Inside was a good-sized bathroom with a toilet, a basin and an actual bath, with a white shower curtain pulled across it.

Without further ado, he shoved his gun under his arm and began to relieve himself. As he felt the tension flow out of him, he looked over at the closed shower curtain to his immediate right with a sinking feeling. He'd forgotten to check behind it! Staring at its dull plastic whiteness he could feel the tension return. If there was a French drug-dealing gangster hiding there, with a semi-automatic machine gun pointing at his head, this was probably the last time he'd ever have to use a toilet. Blood drained from his face, and without moving his head, he put his manhood away and, ever-so-slowly, reached for his gun. With exquisite care, he pushed the barrel round the edge of the curtain and gradually eased it back.

He let out a sigh of relief.

There was nobody there.

But then he noticed that the bath itself was full to the brim of brown packets similar to the one they'd seen near the Jacuzzi, and on top of those were two black holdalls. He put the gun down and unzipped one of them.

'Well, bugger me!'

Then he unzipped the other.

They were both stuffed full of neatly bundled 500 Euro notes. There were loads of them. And as he picked up a couple to stare at, he saw that underneath, lining the bottom of the holdalls, were a number of small pouches, tied off with cords and marked, "BANQUE DE FRANCE". He dropped the notes and pulled one of the money pouches out. It was really heavy, so he dumped it in the sink to take a look inside.

'Jesus Christ! It's full of gold!'

He picked out one of the many solid gold sovereigns and, again, held it up to stare at.

'Right, we're having this lot!' he said to himself, and having completely forgotten about the possibility of being drilled full of holes by hidden gun-slinging, drug-dealing gangsters, he went off in search of some sort of a container to transfer this newly discovered treasure onto the Victory.

It wasn't long before he found just the thing. Lying on the opulent bed built into the boat's bow was a half-unpacked vintage brown leather luggage trunk, with a gold lock and matching hinges. It must have been worth a few quid in itself.

'Perfect!' he said, and threw all the remaining clothes out onto the floor, heaved the lid closed, and dragged it off the bed and along the corridor to the bathroom. There he began transferring the contents of the bath into the trunk.

As soon as he'd finished, he closed the lid and dragged it back into the main cabin.

'Where the fuck have you been?' asked Will, who'd since returned with Peter, who was doing his best to patch Cate up.

'You'll never believe what I've found!' and he continued to drag the trunk until it was right in the middle of the cabin where he flung the lid open.

'How about that!' he exclaimed.

'What is it?' asked Cate, who couldn't see from where she was lying.

'Oh, sorry,' said Cannonball. 'It's basically a shed-load of money, gold, and drugs!'

'I've gotta see this,' said Cate, and used Peter to help her to stand up on one leg.

Will, Peter, and Cate just stood there and stared at it.

'We can't keep it!' said Peter.

'Of course we can keep it!' said Cate. 'I didn't take two bullets for nothing; and anyway, who's going to stop us?'

But at that precise moment they heard something that sounded like a giant fog horn.

'That's another ship!' said Will. 'Quick, hurry! We need to get the trunk and Cate back on board the Victory, and sharpish.'

Peter took Cate's good arm, placed it over his shoulder and helped her to hobble up the narrow staircase, closely followed by Will and Cannonball as they manhandled the trunk up the stairs.

In the cabin above, Deadweight was still lying on top of the two drug-dealing gangster-type Frenchies, plus the one they'd found behind the bar, none of whom were looking very well. With time at a premium Will said, 'Deadweight, Cannonball, just chuck 'em over the side. We really don't have time for them.'

So as Peter continued to help Cate back up to the fly-bridge, Will, Cannonball and Deadweight dragged the three Frenchies out onto the portside walkway, and were about to push them over the side when they saw what looked to be a navy frigate approaching fast.

'They're in a bit of a hurry,' said Deadweight.

'Let's hope they're not French,' added Cannonball.

'Unfortunately they are,' said Will. 'Unless there's a British battleship called La Grenouille, which I doubt.'

'What are we going to do now?' asked Deadweight.

'We'd better keep one of these Frenchies as a hostage, just in case we need something to bargain with.'

'But which one?'

'The one we found behind the bar, with the shiny suit, and the Rolex. He looks like the most important.'

They shoved the other two overboard and Will dragged the small, posh-looking one back into the cabin.

'Right,' he continued. 'Cannonball, Deadweight; you take the trunk up to the fly-bridge and get it on board the Victory, and I'll do the same with this Frenchman. Then I suggest we get the fuck out of here!'

'Sounds like a plan,' said Cannonball.

By the time they'd reached the fly-bridge, they saw that the Victory had been moored up alongside, and Cate was being heaved aboard with both her legs in a double-bowline knot, which was making a good makeshift harness.

'Throw some more ropes down,' Will called up, 'we've got us some treasure and a prisoner to get aboard.'

No sooner had he asked than more lines came cascading into the fly-bridge. Grabbing one, Deadweight tied a quick bowline around the trunk's handle, as Will tied another around their prisoner's waist. Making sure it was secured under the man's arms, he called up, 'HAUL AWAY!' and both the trunk and the prisoner were heaved up, followed by Peter, Will, Cannonball, and Deadweight, who scooted up the lines like over-sized circus monkeys.

Back on board, the French frigate gave them another blast of its horn as it ploughed towards them at what must have been full-speed.

'ATTENTION, HMS VICTORY! RESTEZ OU VOUS ETES, NOUS ALLONS VOUS EMBARQUER!'

'Fuck this!' exclaimed Will. 'Quick, untie us from that plastic French monstrosity. Cannonball, Deadweight; get back down to the cannon. I want that Gin Palace thing lying at the bottom of the Channel. Everyone else, get as much sail up as possible. There's a good breeze for England. We're heading for home!'

A cheer went up as the plastic boat was cast off, and Cannonball and Deadweight legged it down to the cannon they'd been messing about with earlier.

Will, meanwhile, headed over to the prisoner, who'd been unceremoniously dumped besides the trunk on the quarterdeck, and used the rope that was still around his chest to make him more secure. Peter helped Cate up to the poop deck where Crispin had been resting. When Will eventually joined them, they all leaned against the railing that overlooked the quarterdeck and watched as the crew sprang into action, launching themselves up the ratlines to set just as many sails as possible.

'ATTENTION, HMS VICTORY! RESTEZ OU VOUS ETES, NOUS ALLONS VOUS EMBARQUER!'

A huge boom erupted from the lower decks, as a plume of thick black smoke swept over the ship for the second time that day.

'Good work, men!' cried Will. 'They've just put a hole in that plastic boat. Look! She's going down already.'

'Do you think we could put a hole in that other one as well?' asked Cate.

'What, the frigate? No chance!' said Will. 'Unfortunately there's just no way an 18th Century cannonball's going to put a hole in a 21st Century navy battleship, even if it is French! I doubt we'd even dent it!'

A loud whistle passed over the Victory's bow followed by a boom and a huge splash.

'What the fuck was that?' asked Cate.

'They've just put a shot over our bow,' explained Will. 'Looks like they're serious.'

'Well, fuck 'em!' said Cate. 'I for one ain't going down without a fight!'

'Unfortunately we're totally outclassed. They could sink us with one shot, easy!'

'Yes, but would they, Will? I mean, isn't this a really special boat? I doubt they'd have the balls.'

'She's got a point,' said Crispin. 'This is, after all, HMS Victory, and not only that, she's still a Royal

Navy commissioned ship. If they sank us, it would be war! They'd never risk it.'

'Well, it looks like we've got backup,' said Deadweight, staring out behind them.

They all turned to see another frigate fast approaching from the opposite direction.

'Let's hope they're not French!' said Cate.

'No, they're definitely British. It's HMS Arduous.'

'And look!' exclaimed Cannonball. 'There's another boat coming in.'

'British or French?' asked Cate.

'Looks like the British Police!'

'Really?' she asked, trying to see over.

The approaching Royal Navy frigate's loud speaker echoed into life.

'LA GRENOUILLE, THIS IS HMS ARDUOUS, CAN YOU HEAR US?'

'YES, WE CAN HEAR YOU, HMS ARDUOUS.'

'YOU ARE FIRING ON A SHIP BELONGING TO HER MAJESTY, QUEEN ELIZABETH'S NAVY. IF YOU CONTINUE WE WILL BE FORCED TO TAKE IMMEDIATE DEFENSIVE ACTION. DO YOU UNDERSTAND?'

There was a pause as the two ships approached each other, with HMS Victory floating in the middle.

'HMS ARDUOUS, THIS IS LA GRENOUILLE. YOUR MAJESTY'S BOAT, "HMS VICTORY", HAS JUST ATTACKED AND NOW SUNK "LA VIERGE DE LA CUPIDITE", WHICH WAS THE PROPERTY OF MONSIEUR JACQUES MOUTONETTE, THE PRESIDENT OF FRANCE.'

As both vessels slowed, the French frigate continued, *'WE BELIEVE OUR PRESIDENT WAS*

ON BOARD AT THE TIME. THIS ACTION CANNOT BE OVER-LOOKED. DO YOU UNDERSTAND?'

There was another pause in this inter-boat communication, as all parties let that rather unfortunate information sink in.

'Oops,' said Cate.

They all looked down at the Frenchman who Will had tied up and had left lying unconscious in the middle of the quarterdeck, besides the trunk crammed full of drugs, cash and gold.

'Do you think it's him, the French President?' asked Peter, looking even more worried than usual.

'Well, I must admit,' said Will, 'now that you mention it, he does look vaguely familiar.'

Act 3, Scene 4

Voyage scolaire pour les enfants obèses
School trip for obese children

"The course of true love never did run smooth."
A Midsummer Night's Dream, Act I, Scene I

'WHAT'S CHUPPLES up to, Sir?'
'He's turning around. Looks like he's given up, and I can't say I blame him. We haven't seen another boat in hours.'

Capstan and Dewbush watched Chupples' police motor launch, the one they'd surreptitiously been following all day, bear away to starboard before speeding back towards them. As it approached, the boat came off its plane to pass slowly, leaving them to port.

'There's no sign of them,' Chupples called out as they drifted past, 'and we're running low on fuel, so we're calling it a day, and I suggest you do the same.'

He pushed the throttle back on to full power and left Capstan and Dewbush rocking in his wake.

'Do you think we should head back as well, Sir.'

'No, fuck 'em. I don't give a shit what that twat says. Let's give it another hour. They must be out here somewhere.'

There followed another of many long pauses they'd experienced during the course of the day, this particular one being brought to an end by Dewbush asking, 'Would you like another sandwich, Sir?'

'No, thank you, Dewbush, I really wouldn't. I'm not even sure I wanted the first one. What was it again?'

'I think it was cottage cheese, Sir. They all are. Anyway, we've still got loads left, just in case you change your mind,' and helped himself to yet another of the two dozen that had been provided for them by the Solent Police Dinner Ladies Department.

'How about some more orange squash, Sir?'

'And that's another thing, why didn't someone think to give us some tea or coffee? Cottage cheese sandwiches and reduced sugar orange squash! Anyone would think this is a school trip for obese children! Next time they'll give us a packet of Ryvita and some skimmed milk!'

'Don't worry, Sir, I'm sure the Victory will have some coffee on board.'

'Do you think so?' asked Capstan, unable to hide his desperation. He hadn't had any caffeine since that morning's briefing, and was struggling.

'They should do, Sir. The boat's been used as a museum for years, so they must have installed a canteen on it by now. They might even have a souvenir shop!'

There was no response from Capstan who'd been doing his best not to listen or respond to anything his Sergeant had said since they'd left Portsmouth Harbour. And he certainly had absolutely no intention of finding out if, when, how or why HMS Victory might or might not have a souvenir shop.

'If they do,' continued Dewbush to Capstan's misfortune, 'we could get the Chief Inspector a present!'

'That's a brilliant idea, Dewbush. Well done.'

Despite his best efforts, Capstan couldn't help himself, so he added. 'And maybe they'll have a pirate's hat and an eye patch for him. I'm sure he'd like that.'

'Oh, I'm sure he would, Sir. He'd probably enjoy dressing up as a pirate, and it might help cheer him up a little. He does seem to have been a little down recently.'

'Recently? He's a fat, miserable bastard, and always has been. He's not called Morose for nothing, you know!'

'How do you mean, Sir?'

'Never mind, Dewbush. It really doesn't matter.'

This brief intellectual exchange had reminded Capstan just how much he disliked having to talk to his colleague. He was becoming increasingly convinced that two individuals lying next to each other in a coma would have had more stimulating conversations, so he changed his mind and said, 'Chupples is probably right. There's nothing here, and I don't fancy being stuck out on our own like this. Let's spin it around before we lose sight of him and head back to base.'

Just as he finished talking, a thunderous roar boomed out overhead from somewhere beyond the horizon.

'What was that, Sir?'

'How the fuck should I know?'

'I think it came from straight ahead of us, Sir.'

Deep in thought, Capstan looked behind him, just in time to see Chupples disappear from view. He knew that if they continued on now they'd have no guarantee of finding their way back, not without someone to follow.

'Do you think we should take a look, Sir?' Dewbush prompted.

'How much fuel do we have?'

'We've still got loads, Sir. The tank's half full and they gave us a couple of jerry cans as well.'

Thinking that if it was HMS Victory up ahead, firing what did sound very much like some sort of a cannon, then this could be his chance for another promotion. If he was able to bring the Victory back to base single-handed, they might just give him the Medal of Honour to go with the OBE he picked up in the New Year for his heroic actions during the Battle of Bath.

'Sod it!' he said. 'Dewbush, let's push on, full speed ahead. If it's nothing we can turn straight back around, but if it is the Victory, then it might just be our lucky day.'

'Great idea, Sir!'

With mounting excitement, Dewbush eased the throttle up to full power and they started bouncing over the waves towards what Capstan hoped would be medals before breakfast.

Act 3, Scene 5

Bien visé!
Good shot!

*"You pay a great deal too dear
for what s given freely."*
The Winter's Tale, Act I, Scene I

'HEADS OR tails?'

'Heads!'

'Tails. Sorry, old chap,' said Robert, pleased as punch. 'Looks like this just isn't going to be your day.'

Having been flown in his helicopter over to the private golf course he'd bought in Deal, Kent, which hugged the British coastline and provided some challenging, if not downright dangerous, playing conditions, whilst enjoying uninterrupted cliff-edge views over the English Channel, the British Prime Minister, Robert Bridlestock, was about to tee off against his old golfing adversary, Lord Henry Flavourington, the owner of both Planet Communications and Devon; well, most of it anyway.

Having lost the toss, Lord Flavourington was already feeling hacked-off, and bared his teeth at Robert before asking, 'Shall we make it interesting?'

Henry Flavourington had considerably more money than Robert could ever aspire to, no matter how many

Senior Nuclear Scientists he could place with the North Korean Government, or the number of bribes he was able to accept to keep pushing the pro-Fracking agenda, without it becoming too obvious.

Robert pulled out his driver and began to address the ball that he'd already perched on top of his tee. He'd been expecting Henry to use the old, "Let's make it interesting" ploy, in his usual attempt to put him off his game. However, Lord Flavourington didn't know about the recent deal Robert had made with the five main international banking corporations. This one made all his other subversive transactions look like a cake sale held at an old people's home. No, he considered his latest idea to generate as much cash as possible for as little effort to be his finest achievement, his coup de grâce, his Arc De Triomphe; in monetary terms at least, which was all that mattered at the end of the day.

Having dined earlier that year with two other Lords, Lord Basil Wiltshirington, the Chief Justice of the United Kingdom's Supreme Court, and Lord Alfred Oakmore-Thrope, CEO of Her Majesty's Land Registry, Robert had been able to sneak a bill in through the House of Lords that, with one barely discernible signature, had made Canary Wharf a non-taxable place of commercial residence, i.e. a tax haven for global corporations far and wide. This was not only good news for him, as he was paid two billion per bank, sterling, which had made him the fourth richest person in the UK; but as far as Robert could work out it was good for Britain as well, as it made the East End of London the new Mecca for global business and would subsequently inject a huge amount of cash into the British market economy. The only entity it didn't seem to benefit, and which was probably why it had never been done before, was the British Government, who'd lose billions of pounds in tax revenue each year. But Robert really didn't think that mattered too much. The global corporations weren't stupid, and hardly paid a penny in tax as it was. At least this way, all the money they spent on architects, construction, land tax, their employees' hefty salaries and their staggeringly high bonuses, was being kept predominantly within the UK, and not being syphoned off to some tiny island in the middle of the Pacific Ocean.

And so, with a wry smile, Robert replied, 'Jolly good idea!'

He hadn't had the chance to play Henry since the money had been transferred into his brand new Canary Warf "offshore" account, and had been keenly anticipating this exact moment. 'How about making it a million per hole?'

'A-a million…per hole?'

Robert turned around to gaze at Henry with a look of apathetic consternation.'

'Too rich for your blood, old chap?'

'N-no, not at all, b-but..'

'That's settled then!' Robert spun round and whacked his ball, straight down the middle of the fairway, before Henry had a chance to think of an excuse not to play for such a monumental figure.

'GOOD SHOT!' he shouted. 'Even if I do say so myself,' and collected his tee before beaming over at his golfing chum. 'You're up, but you won't match that one I'm afraid.'

Henry was already regretting having agreed to play Robert again. He used to enjoy playing him, back in the day when he'd been easy to beat, when Robert had been a lowly cabinet minister. All he'd had to do then was suggest that they played for a bit of cash, mention a figure with four zeros after it, and the guy would start shaking like a leaf and miss every shot. But since he'd been elected to the top job he'd become virtually unassailable. And this new posturing was above and beyond anything Henry had ever witnessed before. Even Sir Rupert Branston didn't play for a million per hole!

And so, with a hidden grimace, he yanked out his own driver from his golf bag and stomped his way over to the tee.

Just as he was about to take his shot, Robert's phone rang.

'WHAT THE HELL DO YOU THINK YOU'RE PLAYING AT, ROBERT? You know the rules. NO PHONES!'

'Fuck it,' mumbled Robert, as he clawed his new smartphone out from his back pocket.

'That will cost you ten grand. Did you hear me?'

Recognising the caller ID, Robert just said, 'Yes, yes, yes, keep your hair on old chap.' He'd normally just turn it off, or throw it into the nearest bin, especially if it was his Private Secretary, but it wasn't every day that a country's Premier called him, not on his mobile at any rate, and the interruption might also help to maintain Lord Flavourington's current state of furious indignation, which should guarantee an easy eighteen million by end-of-play.

'Bonjour Jacques! How's French presidential life treating you?' Robert asked with his usual boyish charm.

'Robert, what the hell's HMS Victory doing out at sea?'

'Oh, you heard about that did you? Yes, well, apparently some deranged yobs made off with it last night.'

'I don't mean last night, I mean RIGHT NOW?'

'Excuse me, Robert, but are you going to be long?' Lord Flavourington asked, more loudly than was probably necessary. 'I thought we were playing golf?'

But Lord Flavourington was secretly hoping that some major international disaster had occurred, like a meteorite being spotted heading for Europe's largest horse meat factory, or a large sink hole opening under Brussels, and that Robert would be needed back at Number 10, so saving him a possible eighteen million quid, plus a lifetime of being the butt of one of Robert's many hilarious jokes.

'Hold on, Henry, it's the President of France,' said Robert, unable to resist the opportunity to name drop, before returning to his conversation.

'I've really no idea what the Victory is doing right now, Jacques, but I have my very best man on the job who's assured me that he's doing all that he can to locate it and bring it back to England. But that aside, what on Earth's it got to do with you?'

'I'll tell you what it's got to do with me. It's just attacked my fucking boat, that's what it's got to do with me!'

'Listen, Robert, if you can't get off the phone then you're going to have to forfeit the game,' stated Lord Flavourington, making a very deliberate point of looking at his Le Grande Casia De Maskinette diamond encrusted sports watch, that was so lavishly expensive it was unable to tell him the time, but looked great none the less.

'Just hold on, please, Henry, I think the French President is having some sort of mental breakdown.'

Returning to his phone conversation, Robert asked, 'Can you speak up Jacques, I can hardly hear a word you're saying?'

'I said… your HMS Victory has attacked my boat, and despite our very best efforts to dissuade them otherwise, they've just boarded us. Whatever it is that you're up to Robert, you need to call them off, and you need to call them off NOW! I'm in absolutely no position to be searched by the Royal Navy or anyone else for that matter!'

'I can assure you, Jacques, that I have no idea where HMS Victory is or what it is doing, but I promise you that the British Government has absolutely no interest in you, your boat, who you're with on your boat, or what you're about to do to her.'

'I'm not about to do anything to anyone, but my boat is the property of the Republic of France, and under no circumstances are British officials allowed to search it!'

'Listen, Robert, old chap,' interrupted Lord Flavourington, 'you're clearly a bit busy. May I suggest we call it a day?' and Henry lent over and pulled out his ball and tee, before heading back over to his golf bag.

'Just hold on, Henry, for Christ's sake, I'll be done soon! Now listen, Jacques, I've got no idea what the hell you're going on about, but I'm in the middle of a vitally important game of golf, so I suggest you call back another time, and maybe from a landline. I really can't hear a thing you're going on about.'

There was a sudden loud crackle from the other end of the phone, forcing Robert to pull it away from his ear and giving him the perfect excuse to end the call.

'Sorry about that. Henry, I'll turn this damn thing off. Now, where were we?'

'You've just forfeited the game. You know the rules about telephone conversations during a match.'

'Yes, but I'd already teed off. Interrupting play due to an incoming phone call is just the £10,000 fine, not a forfeit.

Henry stood there with his hand resting on the driver that he'd already put back in its bag. He was clearly undecided as to whether or not he should quit while he was at least not down eighteen million.

'Tell you what,' added Robert, 'let's make it for half a million per hole. Would that be more acceptable?'

Henry now felt he had to continue, else he'd never hear the end of it, and at the original figure as well. So he pulled out his driver again and said, 'No, the million per hole's fine,' and forced a grin at the PM through his immaculate white teeth. It was clear that Robert was desperate to play, which in Henry's eyes gave him the upper hand, and besides, a million per hole wasn't that much now that he'd had a chance to get used to the idea. It had just been a bit of a shock, that was all. And anyway, if he could maintain his current state of refined composure he might just come out of the game on top.

Act 3, Scene 6

Êtes-vous Français ou Anglais?
Are you French or English?

"What a piece of work is man! how noble in reason! how infinite in faculty!"
Hamlet, Act II, Scene II

'IT'S HMS VICTORY, Sir!'
'Are you sure, Dewbush?'

'Yes, Sir. It's definitely the Victory, and it seems to be heading our way!'

As the police motor boat continued to chug out towards their newly discovered quarry, Capstan said, 'It's much bigger than I was expecting.'

'But not half the size of those two navy ships though, Sir.'

'No, I'd have to agree with you there.'

'I wonder what they're up to, Sir?'

'I've really no idea, Dewbush. It looks like one of them is French and the other's British.'

'It could be that they're escorting the Victory back to base, Sir.'

'Right, well, if that's the case, then we'll need to arrest them all before they get back in. Any idea how we can get on board?

'Not really, Sir. I suppose if we can get alongside we could climb in through one of the holes, where the cannons are sticking out.'

'What, with my bad leg?'

'Well, maybe I could climb in and then lift you up, Sir?'

They watched in silence as HMS Victory loomed up towards them.

'It really is rather large, isn't it?'

'Yes, Sir. Shall I try and pull alongside?'

'Okay, have a go. I'm going to see if I can talk to those pirate-looking types up there. If we can let them know that we're the police then hopefully they'll feel obliged to tell us how to get on.'

'Right you are, Sir.'

'But I think we'd better not try to arrest them until we're safely on board. For now, let's just say that we want to ask them some questions.'

'What sort of questions, Sir?'

Capstan looked at his subordinate thinking that a giant squid would have a higher IQ.

'I don't know Dewbush, but maybe we can ask them what the weather's like?'

Dewbush gave his boss a quizzical look, and then gazed up at the sky. It was a perfect summer's day with a few clouds and a cool breeze. He had no idea why his boss wanted to ask them about the weather, but was too pre-occupied trying to keep the boat going in a straight line to find out, so he simply replied, 'Yes, Sir. And I'll do my best to get us alongside, Sir.'

As Dewbush eased off the throttle, and the giant man-of-war began to loom up above them, he brought the police motorboat around to match the Victory's speed and started to edge them ever closer to the great ship's blackened hull.

Meanwhile, Capstan could see that there were a number of people all dressed up as pirates, leaning out over the side and staring down at them, so he pulled out his police ID, held it as high as he could and called up, 'MY NAME IS INSPECTOR CAPSTAN, AND THIS IS SERGEANT DEWBUSH. WE'RE FROM SOLENT POLICE. WE NEED TO COME ABOARD TO ASK YOU SOME QUESTIONS.'

One of the pirates from the back end of the ship called down, 'ARE YOU FRENCH OR ENGLISH?'

'ENGLISH!' replied Capstan.

'ARE YOU SURE?'

'YES, WE'RE DEFINITELY ENGLISH! MAY WE COME ABOARD?'

'WELL, OKAY, BUT IF YOU TURN OUT TO BE FRENCH THEN WE'RE THROWING YOU STRAIGHT BACK OVER THE SIDE. COMPRENDEZ?'

Both Capstan and Dewbush nodded with some vigour. The wake from the Victory against their own boat was having an alarming effect, and they were struggling just to stay on their feet.

They watched as the pirates conferred before the same one called back, 'WE'RE GOING TO SEND SOMEONE DOWN.'

A line soon spiralled at them from above, followed by one of the ship's clearly very able, but rather large, seamen, who made it look like he'd spent his entire life climbing up and down the side of an 18th Century ship-of-the-line. But despite his obvious weight, the pirate dropped lightly onto the police motor boat and, still holding on to the line, asked, 'So, you're the police, are you?'

'That's right,' said Capstan, and held up his ID again.

The great hulk of a pirate studied it for some moments before continuing.

'And what is it that you want, exactly?'

'We just want to ask you some questions, that's all.'

'Yes,' added Dewbush. 'We need to find out what the weather's like.'

Capstan gave Dewbush a hard stare, wishing he'd had the foresight to push him overboard five minutes earlier.

'Do you have any food or drink?' asked the pirate.

'Er, yes,' replied Capstan. 'We've got sandwiches and some orange squash.'

'What sort of sandwiches are they?'

'I think they're cottage cheese. Is that right, Dewbush?'

'Yes, Sir, they're all cottage cheese sandwiches, Sir.'

'And you're definitely not French?'

'No, we're British, born and bred!' replied Capstan.

'Are you absolutely sure?' asked the pirate, who leaned in to examine Capstan's facial features. 'There's something very French about you.'

'I promise,' Capstan added, 'I've never even so much as placed a foot in France.'

'I have!' declared Dewbush, with a boastful grin.

The giant pirate man glared down at them both.

'Okay, you can come up,' he said, pointing at Capstan, 'but only if we can have some of your food and drink?'

'Fine by me,' replied Capstan.

Then the pirate looked over at Dewbush and said, 'But you! You're going to have to stay here. We've gone right off French people, and the Captain's given us strict orders not to allow any more on board.

Sergeant Dewbush was now regretting having mentioned his trip to France and so, in his defence, added, 'But I only went there on holiday.'

'For how long?'

'Two weeks.'

'No, I'm sorry, I just can't risk it. You're going to have to stay here.'

With his mind made up, the pirate took the line that he still held in his hand and began to tie a double-bowline knot in its end to make a quick harness.

Seeing what he was doing, Capstan asked, 'I've got a bit of a dodgy leg, will that matter?'

'No, not at all, we've taken up people in a far worse state.'

He then laid the double knot down on the boat's floor and said, 'Right, put your feet inside these two loops.'

'Hold on, let me just grab my stick,' and Capstan ducked down into the small cabin to retrieve it.

On his return the pirate said, 'Okay, now place both feet inside.'

'Like this?'

'Yes, that's it, and then I just pull the loops up, like so, and you hold on to the rope, here! Got it?'

'Yes, I think so.'

'Now whatever you do, don't let go of the rope!'

'Don't worry, I won't!'

'Okay,' and the pirate faced up to the Victory's quarterdeck to bellow out, 'HAUL AWAY THERE, HANDSOMELY NOW!'

And as Capstan was lurched up the ship's side, Dewbush began to feel lonely.

'Good luck, Sir,' he said, as he waved goodbye to his boss.

'I won't be long, Dewbush,' Capstan said, as he tried to stop himself from being bashed against the ship's hull.

'ANOTHER LINE PLEASE!' the massive pirate shouted up. And as he caught that one, he said, 'OK, pass me the food and drink, and don't worry, I'm sure your friend will be fine, unless he does turn out to be French of course. I've seen what our Captain does to French people…' and the pirate stared off into space with a wistful expression, before continuing, 'Anyway, if he is, then you'll probably never see him again, not all in one piece at any rate.'

Act 3, Scene 7

Vous avez dû entendre à tort
You must have heard it wrong

"Brevity is the soul of wit."
Hamlet, Act II, Scene II

'WHAT HAVE YOU found for us, Cannonball?' asked Cate, calling down from The Victory's poop deck.

'I've got me this British policeman, some sandwiches, and some orange squash!'

'Good work, but are you sure he's not…Oh, hold on, I think I know him. It's Inspector Catspam, isn't it?'

After been manhandled over the ship's side, untangled from his harness, and having only just regained his composure, along with his stick, Capstan was being escorted along the quarterdeck towards the stairs that led up to the poop deck, where a number of pirates were leaning over the rail, watching him as if it was his job to provide their afternoon's entertainment. Hearing the all-too-familiar mispronunciation of his name, he stopped and looked up. It was that girl, the one who'd had the body in her bin, and the same one who'd given him a signed copy of her book, after the suicide of her literary agent. She was Cate something, but having got rid of the book by giving it to his wife for her birthday, he couldn't for the life of him remember her surname.

'It's pronounced Capstan!' he said, digging out his ID again. 'From Solent Police.'

'Yes, I know who you are. I'm Cate Jakebury. Do you remember me? You were round at my place when that man was found in my General Waste wheelie bin.'

'Mrs Jakebury, yes, of course!'

'Did you ever find out who that man was, the one in my bin?'

'Er, no, but whoever it was, your neighbour has since been found guilty of murdering him.'

'Oh!' replied Cate, somewhat surprised.

'And how about my husband? Did you ever find him?'

'Um, again no, not that I can remember, sorry.'

'Oh, don't worry, I was just curious.'

'Mrs Jakebury, may I ask what you're doing on board HMS Victory, in the middle of the English Channel, dressed up as a pirate?'

'It's the result of a good night out, I'm afraid. Anyway, get yourself up here. We seem to have found ourselves in the middle of a highly entertaining international altercation.'

Capstan was intrigued, so he limped over to the base of the steps and did his best to make his way up to join her and her pirate friends.

'Can someone please help the poor man up the stairs?' she asked.

'But are you absolutely sure he's not French, Captain?' asked Will.

'Yes! I know he looks French, but he's not. It's his nose, I think. Anyway, give him a hand, will you?'

A few moments later, having finally made it all the way up from the police motor boat to The Victory's poop deck, Capstan was exhausted, and could do little more than prop himself up with the others against the rail that overlooked the quarterdeck, as he caught his breath and found his bearings. After several minutes spent gazing up and around the ship he eventually asked, 'I don't suppose there's a canteen on board? I could really do with a decent sandwich, and a coffee.'

'No, sorry, Inspector, just Evian and the odd dead fish. Here, you'd better have some water at least,' and she passed him the bottle Peter had given her earlier that morning. 'We've been sailing around all day asking boats if they can spare us some food and drink, but none of them have been particularly obliging, so far.'

'You're more than welcome to the sandwiches and orange squash we had with us. Not my cup of tea, I'm afraid,' Capstan said, and took a long drink from the Evian water bottle.

'So, what brings you all the way out here then, Inspector?'

He replaced the lid and wiped his mouth with the back of his sleeve. 'We wanted to ask you some questions about the Victory.'

'Well, you're talking to the wrong person. I've not got a clue about how this thing works. That's my crew's job!'

'No, I meant if you know anything about the fact that it's been stolen?'

'Stolen? Why on Earth do you think it's been stolen?'

'Um, I'm not sure, but perhaps because it's, er, here, out at sea, and not where it's supposed to be, back at Portsmouth.'

'Oh, you must have heard it wrong. It's called sailing, not stealing. We borrowed it last night after we'd had a few, isn't that right lads?'

'That's right, Captain.'

'If we'd stolen it, then it would have been chained up to a post or something.'

'You mean it wasn't locked up?' Capstan asked, with some incredulity.

'Not at all. It was just tied to a few bollards with some bits of rope, so we assumed it would be OK. If someone didn't want it to be taken then I'm sure they'd have put a padlock on it, along with a sign that said it wasn't to be sailed, don't you think?'

Capstan didn't know what to think, as was often the case, so he just stood there, enjoying his new and surprisingly rather pleasant surroundings.

'Anyway,' Cate continued, 'we're taking it back now. Too many Frenchies out here for our liking.'

She looked up at the sails and glanced over at Will. 'We are heading back, aren't we Will?'

'Aye, aye, Captain.'

'It's just that we don't seem to have moved in ages.'

'Well, Captain, unfortunately the wind does seem to have died on us, so progress will be slow, but we do have steerage way at least.'

'Fair enough,' and by way of making conversation she gave Capstan a nudge and said, 'Speaking of French people, that one down there, lying on the floor, is apparently the President of France! And that battleship over on the right, the French one, seems to be under the impression that we sank his boat, with him on it, and are a little upset about it.'

'What about that one on the left?'

'Oh, they're with us. British! But they're a bit cross that the Frenchie ship took a pot shot at us.'

'I see,' said Capstan, who'd already managed to completely forget about why he was there and that he was supposed to be placing the entire crew under arrest before sailing the ship back to Portsmouth, single-handed, for champagne, speeches and medals.

'So we seem to have a bit of a Mexican standoff going on at the moment,' Cate continued, 'which is all rather dull, but we're hoping something might happen; and that reminds me. Will, why don't you pop down and load up some more of those cannons? There's bugger all else going on, and we may as well be ready, just in case things do kick off.'

'Good idea, Captain!' and stood up straight, cupped his hands around his mouth and yelled out to the crew, 'GENERAL QUARTERS! BATTLE STATIONS!'

As an excited commotion swept the ship, and scores of people who Capstan hadn't even realised were there started to climb down from wherever it was that they'd been perched to make their way below decks, he asked, 'If that man down there,' and he gesticulated at the small-looking middle aged chap in a shiny suit, tied up and lying motionless next to a large chest, slap bang in the middle of the quarterdeck, 'is the President of France, and that French battleship is upset because they think you sank his boat with him still on it, then why don't you just tell them that you have him and give him back?'

'It's complicated,' replied Cate, 'but so far today, every time we've tried to communicate with a French ship, it's all gone a bit wrong and we've ended up being pelted by either dead fish or bullets. And as that boat there,' and she pointed out at the ominous looking French frigate, 'has bigger guns than us, I'd prefer not to risk it at this stage, not yet at any rate.'

LA GRENOUILLE, THIS IS HMS ARDUOUS. CAN YOU HEAR US?'

'Oh good, they're starting up again,' said Cate. 'This should be fun!'

YES, WE CAN HEAR YOU HMS ARDUOUS.'

WE'VE HAD A GOOD LOOK AROUND BUT CAN'T SEE ANY BOAT BY THE NAME OF LA VIERGE DE LA CUPIDITE. ARE YOU SURE IT'S MISSING?'

HMS ARDUOUS THIS IS LA GRENOUILLE. WE APPRECIATE THAT YOU'VE TAKEN THE TIME TO CONDUCT A THOROUGH SEARCH FOR LA VIERGE DE LA CUPIDITE, BUT THE REASON WHY YOU CAN'T SEE HER IS BECAUSE YOUR BOAT, HMS VICTORY, SANK HER JUST HALF AN HOUR AGO.'

LA GRENOUILLE, THIS IS HMS ARDUOUS. CAN YOU STILL HEAR US?'

'*Sacré bleu!* MAIS OUI HMS ARDUOUS, WE CAN STILL HEAR YOU, POUR L'AMOUR DE DIEU!'*

WITHOUT SOME SORT OF PHYSICAL EVIDENCE THAT HMS VICTORY DID ACTUALLY SINK YOUR FRENCH PRESIDENT'S BOAT, THEN THERE'S NOT MUCH WE CAN DO ABOUT IT.'

'HMS ARDUOUS, THIS IS LA GRENOUILLE, ARE YOU SERIOUS?'

'I'M AFRAID SO. IT'S NOT THAT WE DON'T BELIEVE YOU, BUT WE DON'T BELIEVE YOU. SORRY.'

'SO IF WE SINK HMS VICTORY WITHOUT A TRACE, THEN THAT WOULD BE OK THEN?'

'That doesn't sound good,' said Cate to Capstan.

'LA GRENOUILLE, THIS IS HMS ARDUOUS.'

This time there was no reply from the French frigate.

'LA GRENOUILLE, THIS IS HMS ARDUOUS. CAN YOU HEAR US?'

'SORRY, WE WERE JUST PREPARING OUR MISILES. YES, WE CAN HEAR YOU, HMS ARDUOUS.'

'IF YOU OPEN FIRE ON HMS VICTORY AGAIN, THEN WE WILL BE FORCED TO DO ALL THAT WE CAN TO DEFEND HER. DO YOU UNDERSTAND?'

'MAIS OUI! NOUS COMPRENONS, HMS ARDUOUS. MERCI BEAUCOUP!'

'Does that mean they're going to shoot at us?' asked Capstan, with a look of growing concern, and a rather more than casual glance over at the four life boats lying on the quarterdeck.

'I don't know,' replied Cate, 'but I'm damned if we're going down without a fight. I'd better see how they're getting on with those cannons.'

Act 4, Scene 1

Oeil pour oeil
An eye for an eye

"The devil can cite Scripture for his purpose."
The Merchant of Venice, Act I, Scene III

'ISN'T THAT your girlfriend?' Lord Henry Flavourington asked the British Prime Minister as they approached the eighteenth tee.

'It's my Private Secretary, Henry, as you well know.'

Robert was winning the round by fourteen holes to three, and was subsequently in too fine a mood to allow his old golfing adversary to put him off as they approached the very last hole.

'Prime Minister, I'm very pleased to have found you,' said Frederick Overtoun, slightly out of breath, having hurried over from the club house.

Robert wasn't quite as pleased to see his Private Secretary as his Private Secretary was to see him, and immediately made that clear. 'What the fuck are you doing here, Freddy? You know you're not allowed! This is my holy place, my temple, my shrine, my tabernacle, my altar, my inner most sanctum, the holy of holies, my sacrarium, la bema, naos, adytum sanctum sanctorum.'

'I'm sorry, Prime Minister, my Latin is still a little rusty.'

'IT'S MY FUCKING GOLF COURSE, AND I
DIDN'T SPEND FOUR HUNDRED AND FIFTY
MILLION QUID BUYING THE BLOODY
THING TO HAVE THE LIKES OF YOU
WALTZING ABOUT IT!'

'But Prime Minister, I've been trying to get hold of
you for hours. The battery on your phone must have
died.'

'The battery on my phone didn't die. I turned the
damned thing off. I can't have that stupid thing
beeping, buzzing and playing the national anthem at
me all the bloody time, especially when I'm trying to
tee off.'

'But Prime Minister, you're the Prime Minister, you
have to make yourself available to be contacted at all
times!'

'Excuse me, but who the fuck do you think you are
telling me how, where and when I should be making
myself available? You're treading on very thin ice
there, young Freddy, and if it wasn't for the fact that
I'm winning by fourteen holes to three, I'd currently
be in the process of beating you to a pulp with my
seven iron before throwing you over that cliff!'

'Yes, Prime Minister. I'm sorry, Prime Minister.'

Robert took a few moments to compose himself
before asking, 'What is it that you want, exactly?'

Having finally been given permission to speak,
Fredrick didn't feel like it, so instead he just stepped to
one side and pointed over the Prime Minister's
shoulder at the English Channel behind him.

Both Robert and Lord Flavourington followed the
line from his finger to the sea, where they could clearly

see dozens of battleships, all steaming their way westwards down the Channel.

'Yes, and…?' asked Robert, assuming it was the British Navy on some sort of training exercise, and subsequently not worth his time, and certainly not worth interrupting his game for.

'It's the French, Prime Minister.'

'What's "the French"?'

'*That's* the French, Prime Minister,' said Frederick, pointing once again at the impressive fleet of battleships.

'What, all of them?'

'I'm afraid so, Prime Minister.'

'And what the hell do they want?'

'It's the Victory, Prime Minister.'

'They want HMS Victory?'

'Sort of, Prime Minister. The Victory has apparently attacked and sunk the boat belonging to the President of France.'

'You mean that stupid floating plastic Gin Palace thing he went and bought himself last year?'

'That's the one, Prime Minister, yes.'

'Damn good job too. I hated that boat! I've never seen anything so pretentious in all my life!'

'But unfortunately, Prime Minister, they seem to think that the President of France was on board at the time it was sunk.'

'Really?'

'Apparently, yes, Prime Minister.'

'Are they sure?'

'They do seem to be quite sure, yes, Prime Minister.'

'That's a shame. I can't say I liked the man, and he had the most God-awful taste in suits, and boats, but death by drowning? Not a fate I'd wish on any man.'

'No, Prime Minister, and it's become apparent that the population of France doesn't seem to like it either.'

'I suppose they don't.'

'And the French Navy is even more upset, Prime Minister. It would appear that they were particularly fond of him, so their entire surface fleet's been called out with the express order to punish those responsible and sink HMS Victory, Prime Minister.'

'Oculum pro oculo, et dentem pro dente,' said Robert, referring back to his knowledge of the ancient language of Latin, as he had a tendency to do whenever asked an awkward question or, in this instance, when he didn't know what else to say.

'I'm sorry, Prime Minister, but would you mind translating that for me?' asked Fredrick. He never liked not knowing what his Prime Minister was saying, especially when the French Armada was bearing down on them.

'I said, "An eye for an eye and a tooth for a tooth." It's what Jesus said to his disciples when he was being nailed to the cross.'

'Actually,' interrupted Lord Flavourington, 'I think Jesus said that when they were stoning the prostitute.'

'Er, I beg your pardon,' said Fredrick, 'but I believe it was Moses who said, "An eye for an eye and a tooth for a tooth". I think Jesus said, "Turn the other cheek".'

'What, when they were stoning the prostitute?' asked Robert.

'Er, no, Prime Minister. When someone asked him what he thought about Moses saying, "an eye for an eye and a tooth for a tooth", Prime Minister.'

'So what did he say when they were stoning the prostitute then?'

'I don't think he said anything, Prime Minister.'

'Didn't he ask, "Who wants to cast the first stone"?' suggested Henry.

'I beg to differ, Lord Flavourington, but I think Jesus suggested that the person who was without sin should cast the first stone,' Fredrick said, with as much respect to his senior as possible.

'Yes, that's right! And because Jesus was the only person there who was without sin, he went first.'

'No, I remember now,' interjected Robert. 'It was Peter who went first because Jesus wanted to draw a picture of the girl being stoned in the sand.'

'Again, I beg to differ, Prime Minister, but I don't think anyone stoned the prostitute. I believe they all went home and left the poor girl alone, and that was when Jesus told her to, "Go, sin no more."'

'Was that when he got her pregnant?' asked Robert.

'I'm sorry, Prime Minister, I'm not with you?'

'You know, from the book, *The Da Vinci Code*, when Jesus got some girl knocked up in secret, and the baby went on to become eternal, and eventually got a job as an Italian investigative journalist.'

Fredrick didn't know quite what to say to that, so he suggested, 'Could we possibly turn our attention back to the French Armada, Prime Minister?'

'Who? Oh, yes, of course. The Bible was never really my thing anyway,' and the three of them turned to stare out at the English Channel again, but by that time it was empty, all but for a single ferry that was probably heading over to Calais.

'They seem to have gone, Freddy. They must have changed their minds. So, anyway, Henry; it's your turn to tee-off.'

'Er,' interrupted Fredrick, 'I suspect that they haven't all gone, as such, Prime Minister, but have more likely just moved beyond our line of sight.'

'Ex conspectu contenderent, quo non extat memoria,' said Robert, as he took his driver out from his golf bag.

Again Fredrick was rather keen not to allow something his Prime Minister said to slip past him due to his poor understanding of Latin, so he asked, 'I'm sorry again, Prime Minister, but I didn't quite catch that.'

'I said, ex conspectu contenderent, quo non extat memoria; out of sight, out of mind.'

'Did Jesus say that as well?' asked Lord Flavourington.

'Yes, he did. It was the bit after he'd told the leper to go back inside the church, so that he didn't have to look at him anymore.'

'The French Armada, Prime Minister?'

'Yes, yes, yes, Freddy, all in good time. Now, whose turn is it to tee off?'

'Mine, I believe.'

'But Prime Minister?'

'Listen Freddy, as I've only just explained to you, my golf course is my inner most sanctum, my holy realm, my adytum sanctum sanctorum; and we haven't finished our game yet. So may I suggest you just bugger off? There's a good chap. We won't be long. You can wait in the club house until I've finished.'

Act 4, Scene 2

Une idée inspirée
An inspired idea

"What's done is done."
Macbeth, Act III, Scene II

'WE'VE PRIMED AND LOADED all the cannons on the starboard side, Cate, so we'll be able to give the Frenchies a decent broadside, as long as we don't have to go-about,' reported Will, after he'd emerged from the ship's lower levels and had joined her on the poop deck.

'Good job,' said Cate. 'What's a broadside?'

'It's when you try to fire all the cannons down one side of the ship at the same time.'

'Excellent!'

'MORE SHIPS APPROACHING!' came the now all-too-familiar cry from the crow's nest at the top of the main mast.

'HOW MANY?' asked Will.

'A LOT!'

'HOW MANY'S "A LOT"?'

'MORE THAN I CAN COUNT!'

'AND WHAT ARE THEY?'

'BATTLESHIPS!'

'FRENCH OR BRITISH?' asked Cate.

'THEY'RE COMING FROM FRANCE, SO THEY MUST BE FRENCH.'

'Looks like we're going to have company,' said Will, as he craned his neck to see what was heading towards them. 'How're your battle wounds?'

'I still can't use either my leg or arm, so I'm not going to be much use in a fight.'

'How did you get hurt?' asked Capstan, who was still propped up against the railing beside Cate.

'I took a couple of bullets from what must have been the French President's bodyguard, although I can't say I knew who they were at the time.'

'We all thought they were just a bunch of drug-dealing Frenchie gangster types,' added Will, in support of his Captain's rather peculiar decision to board the boat in question and slaughter two human beings using nothing more than a 18th Century sword, and in the most grotesque way imaginable.

'I'd no idea you'd been hurt quite so badly,' said Capstan. 'Here, why don't you have my stick? It looks like your need is greater than mine.'

She smiled at him.

'That's very kind of you Inspector, but I'm okay.'

'He has a good point,' said Will. 'I'll get someone to make you something to help you get around.'

'I'm fine, really I am. At this stage I'm more concerned about what those Frenchies have in store for us.'

Will couldn't help but agree with her. 'If it is the French Navy, then it looks like we're going to be out-gunned *and* out-numbered, so with that in mind I suggest we do all that we can to avoid a combat situation.'

'Then perhaps it's time we used our bargaining chip a little more effectively,' Cate mused.

'How do you mean?'

'The French President,' she said, nodding down at the small man in the shiny suit, still tied up next to the treasure chest on the quarterdeck. 'I suggest we haul him up so that the Frenchies can see that we have him as a hostage. If nothing else, it should stop them from firing at us.'

Will smiled.

'Cate, that's an inspired idea!'

It felt good to have her on board as their Captain.

'And while you're at it,' she continued, 'you may as well haul up all those French fisherman. The more French we have in the way of their guns, the less likely it will be that they'll use them on us. And we should also get that treasure chest hidden away downstairs somewhere.'

Capstan was attempting to keep up with what exactly had been going on aboard HMS Victory since the ship had left Portsmouth harbour only the night before.

'So,' he said, 'you've got the President of France, a bunch of French fisherman, *and* a chest full of treasure?' he asked Cate, unable to hide his admiration.

'Er, yes,' she answered, feeling slightly embarrassed. 'We had a busy morning.'

'No kidding?'

With the mention of treasure, Capstan could feel the spirit of adventure course through his adult-hardened veins, which was a feeling he hadn't experienced since he was a boy, when he'd dreamed of becoming a pirate and sailing away to distant shores, far away from anything and everything, but especially Maths, English and over-bearing parents.

'Is there anything I can do to help?' he offered.

'I don't suppose you could give someone a call back at Police HQ, to let them know that we have the President of France on board?'

'Of course, but do we know if he's still alive?' asked Capstan, staring down at the poor man.

'I hadn't thought of that.' She looked over at Will, who was making his way down towards the body. 'OI, WILL! IS HE STILL ALIVE?'

Will nodded and gave her the thumbs up to show he'd understood the question, and on reaching the shiny suited man he prodded him with his foot, but there was no response, so he looked back up at Cate and shouted, 'IT DOESN'T LOOK LIKE IT.'

Capstan thought he'd better offer them his professional guidance, so he cupped his hands together and bellowed down, 'TRY AND GIVE HIM A REALLY GOOD KICK! IF HE'S JUST UNCONSCIOUS THAT SHOULD WAKE HIM UP.'

'WILL DO!' said Will, and looked down at the French President as if he was a rugby ball. He then took five paces back, pretended that he just needed one conversion to win the Rugby World Cup, and then jogged forward to give the body an almighty boot.

'AIE! POUR L'AMOUR DE DIEU! What the fuck pensez-vous que vous faites? Où le diable suis-je et qui la baise êtes-vous? Vous me prenez pour qui ? Avez-vous une idée de qui je suis ? Vous avez des grands problèmes maintenant !   Attendez   que   mon commandant en chef découvre ce que vous avez fait. Et où est le bateau?'

'HE'S ALIVE!' Will shouted, and then added, 'Unfortunately,' to himself.

'GOOD JOB WILL! CAN YOU GAG HIM AND THEN HAUL HIM UP SO THAT THE FRENCHIES CAN SEE HIM?'

'AYE, AYE, CAPTAIN!'

Speaking to Capstan, Cate said, 'If you could phone someone to let them know that we have him and he's okay, that would be helpful. I can't risk my crew being killed just because we accidentally kidnapped the President of France.'

'I'll give my sergeant a call, and he'll be able to phone our boss,' replied Capstan.

He would have offered to call Chief Inspector Morose himself, but he'd been taught during his Graduate Fast Track Police Training Programme never to talk directly to a chief inspector unless absolutely necessary.

'No doubt my sergeant will be able to pass the message on to those responsible,' and with that he pushed himself up straight, and with his stick in one hand and using the other to pull out his phone, he made his way over to the port side railing to try and get hold of his moronic subordinate, who he'd managed to completely forget about for at least half an hour.

'PETER!' Cate called out, and waved to get his attention.

As Peter wandered over to her, she asked, 'How's Crispin doing?'

'Oh, he's okay, but I think you could both do with seeing a medical professional at some point. All I've done is clean and bandage as best I can. Both your wounds could easily become infected.'

Cate wasn't too bothered about herself; she was more concerned about Crispin, who was resting up against the railing but looked paler than she remembered.

'Is there any more wind?' she asked, as she looked up and around.

'Not much, and from what I know it does tend to die off as the sun begins to set.'

'Do you think Crispin will be OK until tomorrow?'

'To be honest Cate, I'm more worried about you! Crispin took a glancing bullet but you took two pretty much full on.'

'I suppose I could do with another drink, but what I really need to know is, can Crispin wait until tomorrow to get some proper medical attention, or should we get him off the boat now?'

'Well, he had some of those sandwiches and that orange squash. I think he'll be fine until tomorrow, but if there isn't a fair wind in the morning, then I'd recommend getting you both off the ship and back to Portsmouth as soon as possible.'

'OK, then we just need to keep the Frenchies at bay until then.' They leaned on the rail to watch the President of France being hauled up the yard arm by the combined efforts of Will, Cannonball and Deadweight.

After a few moments of enjoying their free early evening's entertainment, she asked, 'I don't suppose there would be some black paint on board?'

'There's bound to be some around, somewhere. Why?'

'I was just wondering if it would be useful to make a French banner that we could hang up next to their President to tell them that it's him?'

'Yes, I'm sure we can do that.'

'And maybe it could also say that we don't want him anymore, and that they can drop by to pick him up any time they like.'

'Sure, but I'd recommend we write it in English and not French. We don't seem to have fared too well when we've had a go at French, and now's probably not the best time to risk being misunderstood.'

'Agreed! Can you see to it?'

'Sure, no problem, but what should I write?'

'How about, "This is your French President. We don't want him anymore. Please come and get him."?'

'But what if it isn't the French President after all, and he's actually lying dead at the bottom of the English Channel?'

'I hadn't thought of that. Maybe we should say, "If this is your President, we don't want him anymore. Please come and get him."?'

'Yes, that's better. And we should also say that he's alive as well.'

'You're right. How about, "If this is your President, please come and get him. He's not dead."?'

'But, saying that…' said Peter, as they both continued to watch the person under discussion, who'd now started to swing freely from the yard arm, secured by a thick rope that had been looped under his arms and around his chest. 'What if he's dead by the time they've picked him up?'

'Point taken. You'd better add "yet!" after the "He's not dead" bit.'

'Yes, I think that would cover all angles.'

They watched as the seven French fisherman were dragged up on deck to be hauled up alongside their President, and Cate added, 'And maybe paint an arrow on it pointing at which one we think the French President is. Apart from their clothes, they all look the bloody same to me.'

'Good idea. I'll sort that out now.'

'Thanks, Peter!'

As Peter made his way down the steps, Cate looked out towards where she assumed France must be, and where she could now see a horizon lined with ominous grey shapes, all of which seemed to be growing bigger with every passing moment.

Act 4, Scene 3

Faires les Gros Titres
Headline News

*"The worst is not, So long as we can say,
'This is the worst'."*
King Lear, Act IV, Scene I

AFTER LOSING THE last hole, Robert Bridlestock, the British Prime Minister, drove his golf cart at full pelt over to his clubhouse as he reflected on the game. Having won it by fourteen holes to four, he could hardly complain, especially as he was now fourteen million pounds better off; well, he would be when Lord Flavourington transferred the funds over to his new Canary Wharf offshore account. And although fourteen million wasn't a huge amount, it really wasn't bad for an afternoon's round of golf, even by Rory McIlroy's standards. But despite all that, he still felt he'd been thrown off his game at the last hole by his bloody Private Secretary, and was therefore a million down on where he should have been.

But all that had been largely forgotten about by the time he'd pulled up outside the 17th Century mansion that was now his golf clubhouse, and that used to be the main residence for the Manacle family, who'd made their fortune when they introduced slavery to the civilised world, just after Sir Wilberforce Manacle had patented the new cast-iron chained and lockable wrist holders to which he'd proudly given his name. By the time Robert had heaved his golf bag out from the back of the cart and propped it up against one of the four stone-carved pillars, all he could think about was downing a pint or two, and he headed straight for the bar. However, his Private Secretary, Fredrick Overtoun, who'd been pacing up and down as he waited for him inside, had other ideas.

'Prime Minister?'

'Oh, you're still here, Freddy. How unfortunate,' Robert said as he pushed his way past.

'Er, yes Prime Minister, and I really do need to speak to you, and with some urgency.'

The clear inflexion in Fredrick's voice made Robert stop and turn to stare back at him. It wasn't often that he came over as being quite so desperate for his attention.

'Well, I'm here now. So, what is it?'

'It's the French, Prime Minister.'

Robert sighed.

'Not them again! I thought we'd covered all that.'

'Unfortunately the situation still hasn't resolved itself, Prime Minister.'

'Oh, very well, but can I at least have a drink before we start? I mean it's gone five o'clock, and I have just won fourteen million quid for Christ sake! I think I deserve a drink, don't you?'

'Yes, Prime Minister, and well done. It's certainly good to know that you're fourteen million pounds better off. If I could just leave you with the Evening Standard, I'll go and fetch you a drink.'

'Fine! I'll have a pint of Parson's Tipple, thank you very much. Actually, while you're there you'd better make that two.'

'Yes, Prime Minister,' and Fredrick handed him the newspaper that he'd had biked across, before scurrying over to the bar.

With some reluctance, Robert took the paper to the bar's lounge area and made himself comfortable in one of the studded brown leather armchairs. Crossing his legs, he unfolded the Standard to read the front page.

The headline surprised him somewhat. Being the Prime Minister of the United Kingdom, he was used to reading the odd sensationalist headline, normally during the process of making them up, but this particular one was far and away the most jaw-dropping of the lot, even by his Press Secretary's standards.

"WAR WITH FRANCE!" it said in plain bold letters, so large that they covered the entire front page, and almost too big to read. And so, just in case he'd misunderstood the message, he read it again, but it still said, "WAR WITH FRANCE!" even when he read it upside down. He closed his mouth and looked over his shoulder to ask Fredrick what the hell had been going on in his absence, only to find himself alone, with just his thoughts and the newspaper that still said, "WAR WITH FRANCE!" no matter how often he read it or which way up he held the newspaper when he did so.

But then it occurred to him that just because the headline of a British newspaper said, "WAR WITH FRANCE!" it didn't actually mean the article was about either war or France. Knowing the British press as well as he did, it could just have easily been about the latest Hollywood film that happened to be called

"War With France!" or even a Brit Pop band with a new album of the same name. And now that he thought about it, it was even more likely to be about some wannabe celebrity who'd decided to take the name "War With France" just to get a mention in the press. And so, with these ideas lifting his spirits somewhat, he decided to have a go at reading the first sentence.

"The British Government has confirmed this evening that England is now officially at war with France."

Nope, that still said they were at war with France, and he looked around for his Private Secretary again, who still hadn't shown up with the drink for which he was becoming increasingly desperate.

His mobile phone rang from deep within his trouser pocket. He'd turned it back on again when he'd finished his game, but now wished he hadn't, and did his best to ignore it. Whatever the caller wanted, it was unlikely to be anything pleasant.

With the phone still ringing, and his Private Secretary still off at the bar somewhere, Robert thought that he may as well try to find out just exactly how they'd managed to reach a state of war with a country that they hadn't fought against since Napoleonic times, and all while he'd been playing a round of golf. So he had a go at reading the next few paragraphs.

"This afternoon, HMS Arduous witnessed an unprovoked attack on HMS Victory by a French Navy battleship during a search and rescue mission for their apparently missing President, Jacques Moutonette.

"When asked their reasons for firing a shot at HMS Victory, the French Navy said that their President's boat had been attacked, boarded and sunk by the crew of Nelson's famous flag ship, but despite their very best efforts to clarify such a malicious claim, HMS Arduous was unable to find any evidence to the fact.

"The French Navy, however, is adamant that the crew of HMS Victory has carried out an assassination of their President. They have therefore threatened to sink the Victory with all hands by way of recompense for their loss and have also declared war with England, and our armed forces have been placed on high alert.

"Meanwhile, as the situation rapidly deteriorates, the Prime Minister, Robert Bridlestock, has been reported to be playing golf at his private club in Kent."

Robert turned over the page, but there was nothing about the fact that he'd won his game by fourteen holes to four and was subsequently fourteen million pounds better off, so he turned the paper over to find out how England had been getting on in the Rugby World Cup, just as his mobile phone finally fell silent. But even before he'd managed to find out if England won or lost their game against the New Zealand All Blacks, the annoying ring-tone started up again.

'Oh, for fuck's sake,' he groaned, as he dragged it out from his pocket, slid the icon over to the green phone symbol and lifted it to his ear.

'Robert speaking.'

'Prime Minister, it's Ronold Macdonold here.'

'Who?'

'Ronold Macdonold, Chairman of MDK Industries, Prime Minister.'

'Oh, yes, sorry, old chap,' said Robert, with some relief that it wasn't Madame Hilfner-Brown from NATO, calling to have a go at him for being a war-mongering chauvinist pig-dog bastard, as she was known to do to British Prime Ministers shortly after they'd picked a fight with some virtually unknown third world country. 'I didn't recognise the name.'

'I was just phoning you to talk about your decision to declare war on France.'

'Oh, yes, that's right. Did you like that?'

'Well, it wasn't exactly what we agreed, was it?'

'Wasn't it?'

'No, Prime Minister! I thought you were going to be looking to see if we could do something with Tunisia?'

'Oh, yes, well I hadn't quite got around to discussing Tunisia with anyone yet.'

'So you thought you'd have a go at France instead?'

'I must admit Ron, that after our discussion this morning, I thought you'd have been rather pleased with the current situation?'

'But Prime Minister, I told you to pick a country a very long way away and one that definitely didn't have any weapons of mass destruction!'

'Did you?'

'Well, not in so many words, but that's what I meant. France is right next door, and they've got the most volatile weapons of mass destruction known to mankind!'

'They have?'

'Yes, of course they have, Prime Minister!'

'I'd no idea! What are they then?'

'Nuclear Warheads, you fu… Prime Minister.'

'Now listen here, Ronold MacDoughnut, or whatever your name is, there's no need to take that tone of voice with me. I'm the Prime Minister of the United Kingdom! I don't give a fuck what you're the chairman of. I could have you torn limb from limb by a couple of horses half way through the Grand National and nobody would be any the wiser, so just watch it!'

'I'm most terribly sorry, Prime Minister, please forgive me! It's just that France is…well, it's just so very close, Prime Minister.'

'Look, if it's any consolation, it wasn't my idea. I was playing golf when it all kicked off and I'm not even sure how it did…kick off, exactly, but I can assure you that I'll be doing all that I can to resolve the situation just as soon as possible.'

'And then you'll take a look at Tunisia?'

'Yes, and then I'll take a look at Tunisia.'

'Well, thank you for your time, Prime Minister, and I'm sorry if I came over as being a little…testy, it's just that my family and I have only very recently moved down to Kent, and the estate we bought doesn't appear to have an adequate nuclear bunker, despite what the brochure said, so we're feeling a little…exposed at the moment.'

'That's alright, Ron, I fully understand.' And he did. His own nuclear bunker was buried deep underneath Number 10 and he could access it directly from his bedroom. 'By the way, whilst you're there, I don't suppose you play golf?'

'Actually I do, Prime Minister, but I'm really not very good.'

'What's your handicap?'

'I play off ten, Prime Minister.'

'I play off nine, so we're well matched. You must come down to my golf club in Deal one weekend, maybe after this whole French fiasco has sorted itself out?'

'I'd like that very much, Prime Minister, thank you!'

'Not at all, and I'll have someone send you an email when we know where we are with France.'

'And Tunisia, Prime Minister.'

'Yes, them too,' said Robert, and ended the call just in time to see Fredrick return from the bar with what he hoped were two pints of Parson's Tipple and what looked like a couple of double vodkas that Fredrick must have bought for himself.

'So, what's all this about us going to war with France then, Freddy?' he asked, as his Private Secretary placed the drinks down onto the highly-polished antique glass coffee table in front of them.

'Unfortunately, Prime Minister, it was France who declared war on us, just after four this afternoon, which was why I was trying to get hold of you. Did you manage to take a look at the Evening Standard?'

'I did,' he answered, resenting the fact that he'd actually done something he'd been told to do, and by someone as insignificant as his Private Secretary. 'The French seem to be under the impression that we assassinated their President.'

'That's right, Prime Minister.'

'Is it true?'

'Is what true, Prime Minister?'

'That we assassinated the President of France?'

'Er, no, Prime Minister. We've since learnt that Jacques Moutonette is alive and well on board HMS Victory. Apparently, it was the Victory's crew who fished him out of the English Channel.'

'So why on earth did France declare war?'

'It would appear that although those on board HMS Victory did pull him out of the water, it was actually they who sank his boat in the first place, so placing him in harm's way. And they now seem to have taken it upon themselves to use him as a hostage.'

'And what do they want?'

'They haven't said. All they've done is hang him up so that the French Navy know that they have him.'

'We're going to have to resolve this situation,' Robert said, as he shifted uneasily in his chair.

'I certainly hope so, Prime Minister,' said Fredrick, who lived in Surrey with his wife and two children, and only had an old coal bunker in the back garden, which was only just big enough to fit them all in, but certainly didn't have the space for three months' supply of tinned food and bottled water.

'I mean,' continued Robert, 'we can't very well start a war with France. They're far too close, *and* they have nuclear weapons!'

'Er, yes, Prime Minister, I'm very much aware of that.'

'So, Fredrick, any ideas?'

'About what, Prime Minister?'

'About how we can get back on friendly terms with our French neighbours.'

'None at all, Prime Minister, but perhaps you could have a word with Harold Percy-Blakemore.'

'Who?'

'Your Home Secretary, Prime Minister.'

'I thought he was dead?'

'Er, no, Prime Minister, that was the Education Minister, Harold Spencer-Blacknail.'

'Oh yes, that's right. How did he die again?'

'You remember, Prime Minister, he was killed during that school visit.'

'Blown up by militant school children. Yes, I remember now.' Robert lent forward to lift his pint from off the antique coffee table, drank half of it, and then placed it back down.

'Shall I get the Home Secretary on the phone for you, Prime Minister?'

'Go on, then. We may as well see how the old bugger's doing.'

As Robert picked up his pint again, Fredrick dug out his smartphone, and it wasn't long before he handed it to Robert saying, 'Harold Percy-Blakemore, the Home Secretary, on the phone for you now, Prime Minister.'

'That was quick!' said Robert, as he put down the now empty pint and took the call.

'Harold! How are you? That's nice. And how's that wife of yours?' and as he listened to the reply, he covered the phone and leant over to Fredrick and whispered, 'She's a horny little fuck-bunny, that one!' before returning to his phone conversation. 'Oh, I'm very sorry to hear that. Still, she had slept with half the Cabinet, so you shouldn't be too surprised. Anyway, this "War with France" nonsense. What do you suggest we do about it?'

There was a brief pause before Robert started saying, 'Ah-ha, right, of course, fair enough, yes, sounds good,' followed by, 'I'll give them a call now.' And then, to end the conversation, he suggested, 'Maybe you should give that new internet dating thing a go. I hear it's all the rage these days. Jolly good,' and passed the phone back to his Private Secretary before picking up his second pint.

'What did he say?'

'His wife left him for the Duke of Oxfordshire. No surprises there!'

'I meant about the situation with France, Prime Minister.'

'Oh, that! He said we should give the S.A.S. a call and ask them if they can extract the French President from HMS Victory at night, when nobody's looking. Apparently they're very good at that sort of thing. Then they can hand him back to the French and the problem will be solved. Personally I think it's an excellent idea, don't you?'

'It does sound like a sensible plan, given the circumstances, Prime Minister.'

'Good!'

There was another pause as Robert started his second pint before he asked Frederick, 'I don't suppose you have their number, by any chance?'

'Whose, the S.A.S.?'

'Yes, those chaps.'

'I'm sorry, Prime Minister, I really don't think I do. I can't say that I've ever had the need to call them before.'

'Who do you think would have it?'

'I've really no idea!'

'Can't you look them up on the internet or something?'

'Well, I suppose I could try to Google them.'

'If you could,' said Robert, and as he continued to drain his second pint, his Private Secretary gave full concentration to both his thumbs as he attempted to use his smartphone to search for the S.A.S.'s contact details.

'I think I've got it, Prime Minister.'

'Well done, Freddy! Dial the number and then hand me the phone, there's a good chap.'

'It's ringing for you now, Prime Minister,' and Fredrick handed Robert his smartphone again.

'Hello, is that the S.A.S.? Oh, really? So what are you called now? The S.A.A.B.S.? Oh, okay. Look, its Robert Bridlestock here, the Prime Minister. Yes, that's right. Now I assume you've heard about our current situation with France. Yes, war, I know, who'd have thought it? Anyway, apparently it's all because of those bods on board HMS Victory, and the fact that they're holding the French President as hostage. So, what we need you to do is pop yourselves on board, rescue him, and then give him back to the Frenchies, preferably without putting any bullet holes in him. How does that sound? Excellent! Right, I'll hand you over to my Private Secretary and he'll fill you in with all the boring details. No problem at all, and good luck!'

And with that he handed the phone back to Fredrick, finished his pint and stood up to go to the loo before getting another round in for himself.

Act 4, Scene 4

Opérations spéciales
Special Ops

"What's in a name?"
Romeo and Juliet, Act II, Scene II

'RIGHT EVERYONE, thank you all for coming in at such short notice. For those of you who don't know me, my name's John Harrington-Smith, and I'm the Director of Special Forces for this, the newly formed S.A.A.B.S. Right, I'm now going to hand you over to Tony who'll be conducting this briefing.'

'Thank you, John, and as he said, thank you all for getting here so quickly. Yes, Fred, you have a question?'

'I thought we were going to be called the S.A.B.S.?'

'Er, no, I think we agreed that we would be known as the S.A.A.B.S., but hold on, let me check back through the minutes from the last meeting. Yes, here we are, Frank suggested that we use the "a" from "and", so we sound more like a Swedish car manufacturer.'

'Excuse me, Tony?'

'Yes, Barry, you have a question?'

'Sorry, but unfortunately I wasn't able to make the last meeting, so I was just wondering if you could explain briefly again exactly why it was that the Special

Air Services had to be merged with the Special Boat Services?'

'Er, John,' Tony said, looking back at John Harrington-Smith, 'could you possibly answer that one for me?'

'Yes, of course,' and John stood up from the chair that he'd only just sat down on at the front of the room, and stood beside Tony again.

'Unfortunately, as we discussed in some detail during the last meeting, the current economic climate made it rather difficult for the Government to fund both the S.A.S. and the S.B.S., especially when they think we've seen little action during the last twenty years or so, and it was therefore decided to merge the two together.'

'Thank you again, John. Does that answer your question, Barry?'

'I suppose so, but I really don't like the name. I mean, the S.A.S. sounded great, as did the S.B.S., but, what are we called now, the S.A.A.B.S? Well, it just sounds really boring.'

'Again, we did discuss this at some length at our last meeting Barry, and the S.A.A.B.S. really was the best we could come up with.'

'Couldn't we shorten it to just the Air and Boat Services?'

'You mean so that we become the A.B.S.?'

'Well, yes?'

'We hadn't thought of that one. What does everyone else think?'

'It sounds a bit gay, if you don't mind me saying so.'

'Thank you, Phil. Anyone else.'

'To me it sounds either very gay or like a breaking system used on cars.'

'Thank you Bill. Any more thoughts?'

A hand went up from the back of the room.

'Kevin, yes?'

'I agree with Phil and Bill. It sounds either very gay or very boring. What if we dropped all the "A's" and just went with Special Services?'

A strong murmur of approval rippled through the room as Tony, still standing at the front, clarified the idea.

'So you're suggesting that we call ourselves the Special Services, or the S.S. for short? Unfortunately Kevin, I'm really not sure that would be appropriate.'

'Why's that?'

'Er, because of the Second World War.'

'I'm sorry, I'm not with you.'

'You're probably too young to remember, but the S.S. were an elite force of Nazis who were considered to be the German Army's Death Squad.'

Kevin shrugged his shoulders and looked over at his colleagues around the room, who were all doing the same.

'I still don't follow you, Tony. Isn't that what we are?'

'Well, yes and no, Kevin. Didn't you study World War Two at school?'

'No, sorry. I didn't do History.'

'But haven't you seen any old war films?'

'I've seen Saving Private Ryan, but I don't remember anything about some people called the S.S.'

'No, well, I don't think they were in that film. Let's just say that they had quite a bad reputation.'

'In what way?' asked Kevin again, at a complete loss.

'It's difficult to explain, but they were the most feared regiment of their time and were thought to have killed and tortured huge numbers of people, most of whom were probably innocent.'

Again Kevin just shrugged. 'But isn't that the sort of thing we do?'

'Well, yes and no, Kevin. I mean, the killing and torturing bit is, of course, but we really don't advocate you doing it to innocent people, not in any obvious way, at any rate.'

'So why can't we call ourselves the S.S. then? Personally I think it sounds dead cool!'

There was another strong murmur of approval as everyone in the room nodded their heads, all apart from Tony and John Harrington-Smith standing at the front, who were now staring down at those in the room with some incredulity.

'I'm sorry chaps,' said John Harrington-Smith, 'but I'd have to agree with Tony on this one. Unfortunately the term S.S. has just too many nasty connotations that we could well do without.'

'Well, I like it!' said Kevin.

'Me too!' agreed Fred.

'And me!' added Barry.

'How about we vote on it?' suggested Kevin, and before anyone could say otherwise he asked, 'Hands up if you think we should be called the Special Services?'

Everyone in the room put their hand straight up in the air, apart from the two standing at the front.

'That's settled then,' Kevin continued, and then asked, 'Can we also discuss the new motto? I've had a think about it since our last meeting and I just don't like what was put forward.'

'What was that?' asked Barry.

'By Strength and Guile we Dare to Win,' Kevin replied, with a flat, monotonous tone.

'Oh no, that's bad, that's *really* bad!' said Barry.

Trying to clear his head from the fact that the British Special Forces was now going to be known as the S.S., Tony said, 'Yes, I know it's not the catchiest motto in the world, but with the first old motto being, "Who Dares Wins" and the other being, "By Strength and Guile", it was the best we could come up with.'

'I thought the S.A.S. motto was, "*He* Who Dares Wins"?' asked Kevin, who was a former member of the Special Boat Service.

'That's right, it was,' said Tony at the front, 'but we had to drop the "he" bit when that girl forced us to sign her up.'

'Whatever did happen to Susan?' asked Barry.

'She became a pilot for Corner Cutter, that new budget airline. Apparently they needed someone who could use a parachute, and the money was good.'

'Oh, yes. I remember now. Anyway, going back to the motto, I really don't think, "By Strength and Guile we Dare to Win" is at all suitable. It's about as lame as a duck with no legs.'

'Now that Barry's mentioned it,' said Kevin, 'I'd have to agree with him. It is *really* bad.'

Bill put his hand up and said, 'I agree with Barry and Kevin. "By Strength and Guile we Dare to Win" sounded alright when it was suggested at the last meeting, but now it just sounds cheesy.'

'And lame,' added Barry.

Tony was beginning to feel just a little tetchy. He was supposed to be briefing them on their very first assignment, which was due to take place at zero-two hundred hours that very night. They weren't supposed to be having another marketing meeting.

'So what would you suggest then, Barry?' he asked, with an obvious edge to his voice.

'I don't know. Just something better than, "By Strength and Guile we Dare to Win". Anything's got to be better than *that*!'

'How about, "Who has Strength and Guile Wins"?' suggested Kevin from the back.

'It's better, I suppose, but still not exactly memorable.'

The room fell silent as everyone reflected on the problem.

'If we're now a combined unit formed from both the special air and boat services,' Barry said, 'how about "Who Dares Swims"?'

Another round of approval circulated the room as everyone started nodding their heads again.

Keen to move things along, Tony said, 'Right, hands up who's happy with Barry's suggestion of, "Who Dares Swims"?'

Everyone's hand went up, even John Harrington-Smith, who thought it had a certain ring to it.

'Okay, so we're all agreed. We'll now be known as the Special Services, or S.S. for short, and our new motto is, "Who Dares Swims"?

Everyone was clearly in agreement, so to finalise the discussion on branding, Tony added, 'And is everyone happy with the new logo?'

'Personally I think having two air cylinders with the dagger in the middle works very well,' said Barry.

'Excellent! So, can we finally get on with the briefing?'

Nobody said anything else, so Tony carried on.

'Right! As I'm sure you're all aware, HMS Victory is holding Jacques Moutonette, the President of France, hostage in the middle of the English Channel. I took a call from the Prime Minister this afternoon and we've been given instructions to extract Monsieur Moutonette from the ship. So here's the plan. We'll take two ribs, motor out to the Victory, climb on board, find the President of France, and then bring him back.'

'Is that it?'

'Not quite, Kevin. John Harrington-Smith has also been kind enough to bring in his very own Airfix model of HMS Victory for us to look at. John?'

'Oh, yes, right, I'll get it out.' Harrington-Smith went over to the corner of the room, carefully took out his model of the famous ship from a Safebusy's Forever Bag, and carried it with great majesty to place it down on the classroom table for everyone to see.

'Okay,' continued Tony, 'this is obviously a scale sized model of HMS Victory. The real ship is much bigger, but it does give us an idea of what it looks like. Now, we've been given to believe the President of France has been tied up here. Obviously we're not sure if he'll still be there by the time we arrive, but that is where we're to head for. You should be able to climb up the sides of the ship relatively easily. Reports are that the crew is unarmed, but the ship itself does have one hundred and four cannons. We'll be using our favourite Ingram MAC-10 compact machine gun with suppressors, to help dull the sound of fire; however, we've been given strict instructions not to shoot holes in either the French President or the ship.'

'When do we set off?' asked Barry.

'Zero-one hundred hours, so that we can be at the Victory for zero-two hundred hours.'

Just then, John Harrington-Smith leaned over and whispered something to Tony.

'Oh, yes, I almost forgot,' continued Tony. 'We've been provided with some very special new communication equipment that we think you'll all enjoy. If you could open up the boxes in front of you, you'll find the very latest iPhone, iWatch and blue-tooth ear pieces.'

An audible gasp went up from the room as everyone began to open their boxes.

'You'll notice that they've all been painted a special matt-black colour, and I've been assured that they're waterproof to a depth of two thousand metres. We're particularly excited about the iWatch, as we can use it to communicate with each other via the special pre-installed Skype application. It also tells the time, checks your email, logs into Facebook, monitors your heart rate and calculates how many calories you're burning. It has a built-in GPS navigation system, so that you'll never get lost on a mission again, and if you ever do, we'll be able to find you. These devices are to replace the traditional two-way radio that is, quite frankly, completely out-dated, so I want you all to familiarise yourselves with this new equipment before we leave tonight. Any questions?'

'Does the watch take pictures?' asked Barry, who'd been keen to get one since they came out.

'The iWatch doesn't, no, but the iPhone can.'

'Do you think I'll be able to access my Pinterest account on the iWatch?'

'I believe so, yes?'

'And Twitter?'

'Again, yes.'

'Instagram?'

'I've no idea, but probably, yes.'

'How about LinkedIn?'

'Yes, but this isn't primarily for social media use. This is to enable us to communicate more effectively during an operation, so please focus on its Skype application for now. You can play about with the other features when you return.'

The room fell silent as everyone started trying on the watch to see how it looked on them.

'Right then, and remember, chaps, zero-one hundred hours at the boat station. See you then!'

Act 4, Scene 5

Tuer ou être tué
Kill or be killed

"To mourn a mischief that is past and gone is the next way to draw new mischief on?"
Othello, Act I, Scene III

MOONLIGHT SPARKLED over the flat calm of the English Channel, as two black ribs with muffled engines bounced their way towards the ghostly image of HMS Victory that lay becalmed between two great nation's naval fleets, one belonging to the French and the other the British.

When the ribs were about five hundred metres away from their quarry, they came off their high speed planes and drifted along together for a last minute briefing.

'Okay men,' said Tony, just loud enough to be heard by the crews of both boats, 'you know what to do. Has everyone got their iWatches on and their blue-tooth ear pieces in?'

They all gave him a solemn nod.

'And you're all logged in to Skype?'

They nodded again.

'Right, as soon as we find the French President I want him off that ship, and then it's back to base, sharpish. And remember, no shooting unless absolutely necessary. Okay, let's go.'

The two ribs crept forward again, and after about ten minutes they silently nestled up against HMS Victory's hull, the engines were turned off and the ribs were tied together before being secured to the Victory. The eight men on board just sat there and listened. All they could hear was the gentle lap of water slapping the sides of the three vessels. Nothing else.

When they were certain there was nothing more to be heard, they began to scale the ship's port side in complete silence, like deathly shadows rising from a watery grave.

On reaching the railings that looked out over the Victory's main deck, the eight members of the newly formed S.S. peered out and began scanning the decks, masts and rigging for any sign of movement, but apart from eight bodies being displayed on the shrouds of the ship's starboard side, one of whom must have been the French President, all was still. No sentries, no guards, no nothing!

They looked over at Tony and awaited his instructions, but Tony was thinking that it just couldn't be this easy. Nobody on deck, not even a single sentry? Something didn't feel right, so he spent another few minutes peering into every shadowy corner. Eventually he lifted his hand to give the order to go over, but then he stopped. There was something. Or was there? Over towards the other side of the ship, just underneath where the bodies were dangling. But he really couldn't be sure, so he lifted his left hand up, saw his iWatch blink into life and, making sure his Skype app was on, said, oh-so quietly, *'Movement, far side.'*

A voice came back in his ear. *'Where? I can't see anything.'*

By looking at his iWatch he could tell straight away that it was Barry asking the question, and took a moment to be grateful for this brilliant new technology before answering, *'Behind the starboard side rail.'*

'What does "starboard" mean?'

Being a former S.A.S. member, Barry hadn't a clue about boat-related terminology, and a collective groan went up from around the group.

'The term "starboard",' whispered Tony, *'indicates the right hand side of the ship when facing forwards. We're on the port side. The movement I saw was on the opposite side.'*

'So why didn't you just say "on the right hand side of the ship" then?' asked Barry, feeling confused and more than a little pissed-off at being made to look stupid in front of everyone.

'There's no time to go into that now Barry, but there is definitely movement over on the other side.'

Silence returned as they all peered over, desperately trying to discern what it was that was there, if anything.

Just then, Barry received an incoming Skype call.

'Fuck it', he said, more loudly than he should have, but not with as much volume as the noise his iWatch was making. He stared down at his wrist. *'It's my Mum. Hold on, I'd better take it.'*

'You must be fucking joking?' said Tony, in complete dismay.

'Hello, Mum?' whispered Barry, *'Yes, it's me. I'm fine thanks, but I can't talk now. No, Mum, it's two o'clock in the morning here. Yes, I know. Anyway, how's life in Melbourne?'*

'WILL YOU SHUT THE FUCK UP!' whispered Tony, with as much force as a whisper would allow.

'I'm sorry Tony, but it's my Mum. She's gone to visit Aunt Melissa in Australia and hasn't quite got the hang of time zones yet.'

'Yes, thank you, Barry. But in case you'd forgotten, we're in the middle of a covert military operation!'

'Mum, I've really got to go now, but I'll give you a call tomorrow. Okay, yes, bye then,' and he ended the call.

The entire S.S. unit was now glaring at him.

'What?' he said. *'You don't know my Mum. If I'd hung up on her there'd have been hell to pay!'*

'There'll be hell to pay here too if you don't shut the fuck up!'

Silence returned to the ship's port side and they all, once again, gazed out over HMS Victory's moon-lit deck.

'OK, I can't see anything now. I suggest we go, but keep your heads down.'

The moment they started climbing over the rails, bullets sliced through the air around them and Barry disappeared back over the side.

'SHIT, SHIT, SHIT,' cursed Tony, as he jumped to the deck, fell flat on his face, and started to provide covering fire, giving his men precious time to find shelter.

'No need for silence now chaps,' he called out. 'It's "kill or be killed" time!'

'You know, that should have been our new motto,' observed Kevin, through a wistful but savage grin, as he flung himself down on the deck besides Tony.

Seeing that everyone had found cover, and with the gunfire having abated, Tony gave the order, 'Move in, men, and secure the French President, but don't shoot him, for Christ sake!'

'And try not to hit the ship either,' added Kevin, before springing to his feet and pelting over towards the main mast; but he didn't make it, taking a bullet straight to the head which sent him spinning around in a cloud of sprayed blood before falling back to the deck.

Having witnessed another of his men go down in action, Tony leapt up and charged over towards the forecastle, where he leapt up the steps and flung himself over to the starboard side. With no bullets chasing after him he peered over the railings. There he could just about make out a number of shadowy figures, all holding very similar positions to where they'd been just moments before when Barry had taken his rather ill-fated Skype call, but on the opposite side of the ship.

Tony aimed his Ingram MAC-10 at them and let out a continuous stream of bullets. Most of the figures fell back into the water. With his enemy's position now compromised, those remaining surged over the side and onto the main deck and started spraying the ship with bullets. Tony crawled over to the base of the foremast, and from what was a commanding position, started taking out those of the opposing force he could see, one man at a time.

And as the ship slowly began to fall silent again, and with his heart pounding in his ears, Tony lifted his hand to wake up his iWatch.

'Report in everyone,' he said, but there was no response. He put a hand up to his blue-tooth ear piece to push it firmly against his ear, and with greater urgency demanded, 'Everyone, report in!'

Still nothing.

'Shit!'

It looked like he was the only one who'd made it.

But had he?

It was then he realised he'd been hit after all, and as was often the case during the heat of battle, hadn't even noticed. He reached down to his left leg's calf muscle as he felt a delayed pain tear up through his body. Blood was pumping out of him, he could feel it spurt out over his fingers. Hot, wet, sticky blood. The bullet must have sliced open one of his main arteries.

'Shit!' he said again.

He tried to stand but the deck spun around him and he crashed back down. He looked at his iWatch to call for help, but his vision was fading in and out and the screen was just too small for him to focus on. He realised then that he'd made a massive mistake. It had been his idea, and his idea alone, to ditch the traditional two-way radio in favour of more up-to-date technology, but he realised now that they should have tested it in the field first, and certainly before using it during an actual covert mission. The iWatch may have been okay for civilian use, and possibly even for normal military personnel, but for special ops it had been a wholly misguided idea, and on that fateful realisation, he passed out.

Act 5, Scene 1
Tous sont morts, Capitaine
They're all dead, Captain

*"When sorrows come, they come not
single spies, but in battalions."*
Hamlet, Act IV, Scene V

THERE WAS a gentle knock at the Captain's door,
and Peter's head poked through the gap.

'Are you awake, Cate?'

'No!'

A moment's silence followed before she asked,
'Why?'

'Oh, um, well, it, er, seems like there was some sort
of a disturbance on board last night, and we thought
you'd be interested.'

'I thought I heard something going on. What
happened?'

'Well, I think you may want to take a look for
yourself.'

'Can't you give me the gist?'

'Um…'

'Okay, give me five minutes,' she said, and the door
closed, leaving her to enjoy the comfy feeling of being
snug and warm inside her rather strange coffin-shaped
bed.

A few minutes later curiosity got the better of her
and she attempted to climb out of the box, but only

then remembered that she'd taken two bullets just the day before, and Peter had had to help her get into the bed, so it stood to reason that she'd need his help to get out of it.

'PETER!' she bellowed.

His head appeared around the door again.

'Help me, will you?'

'Oh, yes, of course. How are your injuries anyway?'

'No doubt they'll feel better when I'm out of this damned coffin,' she moaned as he helped lift her out.

'Right, you can sod off now,' she said. 'I need to get dressed.'

'Yes, um, right, well, I'll be waiting for you outside, if you need me.'

'I'll cope,' she said, but he didn't move.

'Bye then!' she added.

Momentarily transfixed by the current love of his life standing in front of him in her bra, pants and bandages, Peter had to forcibly shake himself before he could start backing himself out towards the door.

'I'll be waiting outside,' he said again, with an embarrassed smile before ducking out and closing the door after him.

With him gone she began to slowly put on the only clothes she had - her pirate costume - and after several minutes of muttered cursing, she managed to make herself presentable and stepped over to one of the cabin's windows to take a look out.

The view was very similar to that of the evening before: an abundance of sea, sky, and battleships of various shapes and sizes; so she fetched her sword which had been propped up against her bed and sliding it back into her belt, made her way out onto the main deck.

Peter and Will were waiting for her outside.

'So what's all this about then?' she asked.

Will took it upon himself to answer.

'It would appear that we picked up a few additional passengers last night, Captain.'

'Oh, really? Who are they?'

'We're not exactly sure.'

'How come?'

'Well, it would seem that none of them can actually talk.'

'Why? Are they not human?'

'Oh, they're human alright.'

'Then what the hell's wrong with them?'

'They're all dead, Captain.'

'They're all what?'

'Dead, Captain.'

'Sorry, I'm confused. You're telling me that we picked up some new passengers last night but they're not like normal passengers because they're dead?'

'That's right, Captain.'

'So how did they get on board then, and don't tell me that they're a bunch of Zombies!'

'I don't think they were when they came on board, Captain, but it looks like they died in the process of boarding.'

'What on earth are you talking about?'

'Well, Captain, if you could look behind you, I think you'll get a better idea.'

She spun around to see three dead soldier-types, all dressed head-to-foot in black and lying in congealed pools of darkened blood besides the ship's great wheel.

'Who the fuck are they?' she asked, somewhat surprised. She was used to seeing the odd dead body before breakfast, but three at the same time was a bit much, even for her.

'We've had a look over them and two have S.B.S. badges on their berets and the other has an S.A.S. badge. So we're assuming they're special forces.'

'Oh!' said Cate. 'I've heard of the S.A.S. before, but what's the S.B.S.?'

'Special Boat Service, Captain. They're like the S.A.S. but are trained to operate on the water,' replied Will, who was clearly doing his best not to look at the bodies.

'I see. And are there any more of them?'

'Yes, Captain. Quite a few more, in fact. We found them lying all over the quarterdeck when we woke up. We even discovered one up on the forecastle.'

'And they're all dead, are they?'

'Every last one of them, yes, Captain.'

'And I assume they're all British?'

'Well…'

'They *are* all British Will, and not French! You know we have a strict rule about not allowing any more French people on board?'

'Yes, Captain, I am aware of that, but it would appear that some are from the B.F.S.T.'

'And what's the B.F.S.T. when it's at home?'

'It's the French Special Services, Captain. The Brigade des Forces Spéciales Terre. They're like the S.A.S., only French.'

'And did anyone give them permission to come aboard?'

'No, Captain, absolutely not! They snuck on last night, without asking.'

'Well, then, I suggest you identify all the French ones and throw them back over the side.'

'Yes, Captain!'

'But take their weapons first. At this rate we may need them.'

'And what about the dead British soldiers, Captain?'

'Oh, we'll keep them for now, but again, take their weapons, and hand them out to anyone who may have some vague idea about how to use them.'

'Yes, Captain.'

Following orders, Will went off to strip all the dead special forces soldiers of their weapons and then to dispose of the French ones over the side.

Cate turned to Peter. 'Do we have any idea what the military was up to?'

'It's difficult to know for sure, but at a guess I'd say they were after the French President.'

They both looked up to see the President of France still hanging from the yard arm, next to all the French fishermen.

'Oh yes, I'd forgotten about him. But if that's the case, why didn't they just take him? They must have known we didn't want him. I mean, we even had that banner put up saying so.'

'I really don't know,' Peter replied. He was about as mystified as everyone else. 'It must have been some sort of communication mix up. The French Special Forces must only speak French, and not English like the rest of us, and the ship's been riddled with bullets, so they must have had some sort of disagreement about something.'

'Yes, that sounds familiar. Anyway, to change the subject, how are all our navy friends doing out there?' and she gesticulated towards the myriad of naval vessels that now seemed to be surrounding them.

'Very much the same as yesterday evening. There's an armada of French battleships over there, and there's a bunch of British ones on the other side.'

'Let's take a look, shall we?' and she put her arm over his shoulder and he helped her up to the poop deck for a more elevated view.

'Morning, Inspector!' she called up to Capstan, who was leaning against the poop rail.

'Morning, Cate!'

'Did you sleep well?' she asked, as Peter helped her up the steps.

'Best sleep I've had in ages, thank you! How's your leg?'

'Bloody painful; which reminds me. Peter, fetch me something to drink will you? And I don't mean water!'

'Yes, Captain!' Peter said, and after propping her up against the poop rail besides Capstan, he scampered off to find her medicinal bottle of rum.

'So, Inspector, what's your plan for the day?'

'I'd really like to stay here, if it's alright with you? I can't say I'm missing my normal job, and the battery on my phone's died, so my boss can't get hold of me, which makes for a very pleasant change.'

'Well, you're welcome to stay for just as long as you like.'

They leaned against the poop rail to watch Will and his men dispose of the French Special Forces overboard, and when he'd completed that rather irksome task he came bounding up to see them.

'All the French army-types have been discarded, Captain, and we now have our own little collection of machine guns and explosives.'

'Good work, Will!'

'We also found some supplies of food and water on them.'

'Excellent! Dispense what you have to the crew, but make sure Crispin gets something first. How's he doing, anyway?'

'Oh, he's fine. I think he'll be up and about as normal at some point today.'

'That's good news indeed! So, Will, what do you propose we do about all these bloody French battleships? We can't have them loitering around here all day not doing anything interesting. If nothing else, they're spoiling my view.'

'I'm not sure that there is anything we can do about them, Captain.'

'Well, this is all rather tedious,' she said, and let out a heavy sigh.

Seeing Peter return with her bottle she called out, 'Ah, my medicine. Praise the Lord!'

'Here you go, Captain.'

'Thank you, Peter,' and she unscrewed the cap and took a few hearty swigs.

'Right, that's breakfast sorted.'

Will glanced over at her and asked, 'Would it be okay if we had a go at firing off some more of the cannons? We could really do with the practice.'

'Good idea there, young Will, and it will give the rest of us something to look at apart from sea, sky and boring-looking French battleships.'

'Thank you, Captain!' and with a beaming smile,
Will set off below to play with some of his new toys.

Act 5, Scene 2

La pénétration est la meilleure forme d'attaque
Penetration is the best form of attack

"How bitter a thing it is to look into happiness through another man's eye."
As You Like It, Act V, Scene II

THE BRITISH PRIME MINISTER, Robert Bridlestock, stood in the middle of his office addressing an imaginary golf ball with a seven iron. In the far corner of the room, and just about as far away from the Prime Minister's rather erratic swing as he could position himself, stood the Home Secretary, Harold Percy-Blakemore. Over in the opposite corner, beside the PM's desk, stood the Defence Minister, Gerald Frackenburger, and hovering by the office door, as he was accustomed to, was Fredrick Overtoun, the PM's Private Secretary.

They were all listening to the telephone conversation the Defence Minister was having with John Harrington-Smith, the Director of Special Forces, who'd been put on speaker phone.

'Are you sure?' Gerald Frackenburger asked.

'Unfortunately, yes,' replied John Harrington-Smith.

'But couldn't they simply have got lost on the way home and be running a bit late? After all, the English Channel is quite a big place, isn't it?'

'It's not that big, Gerald, and besides they all had the latest iWatches with both Skype and GPS tracking, so unless they all took their watches off, left them on board HMS Victory and then decided to go AWOL, I suspect their mission failed and they've all been killed.'

'You're being a little over-dramatic, aren't you, John? They could have simply been taken prisoner.'

'Again, it's unlikely, Gerald. Their iWatches have built in heart rate detectors which we were monitoring, but they all flat-lined one after another, shortly after two o'clock this morning.'

'So you're telling us that our nation's very best special forces, a crack-combination of the S.A.S and the S.B.S., known the world over for their ability to do the impossible, "who dares wins" and all that, have been taken out by some students dressed up as 18th Century pirates?'

'As unlikely as it sounds, yes, that is what I'm proposing. Our naval intelligence has also just reported that the crew of HMS Victory have already thrown half the bodies overboard, and they continue to hold the President of France hostage.'

'Jesus Christ!' exclaimed Gerald, for want of anything else to say.

The room fell into a stunned silence, with the only noise being the occasional swish coming from the PM, as he continued to practice his swing.

'Any thoughts, Prime Minister?' asked Harold Percy-Blakemore, the Home Secretary, as he kept a very close eye on the seven iron's club face, just in case it became any more wayward than it already was.

'About what?' asked Robert.

The Home Secretary sighed.

'About the missing special forces and their failed attempt to rescue Jacques Moutonette, the President of France, Prime Minister?'

'No, not really,' Robert answered, his mind clearly focused on other things.

Silence once again descended and after a few moments Robert looked up, wondering why everyone had stopped talking.

'Sorry, are you waiting for me?' he asked, noticing that they were all staring at him.

'We were just wondering what we should do about this situation with France, Prime Minister,' asked the Home Secretary again, hoping that Robert would finally stop swinging his seven iron about quite so vehemently.

'Yes, I know, you just asked me, and I said I hadn't a clue.'

More silence followed, forcing Robert to speak again.

'Listen, Harry, you're the bloody Home Secretary, not me! If you're stuck for ideas then I suggest you ask our Defence Minister who is, after all, standing right there,' and Robert used his club to point at Gerald Frackenburger who was still beside the Prime Minister's desk, in the opposite corner of the room.

'May I go now?' asked John Harrington-Smith from the other end of the phone.

'Yes, you can go now, John,' said Robert, with a voice loud enough for him to hear, 'and thank you for your time.'

'My pleasure, Prime Minister,' and he hung up.

With the conference call now over, and as nobody was contributing anything else to the meeting, the Home Secretary thought he'd better follow his Prime Minister's advice - not something he ever liked to do but, given the circumstances, didn't feel he had much choice - and ask the Defence Minister what he thought they should do.

'I really have no idea!' replied Gerald. 'As far as I can make out it's the Home Secretary's job, not mine!'

'I think not,' retorted the Home Secretary. 'This is a defence issue, not a matter for home security.'

'If we're unable to defend ourselves against the French, then I can assure you it will most definitely become a matter for home security.'

'Well, we wouldn't have to if you could do a better job at "defence"!'

'Well, perhaps I may have been able to do a better job at "defence" if you hadn't done quite such a good job at penetrating my wife!'

'I've never been anywhere near your wife!'

'That's not what *your* wife says!'

'How do you know what my wife says?'

'BECAUSE I'M SCREWING HER, THAT'S HOW I KNOW WHAT YOUR WIFE SAYS!'

'HOW DARE YOU HAVE SEX WITH MY WIFE!'

'YOU HAD SEX WITH MINE FIRST!'

'I DID NOT!'

'YES, YOU BLOODY DID!'

'DID NOT!'

'DID TOO!'

'DIDN'T!

'DID!'

'Now, now, now, everyone *please* calm down!' said Robert, keen to return to thinking about his golf swing without having to listen to some in-house dispute about who penetrated whose wife, and which one of them was first to do so. Besides, he'd slept with both their wives and really couldn't see what all the fuss was about.

'May I propose that, for now, we simply don't do anything? Nothing's actually happened so far. So what if the French are pissed off with us for having their President held hostage by the crew of HMS Victory. They're always pissed off at us about something. If it's not this, then it would be because we beat them at the Rugby World Cup last week, or because of Waterloo, Trafalgar, or Agincourt. Anyway, it's not as if we haven't tried to resolve the situation. We did send in our very best Special Services to extract their precious President from the ship. It wasn't as if it was our fault that the mission failed and they all got themselves killed in the process.'

Prevented, in the nick of time, from having a punch-up, the Home Secretary and the Defence Minister returned to their respective corners.

Delighted to see his words having the desired placatory effect, Robert turned his attention back to his swing.

'I suggest we just wait for something to actually happen,' he continued, as he brought his seven iron all the way back behind his head. When he could just see the club's face from the corner of his left eye he stopped, as he tried to assess whether or not the shaft of the club was parallel with the floor, as it should be;

and in that classic golfer's pose he asked, 'How about some fresh coffee, Freddy?'

Fredrick Overtoun, who now stood with his back firmly against the office door, with his hand resting on its handle, just in case a fight did break out and he had to make a swift exit, was more than delighted to be given the opportunity to leave the room.

'Yes, Prime Minister, right away, Prime Minister,' he said, and disappeared, closing the door quietly behind him.

Act 5, Scene 3

Je ne suis pas certain que c'était une bonne idée
I'm not sure that was such a good idea

"There is nothing either good or bad,
but thinking makes it so."
Hamlet, Act II, Scene II

IT WASN'T long before the first great boom of cannon fire exploded out from beneath them from the starboard lower gun deck, shortly followed by the now all-too-familiar cloud of thick grey smoke that drifted quickly past them on a steadily-freshening breeze, obscuring Cate's view of the French Armada as it did so.

'There's nothing like the smell of gunpowder in the morning,' she said, taking a long deep breath, and another hearty swig from her bottle of rum.

Moments later a missile from the French side screamed through the air, directly over their heads, just missing the Victory's mizzen mast. As the entire crew instinctively ducked for cover, Cate couldn't help but ask, 'What the fuck do they think they're doing?', and was just about to order the Victory into an all-out single-handed attack against the entire French navy when another missile flew past, but higher than the last, and from the British side. That one was followed by an almighty explosion, somewhere amidst the French fleet, but none of them dared to look for fear of having their heads torn from their shoulders by something cylindrical in shape with an armour-piercing explosive tip and which typically travelled at Mach 2.

Having witnessed one of their ships take a direct hit, the entire French navy fired everything they had at the British fleet. Naturally the British followed suit, and the crew of HMS Victory gazed over whatever it was they'd taken cover behind to watch maritime Armageddon erupt all around them.

'I'M NOT SURE IT WAS SUCH A GOOD IDEA,' shouted Peter, over the ear-bleeding noise of ship after ship taking direct hits whilst they all continued firing at each other with gay abandon.

'WHAT WASN'T SUCH A GOOD IDEA?' asked Cate, as best she could over the noise.

'TO LET WILL HAVE ANOTHER GO AT FIRING THE CANNONS.'

'NO, YOU COULD BE RIGHT THERE!'

The missiles were now joined by shell fire, and as the explosions increased, Cate shouted, 'MAY I SUGGEST WE GET THE FUCK OUT OF HERE?'

'I COULDN'T AGREE MORE!' Peter shouted back. 'I'LL GET WILL AND THE REST OF THE CREW, AND WE'LL HAVE A GO AT HOISTING SOME SAILS.'

Peter crawled off to find Will, and as missiles and shells continued to fly over the ship, Cate shouted to Capstan, 'AT LEAST THEY DON'T SEEM TO BE SHOOTING AT US ANYMORE.'

'ARE YOU SURE ABOUT THAT?' he asked, as one particular shell ripped through the air at what felt like inches above their heads.

'NO, NOT REALLY,' she said, and then, 'Bloody French,' to nobody in particular, and began crawling over to lie next to Capstan, so that she could have at least one conversation without having to shout all the time.

'Inspector, I really think we need to get rid of that French President.'

'How do you mean?'

'I was thinking that we could stick him into a life raft and set him adrift. That way the French can pick him up and sod off back to wherever it is that they came from.'

'France,' said Capstan.

'What about it?' asked Cate.

'Where they all came from.'

'Yes, no doubt. But I'm going to need your help, Inspector.'

'To do what?'

'To launch a lifeboat, get the French President in it and then set it adrift.'

Capstan looked down at the four huge wooden life boats that had been secured to the ship's quarterdeck.

'I'm happy to help, but how the hell are we going to get one of those over the side?'

'I've no idea, but I think we're going to have to try. Come on!'

Cate began crawling down the poop steps towards the main deck with Capstan doing the best he could to follow on after her.

Meanwhile, Will, Cannonball, Deadweight, Peter and the rest of the able-bodied crew members were scrambling over decks, masts and ratlines in a desperate bid to get some sail up under increasingly hazardous working conditions. As Cate and Capstan took shelter underneath the prisoners who still dangled from the shrouds, she called to Will as he scooted past on his way over towards the foremast.

He stopped, turned and came back over to them, sensibly keeping his head down like everyone else.

'I think we need to get the French President back to his fellow countrymen,' Cate explained. 'That way, hopefully, they'll all stop shooting at us and each other. Can you help us to get one of those lifeboats over the side?'

Will looked around at the boats in question. They were enormous, but he thought it was possible, as long as they had enough manpower.

'Let me just help them to get that sail up on the foremast,' he replied. 'That one combined with the one already up on the mizzen mast should help to get us clear of this lot and a-head'n back to England. As soon as it's up I'll get everyone back here. Sit tight for now, we won't be long.'

She nodded at him and watched as he continued on his way towards the forecastle, and as good as his word, it wasn't long before he and the crew had the second sail up and were all heading back down to the quarterdeck.

Then the entire lot of them crowded around one of the starboard side lifeboats, untied it, and heaved it off its rockers before manhandling it over to the side of the ship.

'I SUGGEST WE JUST SHOVE IT OVER AS BEST WE CAN, MEN,' shouted Will, in between breaths. 'ON THREE: AND ONE, TWO, AND THREE!'

They gave an almighty shove, the lifeboat slipped over the side and dropped straight down into the English Channel.

'GREAT JOB, LADS!' he gasped, and bent over with his hands on his knees like the rest of those who'd lent a hand.

Cate unsheathed her sword and started cutting the President of France down from where he'd been strung up for around sixteen hours or so and who now, sensing freedom, wriggled and wormed in his rather crumpled, but still very shiny, blue suit.

'I don't suppose we could make him walk the plank?' suggested Cannonball, with more hope than reasonable expectation.

'No time for that I'm afraid,' said Cate. They stood the President on the ship's side, cut the rope that had bound his hands and removed his gag, and before he could start bemoaning his plight to them all in his native French tongue, they pushed him over. Unfortunately he didn't land in the lifeboat, as it had already drifted off behind them, but as soon as he hit the water he got the idea and started to doggy-paddle his way over towards it.

They then did the same with the French fisherman and, forgetting none of them could actually swim, shoved them over to join their President.

'Right then,' said Cate, 'I think we should make way whilst the going's good. Set a course back to England please, Will.'

'Right you are, Captain.' A cheer went up from the crew, as Will, Cannonball, Deadweight and Peter went to man the wheel. And as they did that, Cate and Capstan looked back to where the sea battle raged on as the majestic HMS Victory sailed away, heading for home.

Act 5, Scene 4

Flânerie, ou quelque chose comme ça
Loitering, or something

"Rough winds do shake the darling buds of May."
From Shakespeare's Sonnet 18

'IT'S SIR REGINALD ANTHEM, First Lord of the Admiralty, on the phone for you *again*, Prime Minister,' said Fredrick Overtoun, holding his boss's phone close to his chest as he watched Robert continue to give the Home Secretary and the Defence Minister an impromptu golf lesson in the middle of the office.

'I didn't want to speak to him the first time he called, and I certainly don't want to speak to him now, thank you, Freddy!'

'He says it's become rather *very* urgent, Prime Minister.'

'Yes, but everyone always says that it's "rather *very* urgent", don't they?'

'But I actually think it might be this time, Prime Minister.'

'I doubt that, Freddy, I doubt that. Now, Harry, you have to keep your head looking down at the ball during the follow-through. You keep lifting it up to see where it's gone before you've even hit the damned thing. Try it again, but this time don't move your head at all. Just keep it fixed on the ball.'

'But I don't have a ball, Prime Minister.'

'Yes, well, you'll just have to use your imagination. You do still possess an imagination, don't you, Harry?'

'Er, well, I suppose so.'

He waggled the club a few more times and then looked up and said, 'I'll try it again then, shall I?'

'Yes! There's a good chap,' and both Robert and Gerald Frackenburger stood back to let Harold Percy-Blakemore have another go with the PM's seven iron.

As they watched him address the imaginary ball, Fredrick, the PM's Private Secretary, whispered just behind Robert, 'Sir Reginald Anthem is still holding for you, Prime Minister?'

'WILL YOU SHUT UP, FREDDY? YOU SHOULD BLOODY WELL KNOW BY NOW THAT YOU MUST NEVER SPEAK WHEN SOMEONE'S ABOUT TO TEE-OFF!'

'But... Prime Minister?'

'I SAID SHUT THE FUCK UP, FREDRICK, OR I'LL HAVE YOU ARRESTED FOR... LOITERING, OR SOMETHING!'

After scowling at his Private Secretary for another moment, just to make sure he wasn't going to interrupt them again, Robert turned back and said, 'Sorry about that, Harry. Do please carry on, and remember to keep your head down this time.'

So Harold continued to address the ball, the one he was doing his best to imagine was actually there, and keeping his head firmly fixed on it, he pulled his club back so the shaft lined up parallel to the floor and then brought it down and through, for what looked to be the perfect golf swing.

'That's more like it, Harry, good job! Now, you just need to try it with an actual ball. Hold on, let me get you one.'

'What, you mean here, in your office?' asked Harry as he glanced around at all the mirrors, paintings, and vases.

'Why not? We may as well have a bit of fun, and besides, you can't really know what it's like to play golf until you actually hit a ball.'

Fredrick took the courageous decision to cough loudly and very obviously, as he still clutched at the Prime Minister's phone.

'Hold on boys, I'd better take this damned call first. Put it on speaker-phone, will you please, Freddy?'

Relieved to have finally been able to garner his boss's attention, Fredrick said, 'Yes, Prime Minister,' and turned it on.

The speaker jumped into life with the sound of explosions, shouting and a good amount of background screaming, and over the ensuing noise that vibrated out of it, Fredrick shouted, 'THE PRIME MINISTER'S ON THE PHONE FOR YOU NOW, SIR REGINALD.'

'ROBERT, WHERE THE HELL HAVE YOU BEEN?'

Somewhat surprised by all the commotion, Robert made his way over to the desk.

'SORRY ABOUT THAT, REGGIE, I JUST HAD TO FINISH UP A MEETING WITH HARRY AND GERRY. SO, WHAT'S BEEN GOING ON OVER THERE? SOUNDS LIKE ARMAGEDDON'S BROKEN OUT!' and sent a wry smile to Harold and Gerald, hoping they both got his joke, but neither of them seemed to have done, or showed any obvious signs that he'd even made one, given that it did actually sound like Armageddon had broken out on the other end of the phone.

'*THE FRENCH OPENED FIRE ON THE VICTORY AGAIN, PRIME MINISTER,*' continued Sir Reginald, from on board the British fleet's flagship, HMS Reticent, '*SO WE FIRED A MISILE AT THE OFFENDING FRENCH SHIP IN A BID TO STOP IT FROM REPEATING THE ACTION.*'

There was a pause in the conversation as another massive explosion made the speaker phone lift momentarily off the desk.

'REGGIE, ARE YOU STILL THERE?'

'*YES, PRIME MINISTER, I'M STILL HERE.*'

'YOU WERE SAYING?'

'*SORRY, WELL, AS SOON AS THE MISSILE HIT THEIR SHIP, THE ENTIRE FRENCH FLEET LAUNCHED AN ALL-OUT ATTACK AGAINST US.*'

Sir Reginald seemed to have stopped talking again, so Robert gave him a prompt and asked, 'SO WHAT HAPPENED THEN?'

'*WE LAUNCHED AN ALL OUT ATTACK AGAINST THEM, OBVIOUSLY, PRIME MINISTER.*'

'BUT AREN'T YOU SUPPOSED TO ASK ME FIRST, BEFORE YOU GO ABOUT FIRING MISSILES AT OTHER COUNTRY'S SHIPS?'

'*QUITE POSSIBLY, PRIME MINISTER, BUT GIVEN THE FACT THAT YOU WERE INDISPOSED THE FIRST TIME I CALLED, I FELT I HAD TO MAKE THE DECISION ON MY*

OWN. AND HAVING LAUNCHED OUR FIRST MISSILE I'VE BEEN WAITING ON HOLD FOR YOU FOR AT LEAST FIVE MINUTES, AND UNFORTUNATELY, PRIME MINISTER, WE CAN'T WAIT THAT LONG TO MAKE DECISIONS DURING A BATTLE AT SEA, OR ANYWHERE ELSE FOR THAT MATTER. IF WE DID, WE'D ALL HAVE BEEN SPEAKING FRENCH A VERY LONG TIME AGO, PRIME MINISTER.'

Robert had to admit that the man had a point. As important as golf was, it probably wasn't quite as vital as fending off an all-out attack from Britain's oldest and closest of maritime adversaries, so he shrugged his shoulders and, not knowing what else to say, asked, 'SO WHO'S WINNING?'

'I'D SAY WE HAVE THE UPPER HAND AT THIS STAGE, PRIME MINISTER, BUT BOTH FLEETS ARE TAKING A GOOD POUNDING.'

Harold leant over towards the speaker-phone and asked, 'WHAT'S HAPPENED TO THE VICTORY?' He'd always had a soft-spot for the old man-o-war ever since he'd built an Airfix model of her a few years earlier. 'IS SHE ALL RIGHT?'

'YES, SHE'S FINE. THEY VERY NEARLY HAD HER SUNK AT THE BEGINNING BUT THE CREW WERE ABLE TO SAIL HER AWAY JUST IN TIME TO AVOID ANY SERIOUS DAMAGE.'

A collective sigh of relief went up around the office. Up until that point they'd all taken HMS Victory for granted, but it was only when they'd heard that she'd nearly been sunk by the French that they realised just what a national treasure she really was.

'YOU DID THE RIGHT THING, REGGIE,' said Robert. 'YOU HAD TO PROTECT THE VICTORY AT ALL COSTS.'

THANK YOU, PRIME MINISTER. SHE SHOULD BE SAFE NOW, AND SHE SEEMS TO BE MAKING GOOD PROGRESS BACK UP THE CHANNEL.'

There was a break in the conversation during which they thought they could hear Sir Reginald talking to someone in the background; then he came back on the line, but just said, *'HOLD ON,'* before his voice disappeared into a series of muffled scrapes and noises. Everyone in the room leaned in towards the phone in desperate anticipation of hearing some more news.

'SORRY ABOUT THAT,' his voice came through again, *'BUT IT LOOKS LIKE THE FRENCH ARE PULLING BACK, PRIME MINISTER.'*

'Thank God for that!' said Robert, but they could still hear the sound of explosions and the occasional scream emanating from the background, so for clarification he asked, 'ARE YOU SURE, REGGIE? IT DOES SOUND LIKE IT'S STILL GOING ON.'

There was another pause during which time the phone crackled and intermittently cut out.

'REGGIE, REGGIE, ARE YOU STILL THERE?'

'Yes, sorry, Prime Minister. All the firing's stopped now. Both sides have called a ceasefire.'

'What happened? Why did they give up?'

'It looks like they were able to rescue their President, Prime Minister. The Victory must have set him adrift in a lifeboat at some point. Anyway, they're all now steaming off back to

Calais, as best they can at any rate.'

'Excellent work, Reggie. You've done Britain proud!'

'Thank you, Prime Minister,' Sir Reginald Anthem said, as if it was just another day at the office for him, and he hung up the phone.

'Well, that was all very exciting, wasn't it?' commented Robert, as he stared around at everyone in the room with wide sparkling eyes and an adrenaline-fuelled grin. But everyone else seemed to be more shaken than stirred, so he added, 'It's not every day we beat the French in a battle out at sea!' Still none of them looked as if they were ready to break out the champagne, so he simply suggested, 'Shall we get back to that golf lesson? Gerald, I believe it was your turn.'

'But you said I could have a go with a ball?' protested Harold.

'Oh, yes, that's right. Sorry, hold on.' He strolled over to the golf bag he kept permanently beside his desk, rummaged around in one of its many deep silk-lined pockets and pulled out a brand new golf ball. He then turned around and tossed it over to Harold, who caught it with aplomb before placing it down on the rug.

'Now, don't hold back, Harry, and remember, keep your head down.'

Harold began to address the real-life ball, and as everyone else edged their way back just as far as the physical confines of the office would allow, Robert had a chance to think, and soon realised that this latest victory against their age-old French adversaries would probably, no, would definitely give him the legacy that so many of his predecessors strived so hard to achieve.

He could actually go down in history as the man who defeated France in the twenty-first century, single-handed, if he played his cards right.

As these ambitious thoughts chased themselves through the catacombs of Robert's rather dangerous mind, Harold sliced the ball straight into an antique glass cabinet.

'Good shot!' said Robert, without even looking; and as Gerald picked his way through the various pieces of broken wood and glass to retrieve the ball, Robert turned to his Private Secretary and asked, 'Freddy, will you please call an urgent meeting with the Press Secretary and all his various minions? I want HMS Victory and her crew to be given a very special welcome home. They've done a huge amount for this island nation of ours, and I want the whole of Great Britain to know about it.'

'Er, yes, Prime Minister.'

'And I want the entire crew to be given medals, lots and lots of medals.'

'What sort of medals, Prime Minister?'

'I've no idea. You can ask the Admiralty about that.'

'Yes, Prime Minister.'

'But first things first, we need to think up a name for that battle we just listened to. Any ideas?'

'How about the Battle of Portsmouth?' offered Gerald.

'Or the Battle of Southampton?' suggested Harold.

'Freddy?'

It wasn't often that the Prime Minister asked his Private Secretary what he thought about anything, but this did seem like it was a unique occasion.

'Perhaps it could be called the Battle of the Solent,

Prime Minister?'

'Um, yes, well, none of them sound grand enough. Let's see what the Press Secretary comes up with, but for now I want full pomp and ceremony for HMS Victory's glorious return.'

'*If* they return, Prime Minister.'

'Yes, good point, Freddy!' He turned to look at his Home Secretary and his Defence Minister. 'Harold, Gerald, I don't care which one of you does it, but I want to make sure that the Victory is escorted up the Thames. I don't want them mooring up in Portsmouth again, and I certainly don't want them drifting off up to Scotland. I want them to sail up the Thames, and then we can welcome them home directly outside Parliament House. I think that would work very well, don't you?' he said, turning to Fredrick.

'Yes, Prime Minister. And maybe we could invite the Royal Family as well?'

'Excellent idea, Freddy! I'm sure they can't come, but I suppose we should at least make the effort to invite them. Right,' Robert said, looking down at his Rolex. 'I call that lunch! If you could ask the Press Secretary to pop up to my flat when he's free, we can have a quick chat up there.' In an unusually buoyant mood, Robert bounded out of the office and up to his flat to catch up with the cricket and to see how England was getting on against South Africa at The Oval.

Act 5, Scene 5

Le Butín de Guerre
The Spoils of War

"We have heard the chimes at midnight."
King Henry IV, Part II, Act III, Scene II

CATE LOOKED OVER at Will, who'd just joined her and Capstan up on the poop deck.

'I don't suppose we could take a trip up to London, could we?' she asked him. 'I'm not sure I'm ready to go back to Portsmouth quite yet.'

It wasn't Portsmouth itself that Cate had to be mindful of, but the person whose job it was to investigate her many macabre leftovers, and who was, at that precise moment, leaning against the poop deck rail beside her.

Capstan looked over at Cate, and then up at Will.

'I'll be honest with you both,' he said to them, 'I can't say that I'm in much of a hurry to get back either.'

He was, in fact, far from happy to return to his normal police duties. The idea of having to make conversation with Sergeant Dewbush again, or to put up with being shouted at by his boss, Morose, had little appeal. He was also fairly certain he'd be able to claim all the hours spent on board HMS Victory as over-time, so whichever way he looked at it, the longer he stayed on board the better.

'I don't think there's much for any of us to get back to,' added Will, who'd felt more at home on board HMS Victory than anywhere else he'd lived during his entire life, and he knew that the crew held a very similar opinion.

'So it's agreed then. We'll sail for London, yes?' asked Cate.

'As long as the wind remains as it is, then it should be possible, but it will mean heading back into mainstream society again, and no doubt questions will be asked, especially if Customs decide to take a look inside that treasure chest of ours, which they will, of course.'

'What's inside the chest?' asked Capstan, unable to resist his natural policeman's curiosity.

The question served as a useful reminder to Cate that Capstan was still a policeman, which was something she'd just about managed to forget.

'Oh, nothing important,' she said, with a dismissive wave of her good arm. 'Inspector, I don't suppose you could see if you can find me another bottle of rum, or something similar? This one seems to be nearly empty,' and she drained its remains before adding, 'in fact, it is empty!'

It was an obvious ruse to get rid of him, and he really didn't mind. The last thing he wanted to do was to become involved in what would, no doubt, become a very dull and boring case of illegal contraband, and he was more than happy to let the UK's Customs officials sort all that out.

'No problem, Cate,' he said, but when he was about half way down the poop steps he stopped and turned back to look at them. 'But I suggest that if there's anything dodgy inside that chest, like drugs or something, then I'd ditch it over the side. Money's fine and all that, but I'd avoid drugs if I were you. Just saying,' and he continued to make his way down the steps to leave them to their clandestine conversation.

Cate had a tendency to agree with Capstan. She'd never really been into drugs, even during her student days. Copious amounts of alcohol had always sufficed.

'I think Capstan's right. I suggest we ditch the chest and all the drugs over the side.'

'And what about the cash, and all that gold?'

'Well, we're not ditching that! I suggest we split it out evenly amongst the crew, and by the time we're done, hopefully it won't seem quite so much. Anyway, we can always say that it was our holiday spending money that we just never had a chance to spend.'

'Sounds good to me,' and Will headed off to give the crew their new course, and to divide all the cash and gold up equally between them.

When that was done, Cannonball and Deadweight heaved the chest, the one that Cannonball had discovered on board the President of France's boat and that still had all the bags of cocaine lining its bottom, back onto the main deck. There they added a few cannonballs to its contents and threw it overboard to watch it disappear down into the murky depths of the English Channel, never to be seen again, hopefully, at least not with their DNA smeared all over it.

Then they made their way back to the ship's wheel, from where they'd been called, to continue steering a course for the Thames Estuary and, with a favourable wind, the City of London itself.

Act 5, Scene 6

J'aime cette fille
I like this girl

"All the world's a stage, and all the
men and women merely players."
As You Like It, Act II, Scene VII

'SO, TELL ME again, Freddy, why I am standing
on this floating platform thing and not outside
Parliament House as I requested.'

'It's the Tower Bridge Pier, Prime Minister, and it's
because HMS Victory is what is known as a Tall Ship
so, logistically speaking, it just wasn't possible for it to
make it up the river as far as Parliament House.'

'I'm still not with you, Freddy.'

'It's too tall to go under the bridges, Prime
Minister.'

'Why didn't you say that in the first place?'

'Sorry, Prime Minister. I thought I did.'

'Is that it there?' he asked, pointing directly ahead
of him.

'Er, no, Prime Minister. That's HMS Belfast.'

'So, what does HMS Victory look like then?'

'It has three masts, some sails, lots of cannons and
is made of wood, Prime Minister.'

'Okay, well, tell me when you see it, will you?'

'Yes, Prime Minister. It should be coming around the corner any time now.'

There was a pause as Robert resisted the urge to stand on his toes to see if he could catch a glimpse of it, and with nothing else of much interest to look at he asked his Private Secretary, 'I don't suppose you brought my Golf Club Owners magazine by any chance?'

'Er, no, Prime Minister, sorry.'

Robert's mobile phone rang from inside his Savile Row suit breast pocket.

'I'd better take that, I suppose,' he said, happy for the distraction.

'Robert speaking.'

'It's Ronold Macdonold, Prime Minister.'

'Who?'

'Ronold Macdonold, Chairman of MDK Industries, Prime Minister.'

'Oh, hello again, Ron. How are you?'

'Very well thank you, Prime Minister. I just wanted to personally congratulate you on the outcome with France.'

'That's very kind of you!'

'I also wanted to apologise, Prime Minister. I should have trusted your instinct to go to war with them, and not Tunisia. It was a bold move but one that I think has really paid off. We're expecting to be busier than ever re-arming the British Fleet and our subsidiary ship repair company is going to be kept in work for years to come. Our share price has already risen and, well, Prime Minister, we're all jolly happy, so thank you again!'

'That's quite alright, Ron. It was my pleasure.'

'You know, Prime Minister, it may be that you've come up with a brilliant new concept for managing the economies of international conflict. Your One Day War idea really is quite

remarkable, and highly profitable as well! It seems to not only maximise product consumption but it causes minimal disruption to the normal nine-to-five.'

'Yes, well, I thought it would work,' said Robert, beaming with self-admiration.

'It reminds me a little of this new One Day Cricket thing.'

'That's actually where I got the idea from!' lied Robert with enthusiasm.

'Good for British morale too, no doubt! Anyway, Prime Minister, you most definitely have my vote at the next General Election, and I'll personally make sure your party receives a substantial donation to cover all your future marketing needs.'

'That's most generous of you, Ron.'

'My pleasure, Prime Minister. Well, I won't hold you up any longer. Cheerio!'

Robert replaced the phone in his pocket as he found himself unable to stop grinning.

'That was Ronold Macdonold, Freddy.'

'I assume all is well at MDK Industries?'

'All is very well at MDK Industries, so much so that he says they'll be funding our next election.'

Fredrick looked over at his Prime Minister with incredulous awe. He couldn't quite believe how Robert Bridlestock, a man who should never have been allowed anywhere near Parliament, let alone given the top job at Number 10, always seemed to emerge from each foul smelling cesspit he managed to stumble into not only smelling of roses, but wearing a tailor-made diamond encrusted suit, with pockets stuffed full of fifty pound notes.

'That's good to hear, Prime Minister.'

'I rather thought so. Anyway, where's this bloody ship got too? I can't be waiting around out here all day.'

'It should be here any minute now, Prime Minister.'

'But why's it taking so long?'

'Probably because it doesn't have an engine, Prime Minister.'

'Well, this is all rather dull, isn't it?'

'Yes, Prime Minister, but at least there's a good turn out.'

Fredrick wasn't wrong there. Word had quickly spread throughout the nation's great capital that HMS Victory would be making a triumphant return having beaten the French at sea at what, it had been decided, would be called the Battle of Great Britain, a name the Prime Minister had personally come up with, despite being told that it sounded too much like the Battle of Britain and subsequently wouldn't go down well with the Air Force, or any surviving members of World War Two for that matter. Fortunately, Air Chief Marshall Lord Taylor Highburt Smith was on a cruise in the Caribbean and couldn't be contacted, and a quick look through the National Register showed that everyone old enough to have served during World War Two was, indeed, dead, so it was unlikely that they'd be able to object.

And so the Battle of Great Britain it was, and the River Thames, from Canary Wharf all the way up to The Tower of London, was lined with tourists, commuters and school children alike, all desperate to catch a glimpse of the now famous, for the second time in British history, HMS Victory, along with the man whose leadership and strategic battle planning had seen off the French attempted invasion of our green and pleasant land, our very own Robert Bridlestock, the British Prime Minister. This was how it would be reported by the Evening Standard and given front page coverage by every other national newspaper the very next day, thanks to Robert giving up his valuable time to make a single phone call to the man who owned every British national newspaper, Sir Malcolm Morrisman, along with a personal bank transfer of £2.5 million and the promise of him being made Earl of Shropshire just as soon as the current Earl of Shropshire died.

'I think I can see it now, Prime Minister.'

'Where?'

'You can just see the top of its main mast, and its White Ensign, Prime Minister.'

'Oh, yes, so you can.'

The crowds behind them could see it too, as they all began to cheer and wave the Union Jacks that some highly opportunistic local trader had started to flog out on the streets the moment he'd heard the news.

As the first rate ship of the line, the ship that had helped see off the French at Trafalgar, and now just off the coast of Portsmouth, was guided around the corner by four tug boats, London Bridge's two great bascules began to lift up and slowly separate from each other, making room for HMS Victory to pass unhindered between its two iconic towers.

'That's quite a sight, it really is!' said Robert, feeling almost regal. 'I assume the press are all in attendance?'

'The world's press are very much in attendance, Prime Minister.'

'And they'll be able to get a good view of me welcoming the crew back on British soil?'

'I should think so, Prime Minister.'

'Good show!'

As the ship loomed ever larger, warps were thrown down and caught by those more used to mooring up the London's River Bus service. The pier's galvanised steel gangplank that stood high in the air was lowered down onto the Victory's side and the three British Customs officials, who'd been eagerly awaiting the moment they could search the crew and the ship for undeclared goods, such as money, gold coins, large bags of cocaine and the odd 18th Century sword, put their clipboards under their arms and began rubbing their hands together with expectant glee.

The Victory's miss-fit pirate crew then began to make their way down the gangplank to rapturous applause, waving and smiling as they did.

First to reach the bottom was Cate Jakebury, soon to become known by the press as Cut-Throat Cate, and the moment she placed a foot onto Tower Bridge Pier the nearest Customs official stepped over to her, held out his hand and said, 'Passport, please?'

Seeing this, Robert barged his way forward. *He* was supposed to be the first to greet them off the ship, not the bloody British Customs.

'Excuse me,' he said, pushing the Customs official to one side, 'but what the hell do you think you're doing?'

Somewhat surprised to find himself being man-handled by the British Prime Minister, the Customs official cleared his throat and said, 'Begging your pardon, Sir, but we need to pass the crew through Customs.'

'You'll be doing no such thing!'

'Er…'

'Do you have any idea who these people are, and what they've done for our country?'

'Well, yes, Sir, I suppose so, but they still need to be cleared through Customs, as does the ship, Sir.'

'I'm buggered if they do, and stop calling me "Sir" all the bloody time. I'm the Prime Minister of the United Kingdom! You do realise that, don't you?'

'Um, yes, Sir, I mean, Prime Minister, but we still need to…'

'You need to sod off back to wherever it was that you came from, that's what you need to do! Now mind out the way!' and with one more shove, he pushed him clear and turned to give what looked like a half-bandaged, half-drunk girl-pirate his warmest and most practised, vote-winning smile.

'Welcome, welcome, welcome,' he said, shaking her by the one hand that was attached to a fully-functioning arm. 'You are most warmly welcome back home by a nation that is truly, truly grateful for your brave, triumphant stand against the French. A magnificent performance by you all, and we are so proud, just so proud to have you back here on British terra firma, once again.'

Cate leaned over to Will and whispered, 'Looks like we didn't need to ditch the cocaine after all!' and then turned back to the Prime Minister and said, 'Thank you, Prime Minister. It was our pleasure to serve Queen and Country, as best we could,' and she bowed her head in humble servitude.

I like this girl, thought Robert, *I like her very much*, and as she lifted her head he put his arm around her shoulders and pivoted her around to face the great throng of press, who'd all been strategically positioned along the concrete hard standing above them.

And as flash photography exploded, and questions too numerous, too distant and too stupid to be fully comprehended drifted down, Robert led Cate up the pontoon towards them, showing himself to have an unshakable bond with this perfect Pirate Princess, almost as if she was his very own prodigal daughter, returning home from the horrors of war; battered, injured and completely drunk, but victorious all the same.

Act 5, Scene 7

Un costume et une valise
A suit and a case

"This above all: to thine own self be true."
Hamlet, Act I, Scene III

THREE DAYS LATER, Cate checked herself out of Portsmouth Hospital where she'd been taken by the St. John's Ambulance crew, shortly after meeting the press with the Prime Minister on the hard standing with HMS Victory and Tower Bridge in the background. Despite insisting that she was fine, the ambulance crew weren't convinced, especially after Peter had told them that she'd taken two bullets in the line of duty and had spent the entire time since then drinking 60% proof rum, and not much else.

As she stepped off the number 74 bus and began ambling up Belmont Road towards her house, still wearing the same pirate costume and still carrying her 18th Century sword, she couldn't help but think that it seemed like a very long time since she'd last walked up here, but it really wasn't. So it was hardly surprising that nothing much had changed. The houses that were having their lofts converted were still having their lofts converted, the front gardens that were being excavated to be replaced with driveways were still being excavated to be replaced with driveways, and the section in the road that was being dug up to fix some pipe, or cable, or whatever it was that had broken was still there, waiting to be filled back in again. The only thing different, or at least unusual, was that there was a young-looking man in a dark three-piece suit, sitting on the low garden wall directly opposite her house, reading the Financial Times. Seeing someone sitting on a wall wearing a three-piece suit wasn't unusual in itself, but she could never recall having ever seen anyone in Portsmouth reading the F.T. before. It just wasn't a "Portsmouth" sort of a newspaper.

Anyway, she had more important things to think about than men reading finance-related newspapers opposite her house; she had a book to write, and she was desperate to get started on it.

Entering her home, she propped her sword up against the wall and retrieved all the flyers, letters and the Portsmouth Post from the floor before dumping them all on the cabinet underneath the hall mirror. Then she made her way through to the kitchen to make herself a coffee, and as the kettle boiled, she went into the dining room to dig out her laptop that she'd left in there somewhere. When she found it, she opened it up, turned it on and entered her password before leaving it to do its thing while she returned to the kitchen to finish making her coffee.

Returning to the laptop, she sat down, found the book folder she'd named, "Blown Away" and opened the Word document inside to reveal what she'd written so far, which was the first chapter. So, underneath that she wrote "Chapter Two" and stared down at the blank white space underneath it before letting out a heavy sigh.

'I'd better check through the mail before I start,' she said out loud to herself, and went back into the hall.

Rifling through the pile of letters, she could only find one that she didn't recognise as being either a bill or an invitation to switch her broadband supplier. So she took that one solitary letter, along with the Portsmouth Post, into the dining room and sat back down.

Opening up the paper she looked at the front page and smiled. The main photograph was of Inspector Capstan being presented with not just one, but two medals by the Prime Minister, right outside Number 10 Downing Street. And the bold headline underneath said, "Local Police Hero Honoured by PM". Eager to learn more she folded the paper in half to read the first couple of paragraphs.

"Police Inspector Capstan, O.B.E., who was on board HMS Victory during The Battle of Great Britain, was said to have acted "above and beyond the call of duty", and was summoned to London yesterday to be duly honoured. There, the Prime Minister himself presented him with two Queen's Police Medals for Gallantry and Distinguished Service.

"According to Robert Bridlestock, Inspector Capstan undertook a pivotal role in winning the day for Britain, and was instrumental in carrying out his very own strategic battle plans. When asked what those plans were, or what Inspector Capstan's role was, exactly, the PM was regretfully unable to speak further, due to the restraints placed upon himself and all those who took part by the Official Secrets Act. However, he went on to re-state that Inspector Capstan had played a significant role, as had the rest of HMS Victory's gallant crew."

Cate chuckled to herself and put down the paper before staring at her laptop's screen, where the big white space continued to stare back at her. But with no immediate inspiration as to which fine selection of words she could choose to fill the space up, she picked up the letter instead.

On opening it, she found it to be from a firm of solicitors called Blackthorn & Buggledown, a name she vaguely recognised, but couldn't remember from where; and so with her curiosity aroused she started to read.

"Dear Cate Jakebury,

I am writing to inform you that despite the authorities' best efforts, they have been unable to locate your husband. It is therefore, with deep regret, that as it has been over six months since he went missing, we have to inform you that he has now been legally classified as dead.

We have subsequently been in contact with his life insurance company, in accordance with his wishes, to make a claim against his policy; and they have since released the sum of £1,543,742 which has been placed in our client account.

We would like to invite you to the reading of his last Will and Testament, of which you are the sole beneficiary. If you could contact us at your earliest convenience to arrange a suitable time to attend such a meeting, we would be very grateful.

Do please be aware that, after the reading, if you would like the sums of money to be transferred into your bank account, you must bring with you your relevant account details along with a current passport for formal identification purposes.

We very much look forward to hearing from you soon,
Yours sincerely,

Daniel B. Buggledown, Esq."

With her mouth hanging open she read it through again, stood up, walked around the room, and sat back down to re-read it, just in case she'd mis-understood its core message; that being that her late husband, the one she'd murdered outside their house with the help of a frozen leg of lamb, a postman, and a General Waste wheelie bin, had been insured for over £1.5 million, and all that money was, at that precise moment in time, sitting in a solicitor's account, waiting for her to collect.

She was just about to phone their office to make the appointment when she remembered that her passport was still inside her suitcase, the one she'd left behind at the pub, just before boarding HMS Victory all those days ago.

She looked back at her laptop, opened up Google and typed in, "Badger and Hamster pub, Portsmouth". The name came straight up, along with its number, and so she popped back into the hall to retrieve the phone.

Resuming her seat at the table, she dialled the number and listened to it ring for a few moments before a girl answered saying, *Badger and Hamster, how can I help?'*

'Oh, hello, it's er, Cate Jakebury here. I think I might have left a, er, suitcase with you, four or five days ago now, after the, er, student's pirate party. I don't suppose it's still there?'

Is it a large silver one?'

'Yes, that's it!'

It's still here. I popped it behind the bar for you. You can pick it up any time.'

'That's great! Would it be okay if I came over now?'
'Sure, no problem.'
'Perfect, thanks again,' and she hung up.

Finishing her coffee, she closed the laptop and made her way out the front door, picking up the car and house keys on the way. She closed and double locked the door behind her, and made her way down the path towards her car. But as she did, she couldn't help but notice the man who'd been reading the Financial Times on the other side of the street stand up and cross the road to head over towards her.

This doesn't look good, she thought. After her many adventures on board HMS Victory, coupled with the various bodies she'd left behind prior to that, she had way too many skeletons rummaging around her closet not to be highly apprehensive of a rapidly approaching man clad in an immaculate dark three-piece suit and armed with a highly suspicious looking copy of the Financial Times, so she hurried around to the driver's side door, trying to avoid catching his eye.

'Mrs Jakebury?' the man called out.

'Possibly,' she answered. 'Who wants to know?'

The young man popped his newspaper under his arm and pulled out a wallet from his back pocket, and from that he extracted a crisp white business card which he handed to her, saying, 'I'm Plankton, Jeffrey Plankton, MI6.'

'Yes, and..?' she asked, taking a moment to examine the card.

'I've been instructed to make contact with you, Mrs Jakebury, and invite you up to London for a chat.'

'Oh, really, and what would you like to talk about?' she asked, unable to shake a deep feeling of grave suspicion.

'You, Mrs Jakebury, and the possibility of you working for us.'

'Me?'

'Yes, you, Mrs Jakebury.'

'But…why me?'

'I've no idea. I've simply been sent down to make contact. Anyway, that's my mobile number on the card. Give me a call if you're interested and we'll make an appointment,' and he held out his hand by way of saying goodbye.

With some dismay, she shook it, and he turned his head to look over towards the side of her house.

'Nice bin,' he said, and caught her eye with just a hint of a smile. Then he turned and strolled away.

Cate glanced behind her at her General Waste wheelie bin, and then back to watch the man walk down the street.

She looked back at the business card and frowned. She'd never been into all that James Bond, 007 spy stuff. It just wasn't her thing, and she'd certainly never entertained the idea of doing it for a living. She was a writer now, and although not a particularly successful one, she was at least rich, or she would be just as soon as she retrieved her passport from inside that suitcase.

With that thought in mind, she opened the car door, climbed in, started the engine and drove off, heading the opposite direction to the one the man was walking, down towards Portsmouth Docks, and the pub which, hopefully, still had a large silver suitcase waiting for her behind the bar. As she drove, her mind began to think about a possible job working for MI6. If it was something she could do part-time, between going on book tours, then perhaps it could be of interest. Or maybe she could do it at the same time as going on book tours? She hadn't thought of that.

I'll give them a call tomorrow, she thought, beginning to warm to the idea. She had to admit that she did enjoy killing people, and so she supposed it made sense for her to get a licence to do it legally.

'I wonder how much they pay?' she asked herself, as she reached down to turn on the radio that was already tuned in to her favourite station, Radio 4. She then sat back and listened as, by chance, the Prime Minister was being interviewed about the launch of his brand new book entitled, "I, Robert". Apparently, in it he shared his inner most feelings about The Battle of Great Britain, and why he made such a good military tactician. His book also promised to explain how he considered winning a decisive battle out at sea was very similar to beating someone at golf, in that you just needed to make the correct club selection, and then keep your head down during follow-through.

ABOUT THE AUTHOR

HAVING BEEN BORN in a US Navy hospital in California, David spent the first eight years of his life being transported from one country to another, before ending up in a three bedroom semi-detached house in Devon, on the South Coast of England.

David's Father, a devout Navy Commander, and his Mother, a loyal Christian missionary, then decided to pack him off to an all-boys boarding school in Surrey, where they thought it would be fun for him to take up ballet. Once there, he showed a remarkable aptitude for dance and, being the only boy in the school to learn, found numerous opportunities to demonstrate the many and varied movements he'd been taught, normally whilst fending off attacks from his classroom chums who seemed unable to appreciate the skill required to turn around in circles, without falling over.

Meanwhile, his Father began to push him down the more regimented path towards becoming a trained assassin, and spent the school holidays teaching him how to use an air rifle. Over the years, and with his Father's expert tuition, he became a proficient marksman, managing to shoot a number of things directly in the head. His most common targets were birds but also extended to those less obvious, including his brother, sister, an uncle who popped in for tea, and several un-suspecting neighbours caught doing some gardening.

Horrified by the prospect of her youngest son spending his adult life travelling the world to indiscriminately kill people, for no particular reason, his Mother intensified her efforts for him to enter the more highbrow world of the theatre by applying him to enter for the Royal Ballet. But after his twenty minute audition, during which time he jumped and twirled just as high and as fast as he possibly could, the three ballet aficionados who'd stared at him throughout with unhidden incredulity, proclaimed to his proud Mother that the best and only role they could offer him would be that of, "Third Tree from the Left" during their next performance of Pinocchio, but that would involve him being cut down, with an axe, during the opening scene. Furthermore, they'd be unable to guarantee his safety as the director had decided to use a real axe instead of the normal foam rubber one, to add to the drama of an otherwise rather staid production.

A few weeks later, and unable to find any suitable life insurance, David's Mother gave up her dream for him to become a famed Primo Ballerino and left him to his own devices.

And so it was, that with a sense of freedom little before known, he enrolled himself at a local college to study Chain Smoking, Under-Age Drinking, Drug Abuse and Fornication but forgot all about his core academic subjects. Subsequently he failed his 'A' Levels and moved to live in a tent in Dorking where he picked up with his more practised skills whilst working as a Barbed Wire Fencer.

Having being able to survive the hurricane of '87, the one that took down every tree within a fifty mile radius of his tent, he felt blessed, and must have been destined for greater things, other than sleeping rough during the night and being repeatedly stabbed by hard to control pieces of metal during the day. So he talked his way onto a Business Degree Course at the University of Southampton.

After three years of intensive study and to the surprise of just about everyone, he graduated with a 2:1 and spent the next ten years working in several incomprehensibly depressing sales jobs in Central London, before setting up his own recruitment firm.

Seven highly profitable years later, during which time he married and had two children, the Credit Crunch hit, which ended that particular episode of his career.

It's at this point he decided to become a writer which is where you find him now, happily married and living in London with his young family.

When not writing he spends his time attempting to persuade his wife that she really doesn't need to buy the entire contents of Ikea, even if there is a sale on. And when there are no items of flat-packed furniture for him to assemble he enjoys writing, base-jumping, and drawing up plans to demolish his house to build the world's largest charity shop.

www.david-blake.com

Printed in Great Britain
by Amazon